LISA MARIE RICE

MIDNIGHT
Renegade

Midnight Renegade ©2019 by Lisa Marie Rice

Published by Lisa Marie Rice

Cover Design & Formatting
by Sweet 'N Spicy Designs

One

The foothills of Mount Hood, Oregon
June 12

She can barely see, barely breathe, barely control the vehicle as she drives up the cliff road. The road has loose gravel that makes her vehicle slip and slide. Where she lives, it's not like that. Roads are smooth, not gravelly.

Where is that? Where does she live? It's gone, the only thing in her head is fog and pain and determination.

Matt Walker. That is her goal. A who not a what, she has to remind herself. Everything in her head is gone except for the name and the numbers. She can't even remember what the numbers are for — just that they need to match the numbers on the screen on the dashboard of the vehicle.

GPS numbers, she suddenly realizes in a flash of clarity. GPS numbers mean something, no … mean some*where.*

It's too hard to grasp, too hard to hold on to. All she knows is the gusts of wind on a blustery day, the pockets of loose gravel, the hairpin bends in the road. All she knows is that there's somewhere she must get to, someone she has to see. Someone who maybe can help.

Because she needs help desperately.

She is driving too fast, is barely in control. Her head is pounding, her vision is clouded, her wrists hurt. They kept her in shackles and the skin of her wrists is torn and bleeding and bruised.

The fog in her head billows and thickens, she cannot hold on to any thoughts.

The road makes a sudden bend and she takes the curve at the last second, back of the vehicle fishtailing. A rainstorm is coming, a slanting gray sweep of it visible in the hills. Tendrils of rain are already reaching the road. Soon, visibility will be down to a few feet. The road is incredibly dangerous. There is sheer rock to the right of her and a steep cliff edge to the left.

Slow down, she tells herself. But they might be following her. Probably are. Whoever held her was smart and tech-savvy. She remembers almost nothing but she does remember being in a room that required retinal scanning, remembers an IV pumping something into her veins, something that made her brain as foggy as the sky.

Maybe even now there is a drone overhead.

She bends forwards, looks up at the sky, but all she can see is black thunderhead clouds. If there's a drone, it's invisible.

She checks the number written on her biceps, then the number on the GPS. Close. She is close. She shakes her head sharply, as if waking herself up, as if she can clear her mind with the motion.

When she gets to … whoa … she can't remember his name any more. To … him. When she gets to him she will be safe. For now, all she can think about is those GPS numbers and how she is getting closer, closer …

Damn! Something dark and big at the corner of her eye and she slams on the brakes and twists the wheel. A deer. She feels the thump of the right front fender, the back wheels hit loose gravel and the vehicle starts sliding, moving in a horrible kind of slow motion.

She's a good driver but her reflexes are slowed by the drugs, by her ordeal. She tries to get back onto the road, but the back of the vehicle juts out over the cliff edge. She guns the accelerator but it's too late. In a horrifying slow motion that is in reality just a few seconds, the vehicle tips backward into the abyss.

There is nothing she can do but hold on to the seat belt as the vehicle picks up speed down the cliff toward the rushing river at the bottom, rolling over and over, the sounds of grinding metal and shattering glass loud in the cabin. Over and over and over, rolling down the hillside, each roll a bone-jarring crash, gashing her forehead, her arms against jagged metal.

After what feels like hours, the roll comes to a halt, the sudden silence disorienting. Her senses slowly start coming back online. She can hear the sound of rushing water and there is a terrible smell.

The sky is on the ground.

It takes her long moments to realize that she is up-side down, hanging from the seat belt, looking at the ceiling. She watches, dazed, as red drops collect on the ceiling. Blood. Her blood. Not gushing, dripping. So she hasn't severed an artery. But it is a lot of blood, none-theless. She has to get out, has to staunch the blood be-fore she passes out.

And that smell ... the memory of that smell tickles her brain. It reeks of danger, invokes fear.

She beats back the air bag, powder misting the air, unclasps her seat belt and falls to the roof, lying crum-pled there for a long moment, dazed. It's the smell more than the pain that makes her move. The vehicle's roof is strong, only slightly dented. The window has shattered with shards inside and outside. She winces as she crawls through the window. The cuts are minor, without much bleeding. Her head, however, is dripping blood. She has to clear her eyes with her hand to look around.

She's in a valley, cliffs rising steeply to either side of a rushing river, steel gray and in full spate. The water is loud as it rushes over boulders, spray rising high. She rolls over several times toward the water, too weak to stand up.

The river runs high and fast. Scary, but not as scary as the vehicle. Too stunned to think it through, she acts on instinct, rolling into the water. She's a strong swim-mer, but she's so weak she can only manage a few strokes, then starts tumbling in the water, half unconscious. Not strong enough to swim, but thanks to some powerful instinct for survival, she keeps her face out of the water.

The rushing river bends and just as it sweeps her away from the bank she hears the massive boom of an explosion, black and red flames soaring to the sky, heat searing the side of her face.

An explosion so big it feels like the end of the world.

And then the river carries her away.

Bogdan Yelchin watched from the road at the top of the cliff as the SUV burned, until there was only the smoking, charred husk remaining of the $40,000 vehicle. It had a gas tank holding almost seventy liters and it had been full.

He should know, because he'd filled it just yesterday and according to his odometer, the bitch that had stolen the vehicle had driven only 34.3 miles.

How Honor Thomas had gotten past the guards, drugged and disoriented, was something Bugayev and Gribkov were going to have to explain to their boss, Ivan Antonov. Yelchin had volunteered to follow the woman but he didn't want to have to be the one to explain any kind of failure to Antonov, who had been known to shoot subordinates reporting failure.

Yelchin didn't care, he wasn't the one who'd let her escape. He'd spent the night at their headquarters in Los Angeles, readying for the shipment that would be offloaded from the *Maria Cristina* in a week's time . He'd flown up early this morning to check on the woman, only to find that she'd escaped.

The woman was simply a tool to keep her father in line. She'd been kept drugged and shackled and they'd filmed her and shown the film to her father. That's all it took. No threats were necessary because she was clearly in their power. The father had to do what they said or else something would happen to his young daughter.

Perfect. In Yelchin's experience, a threat to loved ones worked better than a direct threat.

But now she was dead.

The vehicle down in the gorge was lit up like a bonfire, the sound of the crackling flames rising up the steep canyon. No human shape could be discerned through the black smoke and flames.

Pulling up his powerful binoculars, he studied the terrain down to the riverbank carefully. At times there was a path down, but it was interrupted by a long scree of moraine, then by a line of thorny bushes, then a ridge with a slope so steep it would require gear to navigate.

A sudden squall of rain swept across the river from the sullen black clouds overhead.

He let the binoculars fall down to his chest, thinking hard.

Walking down there was suicide. Glancing up at the

dark sky he saw that a big downpour was coming, which would make part of that descent unnavigable mud.

No. He'd report what had happened, and that the woman was dead, burned to a crisp. There probably wouldn't even be DNA left. Certainly the vehicle itself would provide no information to the authorities. If and when they ever discovered the burned husk deep in the valley.

The daughter was gone. What they would have to do was run the recordings they had over the past days on a loop so her father would be convinced she was still alive.

Maybe it was even better this way because holding the woman, drugged and shackled, was always going to be a slight risk. This was perfect. She was dead and un-traceable.

The area was isolated. Perhaps days would go by be-fore the wreckage was discovered and more days, even weeks, before they could identify the body, if they ever did. The vehicle itself was paid for by a shell company that existed only on paper. Not even forensic econo-mists could track down ownership.

Lightning flashed, forking down to the earth on the other side of the river. Thunder rolled. He watched the slanting gray streaks of a rainstorm in the distance that was coming closer.

Standing here in the cold rain wouldn't do any good to anyone and the weather forecast was for dropping temperatures.

The woman was dead. It was unfortunate that she died before the end of her usefulness but shit happened, as the Americans said.

It was a good expression. Almost Russian in its bleakness.

He turned and got back into his vehicle, backed up and drove off.

The dead woman was a glitch but not a disaster.

Matt Walker cast the line into the water. He'd already caught two salmon, now lying in a basket at his feet. Maybe he could catch a third.

Or not.

He didn't really care. He was living at the Grange, his new company's mountain retreat and it had enough food stocks to last years. Super good food, too. Catching a third salmon wasn't going to change anything.

His teammates kept asking when he was coming down from the mountain to begin his job. Actually, his best friend, Metal, kept asking *when the fuck are you going to stop brooding?*

He wasn't brooding. He was ... reflecting. Hard.

He didn't feel any sense of urgency to come down off the mountain. At times he felt like a 19th-century trapper, only he shaved. Occasionally. There was a Matt Walker-shaped job just waiting for him at ASI, a security company of good guys, most of whom were friends. He had accepted, but he wasn't ready to start yet, and refused any notion of pay.

In exasperation, the Big Boss, John Huntington, decided to just deposit Matt's salary in his bank account so he'd be shamed into coming down and mixing with people. But then Matt had given instructions to his bank not to accept any payments from ASI.

Stalemate.

They ended up compromising. Matt lived at the Grange and in return acted as caretaker. He'd helped his good buddy Nick Mancino out of a scrape a while back. The scrape had been serious stuff and the Grange had been blasted by a drone missile. Matt had overseen and helped with the repair work, donning his toolbelt with relish, grateful for the hard work that took his mind off other things.

He hadn't wanted to be paid a cent, which had annoyed both John and the other Big Boss, former Senior Chief Douglas Kowalski. They gave him a promotion before he even started the job, which he rejected.

Tough shit. They were tough guys, they could live with the frustration. For the moment, Matt was content to live like a hermit in a super luxurious mountain hideaway and nurse his fury.

Every once in a while a buddy from ASI would make it up to the Grange for a beer and a talk. They got the beer.

Seeing people was way down on the list of things Matt wanted to do. He was about done with people.

The outside world didn't hold much appeal. And hell, he had more than enough money in the bank. He didn't have to hurry back to work. His old man had left him a surprisingly large amount. Added to his savings and a few investments, it made him, technically, a millionaire a couple of times over, not that he gave a shit. He'd rather have his old man back. Charlie Walker had known right from wrong and couldn't be bullshitted into mistaking one for the other.

Several freezing cold raindrops fell on his head. He watched as the rain swept down the mountain on the other side of the river, a gray slanting curtain descending from black clouds, the leading edge reaching the river. A few drops spattered his face.

Yeah. Time to get to shelter. Only a crazy man would continue standing out here in the cold and in the rain.

But ... damn. The cool rain felt good.

He'd spent his military life as a SEAL — ten years — in hot, sandy hellholes that smelled of dust and shit, first in Iraq then Afghanistan. This was as far away from that as you could get.

He loved it up here, amazingly grateful for the clean air without the stench of the open sewers of Iraq, surrounded by lush greenery after years of the sere rocky landscape of Afghanistan. The foothills of Mount Hood were paradise and he loved it. Even the rain — so fresh and clean — was welcome.

The patter of drops falling hard on the rocks lining the riverbank grew louder, became a drumbeat. He was getting drenched, nature's way of telling him to cut this shit out, get inside, get dry, get outside a nice tumbler of Talisker .

He lifted his face up to the cold rain for a moment, enjoying the fresh wind, the moment of calm after so many years of back-to-back deployments.

Okay, time to go.

Lifting the rod, he felt resistance. He'd caught something at the last minute. Something big, to judge from the reel spinning out. Huh.

The water boiled white in spots where it rushed over underwater rocks. He pulled hard on the rod but still felt major resistance in the line. Something appeared then disappeared in the river. Something big, pale. What kind of fish was that big and that color?

Then he saw it — a slender arm and a hand. Just a second before it tumbled out of sight.

Fuck, he'd caught a *person,* not a fish! Somehow his hook had ripped into human flesh.

There it was again! Pale gray skin against gray water, caught on a boulder for a moment, water boiling around it. Matt sprang into action without thinking. The part of his mind that had been altered by combat already had a plan by his next breath.

He whipped out his boot knife, sliced the fishing line and dove straight into the water, swimming fast. It was a race against time. Anyone who wasn't a SEAL or an Olympic-level swimmer was going to drown in this water. And he hadn't seen the person actually swim, just be carried along by the rushing water.

He swam in a powerful crawl, keeping his eyes peeled for that pale flash of human flesh. The river took a bend and he swam curving around, keeping to the center of the river where there was a deeper channel and the churning waters were calmer.

A squall pelted his face with icy water and he had to close his eyes for a moment. In BUDS they'd swim ten miles a day using the combat sidestroke but that kept him underwater most of the time. Right now, he had to stay above the water with his eyes open to keep track of the person.

Maybe the body.

The river was snowmelt and freezing cold. How long had the person been in the water? If it was more than twenty minutes, Matt was searching for a corpse, not a living person.

A pale curve of flesh within a white wave ... there! Drifting toward the left-hand bank where a small eddy captured it, spinning it. Matt caught a glimpse of long red hair, a delicate profile, before a wave washed over it.

A woman! This was a woman he'd hooked. Someone who'd fallen into the river and had been tumbling through the rapids for who knew how long.

She was probably dead, but he had to bring her in. Absolutely had to. Something in him couldn't bear the idea of a woman floating down the river to the ocean two hundred miles away. Scraping against rocks and tree roots all the way, she'd be unrecognizable as a human being — just a battered and bloody piece of meat.

Matt lengthened his strokes. In Coronado they'd

mostly trained for endurance, not speed, but he pushed for speed now. He angled left toward her, away from the relative calm of the middle of the river, battling the current, swimming hard.

She spun, disappeared underwater for a second, emerged, and was whisked away by the river again. Matt tried to assess the situation while swimming as hard as he'd ever swum in BUDS. He couldn't see if she was breathing, but her face was often underwater. Jesus, if she was alive, she wouldn't be for long. He put on another sprint, the cold water slowing his muscles. His arms felt like deadweight, like moving boulders instead of limbs.

He pushed again, coming closer. He reached out with one hand, grabbed a piece of fabric, but a strong crosscurrent bore her away again. But just before she spun around he saw her eyes slowly blink. God, she was alive!

SEALs had reserves, deep reserves that had been beaten into them, and he bit into his reserves, finding that place where you can push when there's no more push in you. They were almost half a mile downriver from where he'd been fishing and he knew that very strong rapids were ahead and stretched for a mile or two. Only serious white-water rafters attempted those rapids. If she reached them, she'd be gone, bashed against the rocks. No one in the water could survive those rapids, certainly not someone semi- conscious.

He dug in, pushed for more speed and moments later caught her by the sleeve, then his hand bit into her upper arm, grasping flesh not material. She wasn't conscious any more. Her head lolled on her shoulders as he trod water for just an instant, hooking an arm around her shoulders.

He had her.

Now he had to tow her to the other bank.

Matt didn't wait a second. He was still okay — tired but functional. He could keep swimming for hours. SEALs functioned well even past exhaustion. But she wasn't okay. She wasn't going to survive for very long. There'd be some water in her lungs and she was deathly pale, a terrifying gray-white color.

His right arm hooked under her chin, he placed his hips under hers and set off, legs scissoring powerfully. The current was strong, as strong as the tides at Coronado beach. During Hell Week he swam five and a half miles a day in the freezing Pacific, with sharks, and he'd managed it. He was going to manage this as well. No question he was going to make it — but was she?

The rushing water was loud but his ear was next to her mouth and he heard nothing. He couldn't feel her rib cage rising and falling. He was losing her. At the calmer water of mid-stream he added yet more power, speeded up and rejoiced when his boots scrabbled on rocks. He rose up with the woman in his arms to slip-stagger up the mossy river bank to where there was a flat surface of muddy grass. They were both soaking wet but he couldn't do anything about that. He had nothing warm and dry to cover her with.

She lay lifeless, head turned to one side, chest still.

Matt put two fingers to her carotid, despairing as he felt nothing. Then ... there! A light flutter, faint, barely perceptible. For now she was alive, and she'd stay that way if he had anything to do with it.

But she wasn't breathing.

Placing his left hand on her sternum, he covered it with his right hand and began strong compressions, two inches deep. A hundred twenty compressions, then he pinched her nose, tilted her head back and gave her mouth-to-mouth resuscitation, watching to make sure her chest rose. Thirty more fast compressions, mouth-to-mouth, two big breaths. Compressions, two breaths, compressions, two breaths.

She was still, inert, like a doll.

He didn't let up. He'd seen men come back to life on the field. He wasn't giving up until he got tired and he didn't tire easily. Compressions, two breaths ...

She convulsed, chest heaving without pulling in air. Matt pushed her over to her side as she vomited river water, gasped, wheezed, vomited again. When she'd emptied herself, she lay curled on her side, eyes closed. She was clearly exhausted but her body was coming back from death.

She needed to be warm and dry now. Not about to save her from drowning only to watch her die of exposure.

He placed a hand on her shoulder. He was wet all over and chilled, but his hand must have felt warm, even through the cold, wet material of her sweater. Her shoulder was delicate, fragile and he could feel the chill of her skin.

Her eyes were closed and she was breathing so lightly her chest was barely rising and falling. Head still to one side.

"Hey." Matt tapped her cheek. Not hard, but sharply. Trying to keep her conscious. "Hey, stay with me, ma'am. I need for you to stay with me." He tapped her cheek again, and again. He took her chin and gently turned her face back up. "I'll get you to where you'll be warm and dry, but I'm going to have to carry you. Do you understand me?"

A long exhalation of breath, her eyes still closed. She wasn't responding.

Matt tapped her cheek again, hoping it would annoy her, hoping she'd react.

"Ma'am?" He tried another tack. Have her give basic info. "Ma'am, what's your name? My name is Matt Walker, what's yours?"

Oddly, her eyelids flickered when he mentioned his name, almost as if she recognized it. He tapped her cheek again. "Ma'am?"

She moaned, an animal sound from deep in her chest and then her eyes opened wide and Matt nearly gasped. They were a light gray so luminous they seemed to shine, rimmed by dark blue. Amazing eyes, eyes to get lost in. And it was then he noticed she was ... extraordinarily beautiful. And with those eyes ... he had to shake himself.

Shame washed through him. She'd nearly died and she might still die if he didn't get her back to the

Grange fast. This was no time to be mooning over a beautiful woman.

Her hand shot out and grabbed his arm. Her grip had no strength to it but she held him still. He couldn't have moved if someone had put a gun to his head.

Her lips moved and he frowned. She coughed, tried to speak again, but nothing came out.

Matt moved his head down close to hers. She was shivering, they had to get going, but that icy cold hand and the desperation in those beautiful eyes held him still.

Her weak grip tightened a little and she drew in a deep breath, her first since being resuscitated. She was trembling, her hand shook on his arm. Only moans were coming out of her mouth, but she was trying to tell him something, trying desperately.

"Don't —" she gasped.

"Don't what, ma'am?" he asked, head nearly touching hers.

"Don't let them —" she paused, struggling for breath, for strength.

"Don't let them …?"

"Don't let them catch me." She stopped, breathed heavily. "They'll kill me if … if they catch me."

There were people after this beautiful woman? Wanting to kill her? Cold shot through his veins, an icy rage. *No. Way.* She was under his protection now.

Then he saw something that turned his icy rage into red hot rage. In grasping his hand, the sleeve of her sweater fell back to her elbow. The skin around her wrist was abraded over a large band with scabs halfway up her forearm and around her wrists. An unusual mark but one he was familiar with. He'd seen that mark on kids, a mark he'd never forget.

This woman had been shackled.

Not handcuffed.

Shackled.

To confirm it, he checked her other wrist, which carried the same mark.

She was running from people who'd kept her shackled.

Well, her running was over.

She was watching his face carefully, light gray eyes shifting over his features. He knew what she was thinking. She'd barely escaped with her life from bad guys who'd kept her prisoner. Had she fallen into another bad guy's hands? Because for an instant there, he'd let his rage show and the animal instinct in her — which would be heightened by the danger she'd been in — sounded alarms.

He was dangerous, yes. Not to her, but definitely to fuckheads who would keep a woman shackled. Yeah. Those were exactly the kind of people he was primed to fight.

But right now, reassuring this woman was more important that letting his rage show. He relaxed his features, put on a bland façade.

He held her hand in his. It was slender, strong, icy cold. He made his voice low and soft, as if speaking to a wounded animal.

"Ma'am, we need to get you warm and dry, you are perilously close to —"

"Hypothermia," she whispered.

"Yes, exactly. My company has a lodge not too far from here."

She nodded, light eyes fixed on his. She blinked, blinked again. Her eyes closed, stayed close. She was fading fast.

"You'll be safe there. I can call a doctor —"

"No!" Her eyes flew open. She tried to sit up but didn't have the strength. Matt caught her as she fell back. "No doctor, no hospital. They will look for me there. Please." She coughed, her voice becoming weaker and weaker. "Promise. *Please.*"

He could call Metal, his pal. Metal had been a medic and a damned good one. Lots of soldiers wounded in battle were alive thanks to Metal. He wasn't official and he sure as hell knew how to keep his mouth shut. The Grange had an infirmary that was well stocked.

"Okay, no doctors," he said. He wasn't lying. Metal wasn't a doctor.

"Thank you." Her words were slurring, she was slipping into hypothermia, her core temperature dropping. He had to get her warm and dry as fast as he could.

"I'm going to pick you up now." But she was gone, those remarkable eyes closed, unmoving behind the lids. Unconscious.

Matt had to move fast. He picked her up and moved as quickly as he could to his vehicle upstream, parked on a logger's trail half a mile back, and uphill. She weighed not much more than the packs they carried into battle and he climbed with ease.

Ignoring the slashing icy rain, he watched his step on the treacherous, rocky terrain, slicked with wet pine needles. The last thing he needed was to fall with her in his arms. Maybe bang her head on a rock. She'd been through enough. So he kept his eyes on the ground, switching frequently to watch her face.

To make sure she wouldn't slip into hypothermia and death, but also because watching her wasn't a hardship. Bruised and battered as she was, she was still extraordinarily beautiful.

Get your head on straight, he ordered himself, as if he were his own Senior Chief. He should reinforce that thought with a hearty slap to the back of his head. Just like Master Chief Higgins used to do, bless his rhinoceros hide.

Matt was in a race against time to save this woman's life. He shouldn't be ogling her. Shame on him. He wasn't starved for the sight of attractive women. God no. The place where he would go to work was lousy with beautiful women. It was like they came by the dozen and he saw them every day. His bosses and many of his teammates were married to gorgeous women. Hell, even Metal's fiancée, the company's resident IT genius, was very pretty. Metal thought she was the most beautiful woman in the world and said so often. Loudly.

This woman had the ASI women beat, hands down. He finally reached his vehicle, putting her on her feet for a moment while he fished for the keyfob. It opened with a chirp and he thanked the automotive gods that the keyfob hadn't been destroyed by a dousing in the river.

She couldn't stand on her feet, but that was okay. He held her easily, opened the rear passenger door and carefully, gently, placed her lying down. She didn't move, her eyes were motionless behind the lids. No movement at all.

Not good.

Matt rushed to the back where he held supplies. All ASI vehicles came equipped with weaponry and emergency gear. You could survive a week of the zombie apocalypse with what ASI put in their vehicles as standard gear. There was a thin foil blanket and heat packs. He cracked two heat packs and put them on her stomach and chest, then covered her carefully with the foil blanket.

The engine started right up and he sent rocks and dirt flying as he gunned it. Speed was essential now.

Driving as fast as he could toward the Grange, he connected with his phone via the speaker system, tapping the first number on speed dial on the big screen of the dashboard. Metal picked up on the first ring.

"'Sup, man?" Matt relaxed just a fraction at hearing Metal's deep, reassuring tone. Matt could do emergency medicine but Metal had deep medical knowledge. He'd often flirted with the idea of going back to school to become a doctor but he liked being an operator more.

"Got an emergency. Fished a woman out of the

river, literally. My hook is still in her arm." Her arm was so chilled she wouldn't be feeling any pain. Matt wanted to get back to the Grange and remove it from her arm with disinfectant. "She was in the river, caught in the rapids."

"Weather's bad," Metal answered. "So hypothermia's a real danger."

"Yeah," Matt said, voice clipped. He was driving as fast as he could on the unpaved road. "She's in the vehicle right now, stretched out on the back seat. I put the foil blanket on her, cracked some heat packs and I've turned the heat up to maximum. As soon as we're at the Grange I'll try to get some hot liquid in her if she regains consciousness. Can you come up? She took a pounding on the rocks."

A pause. "Sure. But wouldn't it be better to get her to a hospital?"

Matt's jaw clenched. "I suspect she took a pounding from more than the rocks. I think she was held a prisoner. She gained consciousness for a few moments and begged me to keep her safe. Said that they would kill her if they found her. Begged me not to take her to a hospital. She was half dead and still scared out of her mind."

Silence. "Okay. We're pretty well equipped up at the Grange. Unless she has a compound fracture or internal bleeding, I guess we can deal with it ourselves. She was scared, you say?"

"Terrified. And Metal?" Matt felt his chest tightening at the thought.

"Yeah?"

"She'd been shackled. *Shackled*. You know I recognize the signs."

Metal felt about the mistreatment of women and children the way he did. It was an abomination.

Matt heard a sharp intake of breath. "Be there as fast as I can."

Two

The Grange

She came to slowly, drifting up to the surface from the depths of an ocean. Drifting slowly, slowly toward a distant light. Light and heat and safety, above her. Way way above her. She tried to reach up for the light.

"Whoa. Wake up, ma'am. Breathe."

Someone was tapping her cheek and it was maddening. She couldn't breathe, why was someone tormenting her?

The last air in her lungs left her. Soon she would be forced to draw in a deep breath, the breath that would fill her lungs with water and send her down to her death.

Kicking at the man, trying to hit him. He still dragged her down, he was killing her.

She moaned, a desperate keening sound, fighting the downward pull through the watery depths.

His hands held hers, touched her shoulders and she fought him off, finally drawing a breath and finding air and not water.

She opened her eyes and met the dark eyes of a man she somehow knew, but not the man of her nightmare. Not the man at the bottom of the ocean, with the cruel eyes and the hard hands.

Yet, she knew this man. No, not knew, but he was somehow familiar. Flashes of images — the rushing river, a strong arm holding her up as he swam her across it, being wrapped in a foil blanket, feeling warmth for the first time in forever.

He was holding her hands in a gentle yet unbreakable warm grasp. "You're awake," he said, his voice low and steady. "Good. I couldn't drag you out of the nightmare."

She moved her eyes and saw another man. Tall and strong like this one, but she didn't know him. Oh God, they'd found her!

The nightmare wasn't over! It was even more horrible that she couldn't remember the details of the nightmare, just hard hands and hard eyes. Cruelty and terror and desperation.

She'd escaped and there was no way she'd go back into captivity.

She'd rather die.

She tried to wrench her hands from the dark-haired man but she couldn't. She leaned forward, her voice a harsh whisper. "He found me, he'll kill me! Let me go!" Tugging was useless against his strength but desperation made her try again and again. "Let. Me. Go!" It was like trying to move steel. The last of her reserves left her and she stilled.

The other man, bulging with muscle like the man holding her hands, stepped forward. She couldn't fight him, she had nothing left. All she could do was scrabble with her feet to try to get away but she went nowhere. Desperation seized her. That must have shown in her face because he held up his hands, palms out.

"Stop, please." His voice was low and calm, too. "I'm not going to hurt you, ma'am. My name is Sean O'Brien. My friends call me Metal. I was a medic in the military. My friend Matt here fished you out of the river and he said you didn't want a doctor, didn't want to go to the hospital. But you need medical attention, ma'am, which I'm ready to give you. I repeat, I won't hurt you."

She barely heard the words, but she did hear the tone. Low and calm. The other man — men — their tones had been vicious. Menacing. And their faces, cold and cruel. The man holding her hands — Matt? — and the man speaking — Metal? — had tough faces atop very tough bodies but they weren't threatening her. Either one could crush her and toss her away, but … they were offering help.

Weren't they?

Where was she? She looked around, trying to decipher the environment. An image flashed in her mind. A cold featureless room, a hard cot with a thin foam rubber mattress. Shackled to a wall.

Nothing in the room that could help or give comfort.

Completely unlike the room she was in now. She

was lying on a comfortable bed in a room with stylish modern furniture. Muted earth tones, a sculpture of a bird with outstretched wings on a sideboard, framed landscape photographs on the wall, a large night table. A doctor's bag open on the table.

A whimper escaped her lips and she bit them. Never give anything away. Never show weakness.

She couldn't remember anything except for the defiance she'd felt down to her bones. Why couldn't she remember any details? All she knew was that she'd been held a prisoner by dangerous men and she'd die rather than go back.

The man holding her hands — Matt — leaned forward, looking her straight in the eyes.

"It looks like you were held a prisoner and you escaped. Good for you. You're not a prisoner here. All we want to do is help you. You nearly drowned in freezing cold water. You need heat and medical attention. May we provide that?"

She gave a jerky nod and he nodded back. He let her hands go, walked away and came back with something stacked in his hands.

"You're chilled. I tried to keep you warm but you are still in wet clothes and that's not good for you. You're risking pneumonia, if not hypothermia. That's —"

"I know what hypothermia is," she croaked. And she did. The knowledge blossomed in her head, as if she had an encyclopedia in her mind that just opened to the correct page.

Hypothermia — dangerous condition when the core temperature of the body falls below 95°. When the body loses heat faster than it can produce heat, leading to complete failure of the heart and respiratory systems.

The knowledge was right there in her head.

Those dark eyes were watching her carefully. He held up his hands. "I have dry clean clothes here. The wives of my teammates come up often and they keep a basic wardrobe here. They wouldn't mind. Can you change by yourself? After that, I have a thermos of hot tea and then Metal will check you over. We're just going to have to hope you don't have any internal injuries."

"I don't," she whispered. And she didn't. She hurt everywhere it was possible to hurt but she could tell that it was muscle pain not organ pain. She somehow knew the difference.

He bent his head. "Okay." But he sounded unsure.

He needn't be unsure. "Trust me, I don't have any internal bleeding or serious damage." Somehow, she knew it was true, as if she'd just had a full body scan.

Even those few words exhausted her though. She had to close her eyes, concentrate on breathing.

"Okay," he said again. "Can you change? We need to get you out of those wet clothes fast, they're wicking heat away from your skin. Metal and I will turn our backs. I'm not happy leaving you alone but we can give you privacy." She opened her eyes to see his grim face, frown between black eyebrows. One thing stood out. He was worried — for her. He took her hand and it was the one spot on her body that felt warm. Otherwise she was freezing. He was absolutely right — she needed to get out of these wet clothes clinging to her.

She opened her mouth to say yes but nothing came out. She nodded and he nodded back. She'd given her consent though she hadn't said the words.

"All right. I'm going to help you up."

She nodded again.

Matt pulled gently on her hand, his other hand against her back. She sat up with difficulty, wobbling a bit. But his hand against her back was rock steady.

Her mind was foggy but she knew one thing, not with her mind but with her heart. With the essence of her. She hated feeling this weak, simply hated it. Something told her she was used to feeling strong. And that this weakness was unusual.

It was awful. Unbearable. She didn't quite remember who she was but she knew this wasn't her. She'd survived something, something terrible and it had taken a chunk out of her. This was not her.

She managed to move her legs — it was harder than she thought — and slipped them over the side of the bed.

And collapsed. Or would have collapsed if Matt's strong hands hadn't caught her. He held her against him for a moment, dark face above hers, dark eyes watching her carefully. Where her body touched his, heat bloomed. He was like a furnace. An amazing sense of strength infused her, just for an instant. Like a charge.

The clouds in her head parted for just a moment and she had a memory of him saving her in the water, swimming across a raging river to bring her to the bank on the other side.

He'd saved her life. And he was still saving it.

She couldn't even stand and he was holding her up. She reached back for the bed, muttering "Sorry."

The frown deepened. "Nothing to be sorry for." He breathed out sharply. "Listen, we really need to get you out of those wet clothes. May I help you?"

She looked around at the nice furnishings. Urbane, comfortable and stylish. Not a rustic cabin. Where were they? Weren't they near Mount Hood?

It was too much. She was shivering, exhausted, confused.

The words were there, they just couldn't come out. I need to change these wet cold clothes but I must do it myself. I don't want to strip down in front of two men I don't know, even if one of you saved my life.

But moving toward the stack of clothes made her gasp, wince, a sharp pain like someone sticking a knife in her ribs. Did she have a broken rib? Her side hurt badly. Whoa. Now that she was paying attention, everything hurt. Muscle pain, not internal organ pain, but still.

He saw and he understood. She had the feeling he saw and understood a lot of things.

"I think you should stay still, ma'am. Until we know if you are badly injured."

It hurt to breathe. But she managed to get out, "No internal hemorrhaging."

He nodded. "That may be. But you might have a cracked or broken rib. I'll ask your permission to cut those wet clothes off you and I'll help you put dry clothes on." His dark eyes held hers, serious and steady.

There was so much fog in her head, her world was shaky and her memory was shot. But she'd known violence at men's hands, not so long ago. They had had an evil air, in the old-fashioned sense of the term. They'd been almost soulless and they'd delivered cruelty casually, without thinking. Their eyes hadn't had anything she recognized as humanity.

Somehow she knew cruelty and evil. She didn't know how she knew it but she did. Something in her past, or job …

A sharp pain shot through her head, like someone had jabbed an ice pick into her brain. She gasped, clutched her head with her free hand. The other hand was held in a painless but unbreakable grip.

Matt's face grew even grimmer. "Ma'am?"

"Help me, please." She couldn't get her voice above a whisper. Everything hurt.

Something in her knew it wasn't broken bones or bleeding, but it hurt to move. There was no way she could get these wet clothes off herself unaided.

As if her words were a start pistol, Matt sprang into action. He somehow had shears and gently set about cutting her clothes off her. The entire time, he kept his eyes on hers. He must have excellent peripheral vision because though he moved adeptly and quickly, he didn't seem to see her body. Soon she would be naked.

Naked and wounded. That idea should have made her feel vulnerable, worse than that dark memory of being restrained, though fully dressed, in front of cruel men.

She didn't feel vulnerable.

His entire body language spoke of utter safety. He'd given a sharp glance to the other man, the one who had the weird name of Metal. Metal nodded and turned his back.

Matt took the shears and cut down the front of her sweater, including her bra, then quickly cut the front of her slacks, down the legs. He returned to her torso, lifted the neck of her sweater away from her skin and started cutting from the neck down the left sleeve. He froze, stepped slightly back.

"Metal." His voice was low, urgent.

Metal turned, walked to the bed carrying a medical bag but then he, too, froze.

What?

They were staring at her left arm. She turned and for a moment couldn't figure out what she was looking at. The clouds in her head parted for a moment and she saw clearly what was there.

Someone — was that her handwriting? — had written MATT WALKER and digits, which she recognized as GPS coordinates, on her upper arm.

She stared at the man, the man who'd introduced himself as Matt Walker.

"That's — that's *you*?"

He nodded. "Yup."

What the fuck?

Matt glanced at Metal, shocked. Matt had been a SEAL for ten years. He'd had a new one ripped by the CIA. He'd been betrayed by his government. He thought nothing could shock him anymore, but this did.

His fucking name on this beautiful woman's arm. So astonishing that it distracted his attention away from the woman's slim body. The skin was badly marred by bruises but where there were no bruises she had smooth pale ivory skin, small perfect breasts, a flat little belly.

He'd heroically kept his eyes on her face, but it wasn't easy. But then he was used to heroics and before the blowup of his career, he'd won several medals for valor.

But fuck, not staring at that body — he should get a medal for that.

He heard a noise next to him and saw Metal, who was pretty unshockable, too, looking a little dazed.

Then he got his head out of his ass and realized he was dealing with a wounded, probably concussed, freezing woman who'd been rescued from a river full of snowmelt and he was standing there with his mouth open and his dick in his hand, figuratively.

He should be ashamed of himself. There were a lot of scumbags in this world but his parents hadn't raised one, no sir. They'd tried to drill manners into him. Not much in the way of formal manners stuck, but by God, he wasn't about to disrespect a woman who was wounded.

He had a warm fleece zipup tracksuit and light wool zipup sweater and he had to get her into them. He finished cutting away the wet sleeves, then, lifting the outfit from the foot of the couch, he held it out to her. "May I help you get dressed?"

She nodded and shivered. Yeah, she was freezing. And she looked so weak and vulnerable his heart clenched.

As gently as he could, Matt helped her put on the sweater, the jacket of the tracksuit, then quickly pulled away her pants and panties and slid the tracksuit pants up her long, slender legs. The Grange had everything, including warm woolen socks. Once she was dressed and dry, she lay back with a sigh and closed her eyes.

In the meantime, Metal had taken her wrist and was counting her pulse with a frown. Nobody believed it, but Metal could measure BP via the pulse. Matt had seen him do it countless times.

"BP ninety over sixty. Fifty bpm," he murmured.

"That pressure is low. Pulse, too," she said with a weak voice, without opening her eyes.

Metal shot Matt a glance. When he'd pushed her sleeve up and seen the clear signs of a shackle his jaw had tightened. Metal hated men who beat up on women and kids. Said there was a special place in hell for them. All the men of ASI hated that with a passion.

Matt in particular was filled with fiery rage at the

sight. Unshackling kids had been his downfall and he'd do it again in a heartbeat.

Metal took out a pocket light. "Can you open your eyes?"

Her eyelids flew up and Matt nearly took a step back, but checked himself immediately. Those eyes were not only of an otherworldly beauty but they were keen. In pain, probably concussed, but intelligence shone out of them.

Metal bent over, the light shining in her eyes, first one, then the other.

"Are the pupils dilated? Are they the same size?" she asked and Metal's eyebrows rose.

"Slightly dilated, the right pupil is a little smaller than the left."

"Mild concussion," they said at the same time.

"I think we should take you in —" Metal began.

"I said no hospitals," she said quickly, voice barely above a whisper. She shifted her gaze to Matt, as if he held authority. And, well, he did. He was the one who saved her and he felt responsible. Hell, he *was* responsible.

"Only if Metal gives you the all clear," Matt said. "His word goes."

She nodded. "Okay."

"After which, if you do get the all clear, you agree to take it easy. Rest and eat and sleep."

"God, yes." She closed her eyes for a moment.

"All right." Matt stepped back, let go of her hand, which she been clutching. It was surprisingly hard to do.

Touching her reassured him.

He nodded at Metal, who sat next to her on the bed. He had a stethoscope in his hand. "Ma'am? I'm going to do as thorough a check up as I can, considering you won't let us take you to a clinic."

He stopped, disapproval in his voice. Metal in disapproving mode was pretty scary. Not handsome at the best of times, now he looked like a clean-cut, sandy-haired enforcer and to someone who didn't know him, he looked like he could easily beat you into submission with his pinkie.

She showed no fear, though, none at all. Either she was fearless or she had a sixth sense that Metal would never hurt her. Or hurt any woman.

Metal had a fiancée he loved deeply. She was pregnant and could wrap him around her little finger. It was a good thing she loved him right back just as deeply, otherwise he'd have been in deep shit.

He also had a protective streak a mile wide, like all the ASI guys. Matt loved the company he was going to work for, even though he didn't want to start just yet. He was delighted to join ASI after clashing with a lot of scumbags in the military. It wasn't just the CIA scumbag. There were others. They seemed to proliferate, like rabbits in the wild. Self-serving careerists. Half the time he found himself following orders he found borderline illegal or immoral, sometimes both.

With ASI no one would ever order him to do something he'd disapprove of, and if they did, he'd refuse with no consequences.

So he knew Metal would be his partner in protecting this woman he'd fished out of a river. A woman who'd been shackled, a woman who was running from bad guys.

Here he was, here they were. Protecting her. This is what they did.

Metal ran through a checklist, examined her carefully and concluded that she was bruised and battered but essentially intact. No broken bones, though maybe a bruised rib. Slight concussion.

After asking her permission, he took a blood sample. Carefully stowed it.

She nodded when he finished, as if corroborating that he'd done a good job.

"Now something hot to drink," Matt said, pouring out a cup of hot tea from a Thermos. He held one arm against her back and held the cup in front of her mouth. "Should have done this sooner. Thank God it looks like we were able to avoid hypothermia."

"Yes," she said, leaning back into Matt's arm. She blew on the tea, sipped and sighed. "Good."

It probably wasn't good. Matt knew zero about tea, but it was hot and it had honey and that was what she needed. She was dry, dressed in warm clothes, under blankets and sipping tea. He predicted that she would fall asleep soon.

After she woke up, he'd feed her. He had boiling water down pat, and could make breakfast, though anything else was beyond his abilities. But the Grange was super stocked with fabulous food cooked by the wife of a teammate. Isabel Delvaux-Harris, famous blogger and incredible chef. They had entire freezer lockers stocked with plastic containers of anything anyone could possibly want. He'd nuke some soup and thaw out one of Isabel's five-grain bread loaves.

This woman had been held prisoner, had escaped, God only knew how, and had nearly drowned. Isabel's food would make up for a little of that.

But before she fell asleep...

"Ma'am?"

Her eyes had been closing, dragged down by the thickest, longest eyelashes he'd ever seen. They opened again.

"Yes?"

"What's your name?"

"My ... name?" A look of alarm crossed her face. Her red-brown eyebrows drew together. A hand went to her head. "Oh, oh! Crazy. So crazy. I can't remember. How can that be? Oh man, my head hurts ..."

Matt exchanged a quick glance with Metal. She was making a little mewling sound of distress. God.

"That's okay," Matt said quickly. Amnesia was definitely possible after what she'd been through.

She put the cup down, raised her right sleeve above the elbow, showed them the crook of her arm. "They — they drugged me. Look."

Matt and Metal bent their heads over her arm and, yeah. He'd noticed. The sign of an injection and gummy residue from medical tape.

Metal gently touched the skin. "I saw that. An IV

puncture."

She craned her head, stared at it, closed her eyes, flopped her head back. "Yes."

Matt breathed out his fury.

The CIA kept prisoners pumped full of drugs during interrogations. The drugs would be hung from an IV tree, and the prisoners would be infused for hours, days. No escaping the drugs. A few had been reduced to vegetables, mind gone, drooling sacks of meat.

He leaned a hand on the headboard and bent his head toward her. "Can you try to remember?"

Her hand was still holding her head. She swallowed heavily. "Honor?"

It was a question. Was Honor her name or a quality? "Honor."

"Yes?" she answered, as if he'd called. So it was her name.

"Honor what?"

She whimpered.

Metal tapped him on the shoulder. "I don't think we should push it, man. But one thing — Honor, are you a doctor?"

"Yes." The word came out sure and strong. She didn't know who she was, but she knew what she was.

"Here. Have some more before you rest." Matt gently pulled her up against the pillows and placed the mug of hot tea in her hands. They shook. Before she could spill hot liquid on herself, he cupped her hands while she lifted the mug to her lips. A long sip, another one. A sigh.

Metal placed the back of his hand against her brow. He could tell temperatures as accurately as any thermometer that way. "Ninety seven. Chilled but no danger of hypothermia. Good thing you got her here so fast. It was touch and go."

She sipped again, eyes closed, finally handing Matt the cup. And just like that, sitting up, she fell asleep.

Matt studied the beautiful sleeping woman. A little color had come into her skin. When she'd first arrived the skin of her face had looked like white marble — a dead, still white, veined with blue. Her lips and nostrils had been blue and she looked like she'd already died. Heat inside and out had turned her lips pale pink, the nostrils looked normal and so did she.

The memory loss was probably due to the drugs, not to having banged her head against a rock.

Matt and Metal exchanged a glance. They'd been out in the field together so often they understood each other without words. Matt fished out his cell from his jeans pocket, took a few photos of her and followed Metal out of the room.

"You should keep an eye on her," Metal said.

"On it." Matt showed him the cell screen where Honor was quietly sleeping. The rooms and hallways had video cameras that were kept off when unnecessary. Matt had turned the system on. He'd warred with himself briefly. It was an invasion of privacy of a woman who'd already suffered. But he had to monitor her for her own safety, so privacy had to take a hike.

He was about to invade her privacy again.

"Is Felicity at work?" he asked Metal. Metal's fiancée, IT super genius, was expecting twins and interspersed work with projectile vomiting. Metal begged her to stay home, everyone in the office did, but Felicity maintained she'd rather be busy when not staring into the bowels of the porcelain god. Metal was tough but Felicity was tougher and she won.

Metal's face pulled in a grimace. "Yeah," he said sourly.

"She still hurling?" Matt asked sympathetically.

Metal sighed.

"Can she do something for me?"

"She'd walk barefoot across hot coals for you. Sure."

"Likewise." Everyone at ASI would go to the wall for Felicity. She was super smart, worked hard for everyone and had pulled their nuts out of the fire more than once. He diminished the screenshot of Honor sleeping and tapped a number. An instant later, Felicity's pretty but pale face showed on the screen.

"Matt! How's the Grange? My guy might be stopping by."

"He's here."

Matt tilted the screen so she could see Metal, who waved and frowned. "Shouldn't you be lying down?"

Felicity rolled her pretty blue eyes. "No, mom, I'm at work."

"There's a cot in the back room, you could —"

"Matt." Felicity smiled, showing all her teeth. She sounded exasperated. Metal could be a little heavy-handed in his concern. "Did you need something?"

Matt nudged Metal out of the way and addressed Felicity. "This is confidential. I think a life might depend on it."

Felicity's face turned sober. "I'm a vault. You know that."

He did. She was of pure Russian blood. Russians kept secrets for generations. Plus she'd grown up under the Witness Protection Program, had done contract work for the FBI and had worked at the NSA briefly. She'd lost her clearances when she joined ASI but she knew how to keep secrets.

"I'm sending some photos of a woman to you. Can you run her through some databases? Her first name is Honor. We think she's a doctor."

He heard faint tapping sounds from off screen. "Got the photos, am running them now. What's the story?"

"I rescued her in the river. She's battered and bruised. Said she'd been kidnapped and I believe her. She has signs on her wrists of having been shackled."

A shocked breath and Felicity's eyes rounded. "Shackled?"

Matt nodded grimly. "Yeah. And signs of IV infusions. We suspect she was administered drugs while being held prisoner. She's frightened to death and doesn't want to be taken to a hospital. Said they'd find her there."

"If clever people were after her, they would."

This touched a chord with Felicity. She herself had been on the run from a man who'd tried to kill her and had chased her to a hospital. She'd barely escaped and had fallen, bleeding and grievously wounded, through the door of a friend. Metal had been visiting and he'd caught her. And kept her.

Matt looked into Felicity's bright blue eyes. "You know how frightened she must be."

"God yes," Felicity said, voice sober and sad. "To be wounded and on the run." She narrowed her eyes and stared at the screen. It was as if she were staring right at him. "But you've got her now, right? She's safe now?"

Matt nodded. "She's safe now and she'll stay that way. Don't worry. I don't care if the hounds of hell are after her, they won't get to her. But we need intel, we need to know what the situation is to be able to protect her, and she doesn't remember anything."

"Amnesia?"

"Don't know. Maybe not. Like I said, I think she was drugged, whether to make her talk or to keep her quiet, I don't know. But I'm hoping when the drugs wear off her memory will return. In the meantime, if I know her name and other info, I won't be blind."

A soft ping and Felicity looked offscreen at a computer monitor. "Okay, here's what I have and I'm sending it all to you right now. Name, Honor Jane Thomas. Physician, internist. Works in the ER of Eastern Memorial Hospital. Single, 31. No criminal record, not even a parking ticket. Excellent credit rating. Doesn't have a

Facebook page, smart girl. Has published two scientific papers, one on hypoxia due to smoke inhalation and the other on emergency treatment of strokes. Owns her own apartment. It's small but in an upscale condo. Contributes to charity, cancer research. I'll have to dig deeper to know more. Here's a photo."

The image of a driver's license photo popped up. It was the woman, Honor. Looking relaxed, beautiful, unsmiling. The hair was deep red in the photo.

"That's her. Dig deeper," he ordered. "And find out if she has any connection to me."

"Come again?" Her eyes rounded. "A connection to *you?*"

"Yeah. She had my name and the GPS coordinates of the Grange written with a Sharpie on her upper left arm."

Felicity's pretty mouth opened, then closed.

"Yep." He felt the same.

"She was looking for you?"

"Seems that way. But she got waylaid by monsters and held prisoner." Well, the monsters weren't getting her back, that was for sure. "I intend to keep her safe but I need to know what's going on."

"Sure." Felicity looked troubled. She knew what it was to have some mysterious man after you and not know why. She'd nearly died at her own monster's hands. A quick glance at Metal showed that he was remembering clearly the snowbound night she fell through the door into his arms, bleeding out. "I'll find out what I can."

"Appreciate it."

"Of course. You know I —" Felicity broke off suddenly, turned sheet white and disappeared. Matt knew exactly where she was going — to the toilet to puke her guts out.

Everyone at ASI felt really bad but there was nothing anyone could do. And she refused to stay home.

"Okay." Metal put a heavy hand on his shoulder. "That's my cue to go. I can't do anything else for Honor. What she needs right now is rest and hot food and drink. She's refusing to go to the hospital, so you can do what needs to be done here. We've got a full stock of drugs up here — ibuprofen, paracetamol, antibiotics, you name it. She's a doctor, she'll know what she should be taking. I gotta go."

Metal was quivering to get going. It was a tossup who was suffering more from Felicity's pregnancy woes — Felicity herself or Metal. He was aging by the day.

In a second he was gone, heading like an arrow down the mountain to Felicity. They'd been planning a wedding but Felicity refused to organize a wedding where she might throw up. "Very uncool," she'd said.

Matt had to agree.

He checked on the bedroom. Honor was sleeping deeply. Who knew how long she'd been kept prisoner? If they were interrogating her, sleep deprivation was a favorite, hugely popular with the kind of people who'd torment a woman. And she'd nearly drowned after being caught in rapids so she'd need to rest anyway.

Let her sleep, he thought. He pulled some food out

of the huge stocks in the deep freezer, prepared another thermos of tea then couldn't stand it any longer. He walked into her room, sat down and took her hand in his.

It immediately soothed him. She was safe here, of course. But she was particularly safe while he was by her side, holding her hand. He had his favorite Glock 19 in a hip holster and his usual Kershaw knife in his boot. He'd checked the perimeter sensors, put the entire system on high alert.

If a fly farted, the sensors would pick it up and he could shoot it out of the air.

Nothing was going to happen to this woman. Nothing.

He settled back in the small armchair he'd pulled next to the bed and sat vigil.

Three

Lee Chamness attached his prosthetic nose, put flesh-colored spacers behind his ears making them stick out, applied special tape to the corners of his eyes to change the shape, put a device in his mouth that altered his jaw-line and put in dark contact lenses. Slid a rubber pregnant belly found in a theatrical props store under his sweater so he looked like he had a pot belly. Those were the basics, what he'd been doing off and on for six months in this Australian city in the back of beyond to establish his identity.

There were lots of things that could be done to defeat facial recognition. Tiny LED lights in the visor of a baseball cap. If he wanted to go full punk, he could have applied CV dazzle makeup that made you look like a member of KISS. Used Hyperface, a scarf made in a special digitalized pattern that mimicked human faces and threw off the algorithms.

47

But as it happened, he wanted to be recognized in *this* persona. An Australian who often travelled to the States. A really unattractive Australian. He looked at himself in the mirror and liked the nerdy image he saw.

Voilà! Ladies and gentlemen, I present to you Martin Stewart, homely mild-mannered accountant who has never, ever been laid.

It amused him to become Martin, to slip through life unseen and unwanted. Ah, one further thing. He slipped out of his Ferragamo loafers and put on a bespoke pair of remarkably ugly running shoes. The sole of the right shoe was invisibly lifted half an inch and there were foam spikes in the instep of the left shoe, giving him an ungainly gait.

He'd tested the set up, running video footage of himself through a mirrored copy of the CIA's facial and gait recognition system, which as far as he knew was the most powerful in the world. First, he'd paid very good money to a hacker in Bangkok to wipe his data from the CIA data banks.

Zip. The facial recog system gave the cyber equivalent of a shrug.

He knew his gait had been in the system, as was the gait of about seven million people, and that too came up blank, wiped. Only Martin came up in another database, Homeland Security. Martin Stewart, the poor schlub accountant, who travelled often to the US.

Martin had a deep legend. He'd been born in Hobart, Tasmania and now lived in Perth, where he ran a small one-man accountancy business. The business was registered, paid its taxes, the office was a room in a flat he owned and the phone was answered by someone in India. The credit cards made out in the name of Martin Stewart were genuine and had records of low-level spending.

His passport was genuine, too.

It had to be.

Little-known fact. Australian passports were the most secure, hardest-to-forge passports in the world, with floating images of kangaroos and the intaglio on the inside cover made of five colors instead of the usual two. Consequently, border officials stamped Australian passports without a second glance.

Chamness had gotten his real passport using his fake identity many, many years ago, in his early days with the CIA, deepening his identity with each iteration of the passport, building up his legend. He even did a very credible Australian accent. He had done it as insurance and now he was cashing in on the policy.

He had to work hard not to get overconfident and sloppy because when he travelled as Martin, he felt invisible. Like one of those superhero movies where the superpower was being able to pass through crowds unnoticed.

When he arrived in LA he would ditch Martin Stewart, like Clark Kent ditching the glasses and the suit. Until he had to fly out again, which he would, as Martin. No record at all of Lee Chamness flying into or out of the US.

He would fly out fifty million dollars richer, though.

He would fly to Mexico City and then to Sydney, then on a German passport via a private jet to Bali, just another sex tourist. And then on his yacht to his own private island, where he would live under the radar in luxury forever.

The hardest thing about this was flying coach. Insignificant, frumpy, overweight Martin would stand out like a sore thumb in business.

When this was over, he would not only never fly coach again, he'd never fly commercial again.

He was a week from becoming insanely rich but for now he was still modest, unassuming Martin Stewart. He even took a bus to Perth International Airport. This one last time.

When they called his flight, he boarded, turning right for coach for the last time in his life, looking with dismay at the crowded seats of ugly, fat people up ahead. The back of the plane already smelled of suet and sweat and cheap perfume.

He shuddered. Never again, never ever again.

The Grange
June 14

She was used to waking up quickly, fully alert. She knew this about herself, without quite knowing why.

But this was different. It was like being underwater, swimming toward the surface far above but weighed down by chains.

She'd swim up, seeing light ripple on the surface, up where there was light and air, only to sink again under the weight of steel. Desperately trying to rise, being brutally yanked down.

Up toward the light, that's where she wanted to be, needed to be, but it wasn't working.

A hand reached down, broad and strong, and took hers, towing her gently up. She broke the surface on a gasp, disoriented.

"Good morning, Honor," a deep, low voice said. "Are you feeling better?"

She wanted to panic. In unfamiliar surroundings with an unknown man sitting next to her, holding her hand. Her heart pounded. The last thing she remembered was escaping from 'them', trying to run but stumbling because she'd been pumped full of ...

What?

But that had been some time ago. A few ... days ago. Hadn't it?

This room, unfamiliar, yet — she'd been here before. She'd slept and woken up. Hadn't she? And this man, this stranger, he wasn't a stranger. She remembered —

"You saved my life." It wasn't a memory so much as knowledge. She'd been running, then drowning and then she was safe.

He was a big man, tall even sitting down, broad

shoulders extending beyond the chair back. Shaggy dark hair almost touching his collar. Dressed in black — black long-sleeved tee, black jeans, black boots. Hard face.

She'd been held prisoner by men who had that look. She didn't remember them individually but she remembered being their prisoner. She'd observed them carefully — the memory of that was coming back. They'd been cruel and vicious, almost inhuman.

Their body language had revealed who they were. They'd ogled her, eyes lingering on her breasts and crotch, sexualizing her captivity. Restless, fingers twitching, jaws clenching and unclenching, eyes constantly roving.

This man was the opposite. He sat calmly, unmoving, dark eyes fixed on hers. Absolutely nothing like her jailers.

He moved his torso forward, slowly, resting one elbow on one knee, one hand still holding hers.

"Are you starting to remember what happened? How you came to be in the river?"

Honor closed her eyes, a blinding headache building behind them. Spikes of jagged pain dug deep inside her head. Since when did thinking hurt? All she saw were flashes. The cruel men, being chained up, escaping … how did she escape?

Her head hurt so much. There was a mewling sound. She looked around wildly. There was only Matt in the room, face grave, dark eyes sad. That horrible sound … it came from her mouth. She sounded like a wounded animal.

"Never mind." Matt gently squeezed her hand then withdrew it. "I have some hot food, excellent food actually. We have a lot of it here. All prepared by Isabel Harris."

That name … she blinked. "Isabel Delvaux-Harris … the food blogger?"

He nodded. "The very same. She experiments up here, holds courses up here. So basically anything you might want, we probably have. I can nuke whatever you want. The only thing I personally can make for you is some more hot tea. Do you want to get up or do you want me to bring it in on a tray?"

"Get up." Oh God, yes. Stand straight, walk to food prepared by Isabel Harris's hands! Most people would walk over hot coals barefoot to eat something cooked by her. She swung her legs over, tried to stand. Her knees shook, legs shook.

Standing, the easiest thing in the world until you couldn't do it.

He caught her by her arms before she could fall.

"Easy there, Honor. Let me bring you a tray. Maybe tonight you can eat dinner at the table."

Tonight. "What time is it?"

"Noon. You'll be hungry because you slept past breakfast time. I didn't have the heart to wake you up. Dinner will be any time you want it."

Time, the concept of time, rushed back in. She'd been here days. She met his eyes. "I escaped."

"Yeah. Got that. You must have been very smart

and very brave. You were shackled. I've seen the signs of that before. Getting away must have been hard."

She looked at her wrists and registered the bruises, the chafing. She held her hands up, the memory of weights on them rising up in her head. She'd been shackled … to a wall. The memories rushed in a crowded jumble. "You're right," she said slowly, shaking her head to get rid of the cobwebs, though it didn't help. "So hard to think."

It was horrible, not being able to think straight. It made her feel unmoored from the world.

He put a hand over hers again and she was astonished at the comfort it gave. His dark hand was strong yet gentle and it felt like just a little of his strength passed from his hand to hers.

"Don't push it. You were drugged. You have signs of an IV. Metal took a blood sample and should be getting results soon. Today, probably."

"I remember." She stretched out her arm, looked at the crook of it. The information was there, right in her head. "Judging from the size of the hole, it was a cannula. Which means an infusion of whatever I was given, over hours or possibly days. No wonder I can't think straight."

Matt rose and for a second she panicked. His presence was immensely reassuring, like having a guard wolf looking out for you. A few more clouds cleared away, and there was the memory of him swimming strongly against a river in full spate to carry her to safety. "Are you going?" she tried to keep the panic out of her voice.

"Just to get you something hot to eat and to drink. It will do you good."

It would. She knew that. Knew it with her heart and her head. Knew precisely that a person who'd skirted hypothermia needed warmth, hot nourishment, bed rest, all things this man was offering.

But ... she also didn't want him to go. The room she was in was beautiful but large and with shadowy corners. Nothing at all was familiar. Something was wrong with her head, she kept catching at thoughts and memories and they slid away, like trying to catch fog with your hands. The one thing she could catch, hold onto, was this big man who'd saved her life.

Holding on to his hand felt like holding on to a life-line.

Something in her told her she wasn't a needy woman but right now she'd do anything to keep him right here, anchoring her shadowy world.

He seemed to understand. How could that be? But he was just standing by the side of her bed, her hand clutching his, patiently waiting.

She was brave, strong. Wasn't she?

She let go of his hand and he stepped away. "I'll be right back," he said and she nodded, clutching the duvet tightly to keep from calling him back when he walked out the door.

Panic. Her heart raced, breathing fast and shallow, prickling under the skin. Classic signs of overwhelming fear which she didn't recognize as a normal response from her body. She didn't panic, ever. Except, right now, she was panicking.

Her job — then the thought vanished. But she'd had glimpses of her job — fast-paced and dangerous, requiring steely nerves. What was her job?

Fog.

I am self sufficient, she thought. *Not dependent on anybody. I don't need anyone to keep me safe.*

She repeated those words over and over and felt slightly better, but her whole body gave a surge of joy when Matt walked through the door carrying a big tray.

The sound of her breath whooshing out in a relieved sigh was loud in the quiet of the room. She was appalled at herself but it didn't make her relief any less strong.

He walked to her bedside, pulled down two flaps, turning it into a bedtray, shook out a big cotton napkin and placed it on her lap.

"Okay." There was a crease in that dark, rough face that might have been a smile. "Here's what we have. I just pulled some stuff out of the freezer but if there's anything you don't like, I can find other stuff. There's actually a list in the central computer, organized by categories and ingredients. So far I've fed you soup and bread and you've seemed okay with that. But if there's anything else you want, we probably have it."

"Wow." She didn't remember much about herself but she remembered she was pretty useless in the kitchen.

"Yeah, Isabel is pretty thorough. And we have an OCD gear guy, Jacko, who has taken it upon himself to prepare this place for the zombie apocalypse or a virus that kills 80% of humankind, take your pick. So he has started listing survival stocks, and that includes food."

"Pretty useful when civilization collapses," she murmured. "Which it will, any day now."

"Totally," he agreed and that dent in his cheek grew larger. "So, back to us. I chose, as you can see, to nuke a bowl of white bean soup and I heated up a small loaf of whole wheat bread. Sort of boring choices but I didn't know what your stomach could handle."

Her stomach chose that moment to growl loudly.

"Well, I think we got a vote of approval." The crease in his cheeks deepened even further.

The smells coming from the tray were divine. "I feel like I haven't eaten in days."

"Maybe you hadn't before I fished you out of the river." The smile completely dropped from his face and his voice was deep and serious. "You were held a prisoner. You were certainly shackled and drugged. People who can do that aren't usually good hosts." He looked her deeply in the eyes. "Are you starting to remember anything?"

She considered. "Not much. Just a few flashes, and more about my life than the last couple of days. Or weeks. Or … months?"

Matt shook his head. "If you'd been a prisoner for months I think you would have been in worse shape than you are. There would have been some muscle atrophy. I wonder what they gave you."

"Could be any number of drugs," she said, bringing

the bowl closer, picking up the spoon. "Midozolam, Thiopental. Ondansetron, with different stable target concentrations. There's a whole pharmacopeia of drugs that can induce compliance and memory loss." She put the spoon in her mouth and nearly sighed with pleasure. God, it was good. Earthy and dense and flavorful. She looked back up at him. "What?"

"I don't know many people who could guess at a drug regimen. You have specialized knowledge." He squinted at her. "Ring any bells?"

She blinked. "Some. I guess." The information had been right there, at her fingertips.

"Eat now," he ordered. "We'll talk about it when you've got something warm and nutritious in your stomach." It was a command, couched in reasonable terms. Since it was reasonable, she dug in.

"Delicious," she said after a few spoonfuls.

He nodded his head. "It's got bacon. Anything with bacon is good."

She frowned and poked with her spoon. "I think it's pancetta."

"Huh. Something else about you. You're a foodie."

She finished the soup, mopping up with several bites of the amazing bread.

"There's more," he offered and she consulted her stomach.

"I think that's about all my system can handle now." She reached for the steaming cup he'd put on the tray and sipped. "Mm. Lady Grey, my favorite."

He cracked a smile or as much of a smile as that

craggy face could manage. "The tea shelves are stocked better than the bar. Full of different types of tea, including Lady Grey, which I'm told is good."

"Delicious."

"I'll take your word for it. I'm a coffee and beer man myself. So." He leaned forward, elbows on knees, big hands dangling. "Metal and I did some research. Please don't think we were invading your privacy but I think it's important to know who you are to figure out who might be after you."

"Well, unless I somehow turn out to be a serial killer or an arms merchant or a politician, I can't fault your reasoning. Did you guys find out who I am?"

He dipped his head. "We did, with the able help of Metal's fiancée. You're Honor Thomas. Dr. Honor Thomas. I was hoping you'd remember on your own when you were talking about the drugs you might have been given. You work in the emergency department of Eastern Memorial Hospital. Does that sound right? "

Some of the words reverberated in her. Some not. She stared at him, trying to order her thoughts and feelings. "It … does. But it feels like a faraway world." Images of a busy hospital filled her head, moving fast, blood and adrenaline. She frowned. "How can I not remember clearly my own life?"

"You might have been drugged for days. Be thankful they didn't zap your medical degree right out of your head."

"Right now I'm glad I don't have to practice medicine. My whole brain is a fog." Please God, let there not be permanent damage.

He held up two long fingers. "How many fingers?"

She smiled. "Three."

He smiled back. He was … attractive when he smiled. It was a rough, tough face with harsh angles, a tight mouth, unused to smiling. But when he did smile, you could see that his features were clean and regular.

He took her hand, the forefinger crossing her wrist. What he thought of as a discreet way of taking her pulse.

Did he have the wrong woman. She knew all the ways to check a patient out without seeming to do so.

She was feeling much better, though. How many days had she been here? Two days? No, three, counting the day he'd saved her life . But that day was almost lost to her. All she remembered was terror and ice.

"How are you feeling?" His voice was soft.

"I think you've asked me a gazillion times now."

The smile deepened the creases in his stubbled-covered cheeks. "Gazillion and one. How are you feeling?" He was trying to keep it light but his eyes searched hers keenly.

He didn't need to watch her so carefully. She was on the mend. Her mind was still a foggy swamp and it hurt her head to try to remember the past, but some strength was returning. Maybe.

"Better," she answered and then a huge yawn overtook her, enormous and irresistible.

"Okay, Wonder Woman. Instead of sending you out to plow the back forty, maybe you should take a little nap."

"No, no." Another yawn. Her stomach was warm and full and she was warm all over. Her eyes closed, opened, then closed again. She just needed to rest her eyes, just a moment.

Somehow, Honor found herself sliding back down in bed, covers tucked under her chin as if she were a child. She wasn't a child. She didn't need to be tucked in, even if … even if it was a nice feeling.

The next second she went out like a light.

Matt watched her sleep and held her hand because it made him feel better. He stared at her wrists, trying to keep his breathing under control. It was hard because rage filled him every time he saw her wrists.

She'd bled, trying to get out of the shackles. The skin near her hand and further up her forearm, where the iron band had rubbed, was broken and scabbed, signs she'd bled, scabbed over, broken the skin again. It was a cycle he'd seen before, in the young kids he'd rescued back in the 'Stan. They'd chafed against the irons, too. It had broken his heart then and it broke his heart now.

The kids had been shackled to the wall in a broken country where humans had devolved and become little more than wild animals in feral packs called tribes. But

Honor had been held *here*, in this country.

From the little she'd said, her captors weren't far from here. The fuckers had held a shackled woman here, in these United States.

Matt had fought and bled and almost died to keep that kind of barbarity away from his country. And he would fight and bleed to make sure whoever had done this would be caught and punished.

He'd lost a lot of faith in institutions in the past year. He'd been betrayed and punished by corrupt men who worked for his government. But he had absolute faith that he could bring this to the attention of the Portland PD and they wouldn't stop until they brought those fuckers to justice. Portland PD might have its share of fallible men and women but the commissioner, Bud Morrison, was the kind of man who wouldn't let anyone in his command slacken. Bud couldn't be bought, coerced or threatened. If Honor had been held a prisoner anywhere within the Portland police jurisdiction, Bud wouldn't rest until he had her captors behind bars.

One of Bud's best detectives was a former Ranger. Matt had cross-trained with him. He'd joined the Portland Police Department and was, according to Bud, the best cop in the building and a hell of an investigator. Luke Reynolds. If anyone could figure out where Honor had been held, Luke was the guy. And he'd be backed a thousand percent by Bud.

Luke had had problems lately. He'd resigned his position with Portland PD effective the end of the month, after which he was joining ASI. But for the moment he was still a sworn police officer and even afterward, he'd keep working the case since ASI was involved.

Bud and Luke hated bad guys as much as Matt did and they were as relentless as Matt was. Once the men who'd kept Honor a prisoner were caught, they were going down.

So Honor was safe now, and whoever did this to her was going to jail. If it were up to Matt, they'd be going six feet underground.

Still, it gave him comfort to hold her hand.

He studied her face. She was just so beautiful — perfect straight nose, high cheekbones, full lips — even with those pale gray cat eyes closed. There was color back in her face. She'd looked dead when he'd fished her out of the water. He'd seen more than his share of dead bodies and she'd been close enough to death to scare the hell out of him.

He'd pulled her back to life at the very last moment. Remembering that icy white cast to her skin, the utter stillness, that horrible moment when he thought he'd lost her.

He'd watched so many teammates die, some fast, some slow. All badly, because strong healthy young men do not die easy. They fight for life with every fiber of their being.

She'd fought, too. The scars on her wrists proved that. The fact that she'd escaped despite being drugged proved that.

The lines of her beautiful face showed character and determination. This was a woman who'd fight.

Now she was wounded, battered, and didn't have much fight left in her.

No matter, he'd fight for her. He'd stand for her. She wasn't alone.

Matt had no idea when he'd vowed to keep her safe. Maybe when he'd fished her out of the water. Maybe when he discovered she'd been making her way to him.

Didn't matter. She was now under his protection and under the protection of ASI and its operatives. That was how ASI rolled. Matt was one of them, though he hadn't actually started working, and what was important to him was important to them.

ASI was a formidable enemy. Collectively, they had brains and strength and courage. And money and enough gear to start a small war. Some operatives had had private wars going and ASI had always prevailed — against mobsters and criminals and even the head of the CDC. Nick Mancino had helped take down the head of the CDC recently. A man who'd gone rogue and used a deadly bioweapon to make himself rich.

Well, Nick had provided the muscle in taking the man down. His fiancée, Kay Hudson, had provided the brain power. Matt remembered expediting their escape from the Grange, part of which had been blown up by a bomb dropped from a drone. Matt had gotten them out and the entirety of ASI had been mobilized to help Nick and Kay as they went on the hunt.

Matt knew, absolutely, that he would be able to count on ASI and all its assets to protect this woman.

A soft buzz, barely audible. He'd put his cell on

vibrate so it wouldn't wake her up. Matt brought it out and thumbed it on one-handed. A text message from Metal.

Hey bro. Took the sample to a guy I know who owes me a favor or two and expedited the analysis. Our friend was injected with a low dosage of a ketamine-diazepam compound. Ketamine is what they use to fell horses. My guy says that higher doses of ketamine would have been enough to permanently impair her neurologically. He says that he thinks she was injected over the course of days. So whoever held her wasn't trying to get intel out of her, just kept her sedated. Over days. Just the thought makes me mad as fuck.

Matt looked up, stared at the wall, trying to keep his breathing under control. God damn! The picture he got in his head wasn't pretty.

My lab rat says there might be retrograde amnesia, she might have lost her memory of a period before the drugs. So try to find out what her last memory was and work from there.

Matt switched his gaze from his cell to the sleeping woman. So days — maybe weeks — had been wiped from her mind. It was a pharmacological way of wiping their tracks. Yet they hadn't killed her.

Why not?

He looked back at the screen of his cell. Felicity had taken over from Metal, only live. She was concentrated, focused, unsmiling. He held up a finger to the camera. *Wait.* Then got up and walked out of the room.

"Hey Felicity," he said once he was out in the hallway.

"Hey, big guy. I did some digging into Dr. Honor Thomas. She has a top notch reputation at Eastern Memorial, citations up the wazoo, was offered a more administrative job which was considered a promotion with a big raise but turned it down. Likes doctoring. She hasn't been at work since the 6th. You rescued her on the 12th. Six days. She was in the hands of a bad guy or bad guys for six days. Not a happy thought."

He blew out a breath. "No, not a happy thought. Anything else?" Though, being Felicity, of course there was something else.

"Yes. I did some social engineering and got her cell number but it's not traceable. Probably the battery was taken out. Last known location was on her street, just outside her door. Her building has security cameras. The last time she was recorded was the morning of the 6th. She drives a late model Prius, green. Current whereabouts unknown. I got from cameras that she usually takes a bus into work, it's on the direct bus line. On the evening of the 6th, she sent an email to her boss saying an emergency had come up and she had to take temporary leave. The email address is hers but not the IP address. The IP address of where that email originated is registered to someone called Hailey Bosnick, who doesn't exist. Just a ghost, untraceable."

She frowned even harder. Matt could read extreme frustration in her voice. Not much was untraceable for Felicity.

"Dead end," he said.

"Yeah, but there's hope. So, here's the kick. Suzanne came in and heard the name of Dr. Honor Thomas and got really agitated."

Suzanne was Suzanne Huntington, the wife of one of the Big Bosses, John Huntington, aka Midnight Man.

"She knows Honor Thomas?"

"In a way. Turns out Dr. Thomas saved the life of Suzanne's father when he was here on a visit six months ago. Professor Barron was having a heart attack but it was misdiagnosed as a stroke. She intervened and saved his life. You were still OUTCONUS. Once Suzanne realized Dr. Thomas was in trouble she made John and the Senior promise they'd do everything in their power to help." She gave a faint smile. "You know John —"

Matt did. John Huntington was one tough, hard son of a bitch who was completely enamored of his wife. Anything Suzanne wanted she got. Excellent. If ASI had a *personal* stake in protecting Honor, Matt's job was going to be so much easier. They would have helped anyway, but now ...

Felicity nodded. "So, right now finding out what happened to Dr. Thomas is Priority Number One. You've got us all here, Matt. Engines revving. Waiting to help."

"Does she have family?" God. Parents, worried sick.

Maybe … a husband? No, Felicity had said she was single. But she could be co-habiting. He swallowed. If she had a partner, he'd be crazy with worry.

Felicity turned and typed rapidly on another laptop. She had five of them. All going at once. Matt had no idea how she kept track.

She read off the screen, face turned slightly away. "A very small family. No siblings. Mother deceased. Father still alive. So basically just her father."

"Partner?"

More fast typing. "Nope. Doesn't look like it. From the videocams, she goes to work and comes home alone."

Matt let out a breath he hadn't realized he'd been holding. "So she has a father. Has he reported her missing?"

"First thing we checked. No missing person report. So maybe her father doesn't know she's missing because they are not in contact that much."

"Should I ask her when she's feeling better?"

"Mmm," Felicity said and Matt heard the soft patter of her fingers on the keyboard. It was amazing. Her fingers were always a blur. Apparently she'd written herself a little software patch that allowed her to type in what was essentially shorthand but came out in proper English. She typed as quickly as she thought and she was a fast thinker. "Wow. Looking at her cellphone records, she speaks to her father, Simon Thomas, a couple of times a week. For at least twenty minutes a time. Except for the past month. No phone calls this past month."

Matt knew husbands in the field who didn't speak to their wives and kids that often. "That sounds pretty close. Seems weird the calls suddenly stopped." He frowned. "Where does the dad live? What does he do?"

"He lives in Los Angeles where he owns and runs a small but successful shipping company. Quest Line Shipping. It's specialized in delicate or out-of-gauge cargo that requires special care — art works, endangered animals, sensitive electronics, delicate medical machinery, that kind of thing. Quest Line Shipping has an office here in Portland, for no reason I can discern other than the fact that Simon Thomas's daughter lives here."

"So the dad hasn't noticed his daughter is missing?"

"Hmmm." More light clacking. "The guy himself might be missing."

An electric jolt ran down Matt's spine. He sat up, electrified. "What?"

Felicity frowned on the screen. Metal walked up and put a hand on her shoulder. It looked like a catcher's mitt and covered her shoulder from neck to arm. She looked up at him, flashed a smile, then looked back at her screen with a frown.

"I don't have any trace of him in public over the last ten days."

Matt thought about that. "Is he in the news often?"

More clacking. "Not often, no. But enough. Let me try something." She frowned even more fiercely and Metal lifted his eyes from her to frown fiercely in turn at Matt through the screen. It didn't mean anything. If it were up to Metal, Felicity would spend her pregnancy sitting on ten cushions with her feet up. She was devoted to work, though, and everyone admired that about her. Metal admired that too, but she was having a difficult pregnancy and tended to barf a lot. She suffered from hyperemesis gravidarum, which Metal explained meant a pregnancy where you barfed a lot.

Matt was sort of sorry she was working so hard for him, but sort of not. First of all, if the big boss himself — the Midnight Man — had made Dr. Honor Thomas a priority Felicity would knock herself out and there was no stopping her. And once she had her teeth in something she was hardwired to not let go.

And Matt wanted answers, right now.

"Okay." Felicity straightened up in her chair. Her left hand disappeared and Matt was sure she had it curled around her belly. She was starting to show and she had a cute little baby bump. "I hacked into Quest Line Shipping's offices. They have a decent security cameras system, pretty thorough coverage. I took Thomas's photo from the company brochure and ran it through their surveillance system."

Matt blinked. "Well. That was smart."

Metal looked exasperated, rolled his eyes. Of course it was smart. This was Felicity.

Felicity didn't even notice the compliment. "So basically Simon Thomas hasn't been seen since the 2nd of June."

"Several days before Honor — Dr. Thomas — last reported in to work."

Felicity nodded, not having noticed Matt's use of

her first name. But Metal noticed. He stared sharply at the screen and Matt felt, uncomfortably, like Metal was walking around inside his head. Metal looked a bit like a Neanderthal but he wasn't, not by a long shot.

Felicity talked without taking her eyes off her screen. "But — here's the interesting thing. He's been carrying out company business all this time."

"Any biometric data required?" Matt asked.

"Yeah." She smiled smugly. "Just like us."

ASI passes included fingerprints, retina scans and DNA. Though generally speaking, the passes themselves were enough, unless the company was in lockdown, DEFCON 1.

"His cell?"

"In the office. Hasn't moved since the 2nd. Wherever he is, he doesn't have his cell with him. Doesn't mean he doesn't have a cell, though. I hacked into his personal computer and he hasn't sent any personal emails since the 2nd. And he hasn't been in his home since the 2nd. Home camera footage only shows the gardener coming once and a housekeeper every other day. But not him. He's not on a trip because the company system clocks him as using biometric data. He's just disappeared off the face of the earth except for carrying out business dealings."

"So, in essence, we have two family members a thousand miles apart who just dropped off the face of the earth."

"Looks like it."

"But one of them was a prisoner, kept shackled and

drugged."

Felicity lifted her head and looked straight at her monitor, staring straight at him. "Which means the dad could have been held a prisoner too, all this time."

Matt sighed. "Or on vacation in Maui with the girl-friend du jour, guiding the business via intranet."

"No, he logged into his business computers. Right there in Los Angeles. And anyway, he's a widower. Been one since 2011, so he'd have every right to have that girlfriend du jour."

She shrugged, then turned pale as ash and bolted. Matt watched in the monitor as she crossed the great room, her ergonomic chair still spinning.

"Barf time?" he asked Metal.

"Barf time," Metal answered glumly. "Gotta go, man."

"Will be in touch," Matt said and closed the connection.

He checked his wristwatch, which was a compass, a calculator, a stop watch and a tachymeter, had a garotte in the wristband and could blow up a door. It also told the time really well.

Six pm. Time for dinner.

Four

She was half awake when he came back. Something had woken her up and in the silent room she couldn't figure out what it was until the man walked through the door carrying a tray.

Matt. Matt Walker. The man who'd saved her life.

He hadn't been holding her hand and her subconscious had missed that and had woken her up.

"You need some food," he said forcefully, as if she were going to object. Objecting was the furthest thing from her mind. She was ravenous.

He set the tray on the bedside table and helped her sit up, placing the pillows at her back. Honor wanted to tell him she could sit up on her own but it turned out she couldn't, not gracefully. She was pushing feebly with her hands, astonished at her weakness, when he gently caught her under the arms and lifted her until she was sitting against the pillows.

"Thanks," she gasped.

He nodded and picked up the tray, pulling down two flaps at the sides making a bed table. A huge cotton napkin was snapped open and placed on her lap.

He'd done this before, she suddenly remembered. She'd eaten quite a few meals here.

"Everything smells amazing." She eyed the tray and its contents. What smelled like mushroom soup, garlic bread, a small slice of lasagna and — oh God. Was that chocolate mousse?

He smiled faintly. "It should. Everything we have here was cooked by Isabel Harris and frozen. Like I told you. But I'll have you know I am a master nuker, which was my contribution."

Déjà vu. She'd been told this before. Memories were coming back. She paused, soup spoon in hand. "So just to be clear, *everything* I eat here is by Isabel Harris? And you've already told me this?"

"Yep. And yep." He dipped his head in a nod. "Nothing but the finest for you. By the way, I've been given direct orders to treat you like royalty."

Honor frowned. "By whom?"

"By my boss's wife, Suzanne Huntington." He nudged the soup bowl closer to her. "Eat or she'll have my hide. She'd be a scary lady if she weren't so nice."

Honor put the spoon in her mouth and nearly sighed. It was divine. "That's really nice but I don't know a Suzanne Huntington."

"Maybe not by that name. Her maiden name was Suzanne Barron."

"I don't know anyone by that name, either." She frowned. "I don't think I do, anyway."

"You treated her father, a retired professor of

French who was up from Baja California to visit his daughter. Was rushed to the ER. Everyone thought he'd had a stroke but you diagnosed a heart attack and you were right."

Handsome elderly gentleman, very tanned. With diffuse severe pain. Two very beautiful women who were worried sick, mother and daughter.

Matt nudged the garlic bread closer to her hand. "You saved his life. A doctor wanted to treat him for stroke."

She remembered perfectly now. "Strokes and heart attacks sometimes mimic each other. But the treatments are completely different. So the daughter is Suzanne ... Huntington?"

The younger woman had been charming, immensely grateful. Honor had come home the next day to a bouquet of flowers nearly as big as her refrigerator. Suzanne Huntington had invited her out to dinner but work had gotten in the way. They liked each other but they could never get together. When she could, Suzanne couldn't and when Suzanne could, she couldn't.

"That's right. Who is eternally grateful because you saved her father's life. Her husband, my boss, is under strict orders to help you any way he can. Our company has vast resources. They're at your disposal." He bowed his head, like an old-fashioned knight. "As am I."

Wow. "Uh, thanks." She looked him over carefully. He was so formidable, even sitting down. He had an aura of strength and determination built into every line of his body, every line on his face. Her memories were much clearer now. She remembered him battling a raging river, crossing over from one bank to another with her in tow. The river's strength had been terrifying but his strength had been equal to it. She was alive thanks to him.

He bent forward, elbows on knees and without even thinking about it, without realizing she wanted to do it before she'd done it, she held out her hand, palm up. He didn't hesitate, folding his much bigger and stronger hand around hers.

Something tense deep in her bones loosened its iron grip. Something bad had happened to her. The most terrifying thing was that she had no idea what. She'd been attacked, drugged up and she had no idea why. But just the fact that he was holding her hand, somehow transferring heat and strength to her, made things a little better. She could breathe.

He leaned forward a little more and clasped his other hand over the back of her hand, encasing it in a warm strong grasp.

"Can you tell me the last thing you remember?"

Honor blinked. Huh. The last thing she remembered. There was a fuzzy buzzing aura where her memory should be. "The last thing I clearly remember is canceling my talk at an international symposium in Athens because Vesuvius blew up and there was a heavy stream of dense particulate ash over the Mediterranean. My flight was canceled." She was watching his eyes and saw a reaction. "What?"

"Vesuvius blew up two weeks ago. The eruption is

over and flights have resumed their normal schedules."

Oh, man. A deep throb started up in her head. "It feels like just a few days ago. The day before you fished me out of the water. Quite literally." Two weeks had been blasted right out of her head.

"Yep," he said, his voice deep and steady. "That was the 1st of June. It is now the 14th of June. So here's the deal." He leaned forward, so close she could feel his body heat. "A compound of ketamine and diazepam was found in your bloodstream when you arrived. The amount of ketamine found in your system was consistent with you being dosed continuously for six days. Metal says that there would be retrograde amnesia. Do you remember anything at all about being taken prisoner?"

Honor delved deep inside, looking, looking. "No. I remember placing the call to the secretariat in Athens and they said the entire conference was canceled and that they would reschedule in the fall. And they asked me to be back on the program."

"Where were you when you placed that call?"

"In my office. In the hospital," she said promptly. Didn't even need to think about it. She remembered the slight squeak of her office chair. For weeks now she'd been promising herself to bring some lubricating oil to her office. She remembered the sun streaming in through her window and looking out to see fluffy clouds on the horizon. "I ate a chicken wrap which wasn't very good. Then —" she touched her forehead. What did she do then? It felt like she was worried about something ... someone? She couldn't remember her thoughts, she could barely remember the emotions. Her hand dropped. "Nope. Can't remember. It's like a black hole."

"It'll come to you." His hands tightened on hers.

She sighed. "Maybe. For the moment, my brain feels like the Great Garbage Patch in the Pacific — just flotsam and jetsam."

"I've seen the Great Garbage Patch," he said, muscles working in his jaws. "That's not a nice image."

"But apt." A huge jumble of images, most of which were frightening and jagged and no way of telling what was real and what was not. "Anything could have happened in those six days." Her eyes met his. "Anything."

The muscles in his jaw clenched tightly. She was surprised he didn't crack a tooth. "Metal looked you over. Your wrists were scraped raw from shackles, and you had bruises all over your body but from the looks of them, you got them in the river. They weren't old bruises. Metal and I, we didn't check for ..." His throat clicked. He clearly couldn't say the word.

"Rape? You didn't check for rape?"

He nodded. "I'm sorry. We should have. It just felt like a violation of an unconscious woman. But that's stupid. I should have. We should have —"

"It's okay." She searched his dark eyes and found only sorrow and something else. Shame? She didn't know him at all and yet she felt she somehow did. There was some bond she couldn't articulate but it was definitely there. He had nothing to be ashamed of, though.

God knew there was a lot of shame around rape, mostly felt by the victim. She'd seen a lot of young girls and some young boys come into the ER after a rape, shaking and terrified and ashamed. It never failed to break her heart.

"I've treated a lot of drugged rape victims." She met his eyes. "I've been there when they come around after being dosed with a date rape drug — roofies mainly. Whatever was used, there is a vestigial sense that they were violated. They don't remember it, but they know. Every single time. I've seen it over and over again. But I don't think that's what happened to me. Did you see bruising around my upper thighs?"

He swallowed. "No."

"On my hips?"

"No."

She stretched her arms, legs, winced. "From what I can tell, my bruises are on my shoulders and lower legs. And the bruises are recent. I looked at myself in the mirror. The bruises are reddish because of capillaries broken under the skin. They will turn blue and then yellowish in the next few days. Bruising colors follow a set schedule. And everything is consistent with the bruises being from the river. Not a beating while I was a prisoner and not rape."

"You're right." He looked away then back at her. "I was so upset at the thought of you being beaten while shackled, not to mention being ..." He swallowed. "Raped."

"That thought is pretty horrifying to me, too. But the thing is — it looks like I was kept immobile and drugged but essentially unharmed."

Matt nodded.

"Which of course begs the question — why? Why abduct me, shackle me, drug me, for no reason?"

He nodded. "There's a reason. There has to be. Someone went to a lot of trouble and expense and some risk to abduct you."

"Yeah. Only to keep me essentially unharmed. I checked my tongue and eyes. I was kept hydrated."

"Were you ... interrogated?"

"I don't know. I don't remember anything. I was canceling my trip to Athens and then I was driving down a country road, fell off a cliff and fell into the river. I don't remember too much about that, either."

"You had my name and GPS coordinates written with a felt-tip pen on your upper left arm," he reminded her, his voice even, eyes watching hers carefully.

"I ... yes." She'd been so out of it that the significance of that had eluded her. Until now. Now it was like a giant red arrow had come down from the sky and pointed at Matt. Like some kind of supernatural phenomenon. And she had no idea why.

"You were looking specifically for me and for this place when you ran off the road. Do you know why?"

She looked at him with new eyes. Matt Walker. Probably in his mid-thirties. Lean but very muscular. Dark eyes, dark shaggy hair. Not handsome but compelling. Just him holding her hand reassured her at a bone-deep level.

She'd never seen him before, and yet —

"Do I know you?" The question was stupid, but maybe the drugs had knocked out more of her mind than she knew. Maybe she did know him. Why else would she have escaped and run straight to him?

But if she did, wouldn't he have said something?

"No. Never met you before. Never seen you before."

Well, that was that.

They stared at each other for a full minute.

She cleared her throat, exhausted, baffled. "Why would I run to you?"

"I don't know." His jaw muscles clenched. "But you did. You trusted me to keep you safe and I will."

Every line of his body showed determination and strength. She suddenly knew that he'd spoken those words as an oath. He'd do his very best to keep her safe. She remembered him battling the current to bring her to safety on the other side of the river. His very best was pretty good.

Something deep inside of her relaxed, just a little. Something unfathomable had happened to her. She'd been abducted, kept a prisoner for almost a week. She didn't have any faces, she had no information at all on who those people were or what they wanted. It was almost impossible to guard yourself when you didn't know where the danger was coming from. When you couldn't put a face to it.

But now it appeared that she wasn't alone.

She had Matt Walker. And the company he worked for.

Faces … something about faces.

She rubbed her head.

"What?" Matt asked.

"Nothing." She dropped her hand. "I just —"

"You were remembering something."

"I was?" Her head was such a jumble of images.

"Think back a second. What was going through your head?"

Honor wanted to snap at him. *Nothing* was going through her head. Her mind was chaos, unusually so. She knew enough about herself to know that she was usually clearheaded. Her mind was calm and orderly, except for right now. Now confusion reigned, a jumble of images — the freezing water flowing over her face, the vehicle tumbling down the cliff, the explosion, sounds, voices, faces — no!

"You've remembered something," he said. He'd seen it on her face, maybe felt it in the tightening of her fingers.

"Yes, but it's not helpful."

He leaned a little closer. "Let me be the judge of that."

"I never saw anyone's face. There were a few moments when they came in to drug me, when I had a little clarity. They were wearing …" she couldn't remember the word and gestured at her face with her free hand.

"Masks?"

"Yes, only not Halloween-type masks. The knitted

kind."

"Balaclavas? Ski masks?"

"Yes. Exactly. But they had cold eyes. Not human. Not very helpful, is it?" Of all the things to remember, full-face masks was not helpful. Fatigue swept over her. She had a hole in her memory, a big fat black hole and she might never understand why she'd been abducted.

Matt shook his head. "I don't know. They took you in a very professional way. You were heavily sedated, enough to blow a hole in your memory, but I don't think you are functionally impaired. That can't be easy, can it? I mean, you'd have to have knowledge of dosages and human physiology, right? Maybe even have to calculate body mass and put the injections on a schedule, to keep you under but not kill you."

Honor blinked. "Yeah, I guess. Ketamine is very powerful. They could have killed me with it, even accidentally, but they didn't."

"You were dosed intravenously, both drugs, and I imagine you were fed and hydrated, too. The puncture site wasn't infected. All of that that takes some expertise."

She nodded. It did.

"They kept their faces shielded from you. Which means they intended on keeping you alive. Did they speak in your presence?"

Had they spoken? She closed her eyes, concentrating. She'd only been conscious a few minutes, between dosages. If they'd spoken, said anything at all, she couldn't remember it.

"I don't — I don't think so."

"That might actually be a clue. Maybe they are foreign and if they'd spoken you'd have recognized that."

It made a roundabout sense. To the extent that anything at all made sense.

"Eye color?" he said.

Eye color. The images in her head were so fleeting, colored by terror and the drugs. She shook her head.

"How many were there?"

"Two, that I remember. Both men."

Matt nodded. "White?"

"Yes." She didn't have to think. "They didn't wear latex gloves when switching out the IV bags. I think that shocked me on some level. The skin of their hands was tanned but definitely white. Fair even. One had blond hairs on the backs of his fingers and on his forearms."

"That's helpful. Anything else?"

Her eyes closed and she found it hard to open them again.

"You're exhausted," he said. He sounded angry, but not at her, at himself. "I shouldn't be interrogating you. You need to rest."

"No, no. That's okay. I'm not that —" an unstoppable, massive, jaw-stretching yawn overtook her — "tired."

He didn't quite smile but that dent reappeared in his cheek.

"You might not feel tired, Wonder Woman, but I think you need to rest. Metal was quite clear that you needed what he called a 'washout'."

"Total washout of an amount of ketamine that would keep an adult under for over six days could take months."

"All the more reason to start now." He placed a strong arm around her shoulders and eased her down in the bed.

Sleep was a black blanket falling over her. "You'll stay with me?"

It was suddenly important. She wanted him here. With her. In a world where she'd been snatched and pushed down a black memory hole, he was the one stable element in her universe.

Once she was flat on the bed, he took her hand again. A lifeline, a point of warmth in the cold darkness. "I'll be here," he promised, that deep voice almost a whisper. "Rest now."

As if waiting for permission, now that she had it, she tumbled into a deep sleep.

Five

Simon Thomas didn't know where he was except that he was still in LA. They'd taken him ten times, blind-folded, back to his office to send emails he didn't write and make payments via a fingerprint-protected electronic payment system. No one saw them go in and no one saw them go out.

He was a prisoner, had been one for two weeks, and no one knew it. As far as anyone knew, he was mostly hard at work in his office, sending out orders, making payments, even negotiating new shipping contracts via email.

He was lightly sedated, hooded and taken to his headquarters via a company vehicle, a van with a transponder pass. They removed the hood right outside the private entrance to the company compound. The guards never once questioned his driver.

He couldn't even estimate the distance because of

the sedation. No idea how much time passed between the shot and becoming fully awake in his office. For all he knew, he was being held prisoner a ten minute drive away and the drug was fast acting. Depended on the dosage, he assumed.

Honor would know.

Honor. He had a punch to the heart at the thought of his daughter. Whenever he'd shown signs of even a minor rebellion, he'd be shown photographs of his daughter. Walking into the ER, walking out of her apartment building. Grabbing a coffee at a Starbucks.

They pulled out the big guns when he realized that the captain piloting one of his ships, the *Maria Cristina*, wasn't Captain Larry Knowles, who'd worked for Quest Line Shipping for twenty five years. No, it was someone new, someone Simon had never seen before.

Something terrible was happening. He rebelled.

That evening the monitor in his cell switched on, audio off, to show him his daughter shackled to a wall. She was drugged, too. All the time, not like him, via an IV bag hung from an IV tree. She was motionless, her head dangling between her shoulders, eyes closed. All he saw were her eyelashes, so thick they cast shadows from the harsh overhead light. She used to give him butterfly kisses with her eyelashes on his cheek when she was a little girl.

No butterfly kisses afterwards. He'd given her a really hard time when she wanted to study medicine. What the hell had he built a shipping empire for if not to leave it to his only child? But no —

she wanted to be a doctor. Always had, actually, even as a child. He'd just refused to see what was before his eyes.

By the time she'd graduated high school with a perfect 4.0, and he'd called her in to discuss her going to engineering school, or maybe an MBA, she'd coolly informed him that she'd already applied and been accepted at the Oregon Health and Science University in Portland.

He knew why she'd chosen Portland. The OHSU was an excellent medical school but Portland was also a thousand miles away from Los Angeles. It was far away from LA, but not too far away. With her grades she could have gone anywhere to medical school — even Harvard. But — Honor loved him. Even though he'd been mad at her for not following him in the business, she still loved him.

They'd been fighting this last month. His daughter complained bitterly that he wasn't taking care of himself. So, yes, his cholesterol was high and his blood pressure was high. He'd challenge anyone to run a company like his with all the fluctuating exchange rates and abrupt changes in trade tariffs not to have sky-high blood pressure and all sorts of little bombs going off in his blood.

He'd been thrust unexpectedly into heavy debt. Of course he was neglecting his health as he fought for the survival of his company.

Honor got on his case about his health so often he'd yelled at her. Something he was profoundly sorry about now. Now look at her. A prisoner on a bed, shackled to a wall, and all because of him.

She'd been kidnapped by criminals and kept sedated just to keep him in line, because of him.

His cell door opened and closed. He was in a very comfortable room somewhere but he couldn't leave. So it was essentially a prison cell.

Lee Chamness stepped in. Every muscle in Simon's body clenched. When he'd had a heart attack, they'd put sensors on his chest. If he still had them, they would be going haywire, his heart bouncing around inside his chest, loathing and hatred filling every beat of his heart

"Hello Simon," Chamness said as he pulled out the only chair in the room. He tugged at his sharply creased linen trousers so they wouldn't bag as he sat down.

He was a dandy. A soulless criminal planning what Simon suspected was a massive shipment of heroin into the country, a traitor and a monster. But an elegant one.

Simon remembered clearly the day Chamness first walked into his office. There was trouble in his company. Quest Line Shipping was a boutique enterprise. Simon's ships weren't huge container behemoths. They were smaller, with unusual features. His ships could deal with vulnerable livestock, valuable art works, sensitive chemicals, delicate high-tech machinery. His ships had advanced temperature controls, strong gyroscopes capable of contrasting waves up to hurricane strength, several rooms in the hold were equipped to be clean rooms up to the highest standards. If you had something really valuable to ship, Quest Line Shipping was for you. It was a good, albeit risky business, and Simon loved what he did. Until disaster struck.

At exactly the wrong time, two ships had had devastating fires and the insurance company was suspecting arson. Simon would rather have torn out his own throat than set his ships on fire for the insurance money, but the insurance company wasn't so sure.

He was down over ten million dollars at a very delicate moment and up popped Lee Chamness. He looked and talked like a real man of the world, knowledgeable, savvy, connected. Former CIA. Simon had checked and he was the real deal. Retired now, but someone who truly understood geopolitics. Simon understood shipping and Chamness understood geopolitics and represented a consortium of investors — a match made in heaven.

When Chamness offered ten million to become a sleeping partner, off the books, Simon jumped at the opportunity.

Things went well until, a month ago, Simon questioned anomalies in a ship scheduled to sail from Karachi bound for Los Angeles. The *Maria Cristina.*

And then the sleeping partner woke up and turned into a fire-breathing dragon. With scales and fangs and claws. At first, when he realized Chamness was skirting legality for one shipment, Simon pushed back.

Quest Line Shipping was small, but it had a sterling reputation. It also had an B-43 certificate, a little-known and rare certificate granted to only a few transporters that allowed certain ships facilitated entry into sea ports.

Essentially, Quest Line Shipping operated without the close scrutiny other shippers were forced to undergo.

Eleven million cargo containers entered US waters every year, subject to advanced inspection technology and scans for drugs and WMD. Only a couple of shipping companies were allowed to dock solely on the basis of declared manifests and Quest Line Shipping was one of them. Simon found out too late why Lee Chamness had been willing to give him ten million dollars.

By Simon's reckoning, at least ten times that value in heroin could be on the *Maria Cristina*. Once he'd gathered his data and faced Chamness, Lee had simply laughed and said that yes, there was some heroin, but that was nothing. That something bigger was on the way.

And then four very large men had entered Simon's office and one of them had stuck something in his neck and he'd woken up here, in this cell with, horribly, photographs on the table of Honor going about her daily life. And a few days later, a running video of a drugged Honor shackled to a wall.

It was enough to keep him subdued and obedient on the few occasions when they had to go into his head office, to expedite paperwork only he could sign.

Chamness had disappeared and a Russian had taken his place. The man was thin and wiry and looked like a scholar, with small round glasses, creases in his lean cheeks. An athlete's build. The Russian's English was serviceable but he wasn't a talker like Chamness was. Chamness reveled in his schemes, some deep perversion in him that made him feel he was winning by smuggling drugs and maybe something worse into his own country.

The Russian had no emotions whatsoever. It seemed to be purely business for him.

He would come in, question Simon about security measures, make him send reassuring texts to employees and clients, and sign the documents any CEO needed to sign in an ongoing business . All without a spare word.

And in the background, for about ten minutes every hour, the screen would show Honor, shackled and unconscious.

As if his thoughts had conjured her up, the screen switched on and Simon watched his daughter, heartsick that his own weakness had led to his daughter being restrained and drugged and under threat.

Whatever was coming was big. And he and Honor would not survive it. He knew Chamness and the Russian wouldn't keep him alive. Nor would they keep Honor alive.

She looked half dead as it was.

He watched her drugged sleep. Her eyes were active behind her eyelids. Was she dreaming? About to come out of the drug-induced sleep? She was so beautiful, this daughter of his. So beautiful and smart. He was ashamed that he'd tried to stop her from becoming a doctor. She did so much good in the world. It was what she'd always wanted to do — make a difference.

And he'd wanted her to — what? Make money

shipping things to and fro? How did that compare to saving lives every single day?

What had he been thinking? It was as if he'd had a decade-long fever and now it had broken.

His daughter gave a sharp sigh and moved restlessly in her drugged sleep. For a moment, he saw her index and middle finger crossed. She used to do that often when she was a little girl. Fingers crossed for luck. She'd do that before exams, though she always passed with flying colors.

His eyes teared up as he watched her, crossing her fingers for a moment, leg kicking out briefly in a sleep spasm.

He blinked. Wait a minute. He'd seen that sequence before. Crossed fingers, kicking leg. In a moment she'd turn her head on the pillow … there it was! He was watching footage he'd seen before! They had the video footage on a loop!

The only reason to do that would be if they had no more footage to send because … his mind backpedaled, refusing to accept what that might mean.

No, no, no, no. Honor wasn't dead. They had no reason to kill her yet. She was the reason he was under their control. No. Simon would have felt it if Honor had died. He'd have felt it in his bones and blood. He loved her more than anything else and she just couldn't be dead. He refused to even think it.

Which left — she'd escaped. Yes. That was more like it. Honor was smart and brave and somehow she'd found a way to escape and they were just sending him, on a loop, previously recorded video. Like in that old movie with Sandra Bullock.

He had to believe that or his heart would implode.

The Grange

Matt watched her come up, slowly then fast. Watching her come awake was quickly becoming his second favorite thing. His favorite thing was being with her while she was awake.

He watched her through the phases of REM sleep, then deep sleep, then up. She slept well, a restorative sleep. Her face relaxed, the tension gone and it made her beauty more apparent. He'd kept the cove lighting on at very low so she wouldn't wake up in total darkness and panic, intending to go back to his room when she'd fallen asleep.

But every time he moved, her hand instinctively tightened around his. Something deep inside her didn't want him to go. And to be honest, he didn't want to leave her side either. The armchair was comfortable and he was able to snatch combat sleep in half-hour periods, slumped in the chair, holding her hand. He'd slept under worse conditions. He'd slept in fox holes, he'd slept in a tree, he'd slept on the hard steel floor of a loud C-130.

Holding her hand and watching Honor Thomas sleep sure wasn't a hardship.

Her eyes behind her lids were tracking left to right and back again. Her breathing deepened. Suddenly she opened her eyes and smiled at him. An instinctive smile, recognizing him in an instant. The first time that had happened.

She was back.

"Hi," she said softly.

"Good morning."

"Waking up and seeing you seems to be a habit." Then she frowned and looked around, orienting herself. "There aren't any windows. What time is it?"

Matt pressed a recessed button in the nightstand and the wall to her right suddenly … turned on. No other term for it. The wall was a giant screen and it glowed with sunlight. It was several hours after dawn and the sun had topped the dense trees. "As you can see, a little after eight."

She stared. "Wow."

Yeah. A lot of things about the Grange were wow. Including this. Most of the Grange was underground so many of its rooms had walls that became screens broadcasting a number of outside views.

The room glowed and so did she. He pulled his chair closer and looked her over carefully. He told himself it was to assess how she was feeling and part of it was that. Most of it, though, was that he wanted an excuse to stare at the most beautiful woman he'd ever seen.

Her skin had a rose undertone — smooth and perfect and healthy. He remembered all too well that gray skim milk color she'd had when he fished her out of the river. She'd looked dead.

Her head swiveled back to him, shiny red-brown hair shifting on her shoulders.

"So." Matt tried to judge her dispassionately. The whites of her eyes were clear, her hand in his was soft but above all warm. "How are you feeling?"

"Mm. Let me see." She cricked her neck, stretched arms and legs. Felt her own pulse. "I'm feeling *angry*. I want to find the people who did this to me and turn them into the police after beating them up."

Huh. That was good news. Alarming, but good. But any beating up should be done by him and the other ASI guys. Not her. Her hands looked way too delicate to be beating bad guys up. Not to mention that she saved lives with those hands.

"Well, you're right to be angry. But you have a lot of people on your side now and we'll find them."

"Yeah." She slipped her hand out of his, using both palms to sit up in bed. He missed her hand immediately. His palm felt cold. But she sat up easily and naturally, something she couldn't do before. "How many people do you think are involved? I don't think two people could have pulled it off."

"I don't think so, either. Abducting you, transporting you to wherever it was you were kept, keeping you drugged but fed and hydrated — that takes some organizing."

"Yeah." She placed a hand over her eyebrows to shield her from the light. which would have worked if it had been sunlight, overhead. As it was, it didn't help her at all. Matt reached for another button and dialed it down. She smiled. "Thanks. I think my eyes are adjusting still."

He nodded.

"Neat trick, though," she said. "This whole place feels pretty cool."

She had no idea. "How about I show off our food stocks again? You must be hungry."

She stopped, looked down as if consulting her stomach. "Yes, actually, I am. Ravenous, in fact."

"Good sign." He stood. "I'll bring you a tray."

She shook her head and threw back the covers. "I'm not used to being a patient. I think I'd rather eat at a table." She stood, wobbled slightly.

Matt shot out a hand, held her elbow with one hand, put his other hand on her back. They were embracing, chest to chest. She was looking up at him, pale gray eyes huge.

The world ... disappeared. It had never done that. Matt paid attention to everything around him, always. In combat it had saved his life more than once. And even as a civilian he'd never been able to turn off that cool, detached observation mode.

Well, it was gone now. He had no sense of where he was, he barely had a sense of who he was. Every sense he had was concentrated on her, on this amazing woman. She was watching him so carefully, as if he were about to explode, which wasn't too much off the mark.

Because of all the times for his libido to wake up, now was the worst. She'd just escaped abductors, had nearly died. She was traumatized, shaken, stressed.

His dick did not care. It was not a gentle, understanding organ. He was hard as a rock and he wanted her *now*. He hadn't had sex in — he couldn't remember. But it wasn't sex after a long period of abstinence that he wanted, it was this specific woman, and he wanted her right now with a boner that was painful.

His heart hammered, his skin felt hot and too tight, as if he were about ready to break out of it.

His arms were around her, she was clutching two handfuls of his shirt, those pale eyes locked onto his face.

Please don't let her look down, he prayed to a God he didn't believe in anymore.

Her mouth opened and she gasped, as if there weren't enough oxygen in the room. As if the air had been chased from her lungs.

She needed air? Man, he could give it to her, from his mouth. He bent his head and felt her lift a little on her toes. She was barefoot and he had on his combat boots. What tiny little spark of rationality he had left knocked on his head and reminded him not to crush her feet.

His head lowered, he touched her mouth with his and felt a jolt. He lifted his mouth slightly then kissed her again, opening her mouth with his.

She tasted like wine. The good stuff. How that

could be when she hadn't drunk any wine was beyond him. More or less everything was beyond him except holding her and kissing her. He went slowly, because maybe she didn't want this. But her arms went around his neck and her mouth opened wider under his and yes, she wanted this. Maybe a millionth as much as he wanted it, but still.

There was welcome in her. Her mouth slowly opening under his, her arms around him in a warm embrace, her tongue meeting his. It was almost electric, that moment, a crackle of energy passing between them. So intense he lifted his head. She looked surprised and aroused. Matt had to work to keep breathing normally, to not crush her to him.

What he really wanted was to push her back on the bed, climb on top of her and taste every inch of her, touch everywhere. Strip her fast, open his jeans and Jesus, just slide right into her.

But he couldn't do that. *Take it slow*, he told himself. It was hard. Every muscle was tense with desire, his hands wanting to hold her so tightly he was afraid he'd hurt her. Against her back, he opened his hands so he wouldn't clutch her.

Suddenly, everything had to be coordinated. He had to remember to breathe, to not grab her, to not throw her on the bed.

But another kiss, yeah.

His eyes were closing and so were hers, when they both heard a loud noise, like metal imploding, followed by a rat-tat-tat sound. Which could almost have been gunfire, but wasn't.

Honor's eyes blinked and she fell back down on her heels, looking lost. "What was that? Are people firing guns?" she whispered. Stepping back, she loosened her grip on his shirt. Matt missed her body heat immediately.

On instinct, he took her hand and kissed the palm. He'd wanted to kiss her again and had missed his chance. This would have to do.

But first, he had to reassure her. He didn't often smile, and particularly these past few months there'd been nothing to smile about. He felt like his cheeks would crack when he tried on a smile for her. "No, it's not gunfire. If it had been, I'd have rushed you to our safe room. There was ... an accident a few weeks back and we're rebuilding."

An accident was one way to put it. A drone missile attack was another way. His good buddy Nick Mancino and his woman, Dr. Kay Hudson, had nearly been killed by a drone. But in combat, unlike in horseshoes, close didn't count.

And they'd killed the bastard in the end.

Always a good thing.

She was looking up at him silently. He stared back. She was an eye magnet. Every time he looked at her he noticed something new. Like her eyes. That pale luminous gray with a rim of darker color. They were like spotlights, or tractor beams in old sci-fi movies. And her hair. It wasn't just red. Auburn, a chick would call it. In the bright light of the wall screen, there were a thousand colors in her hair, from pale blonde to dark brown. Her hair was completely natural because there wasn't a hairdresser in the world who could create that color .

There were intelligence and character in that face. She looked young and was. Thirty one was young nowadays, but she also looked seasoned, like she'd seen a lot. He knew what that felt like.

He couldn't tear his eyes from hers.

Whoa.

He'd been staring for a long time. Not cool. And she'd said she was hungry, and here he was, keeping her from food.

Matt stepped back a step because it was either step back or step forward.

"I brought you some clothes to change into ." He waved at the foot of the bed where he'd put some folded clothes. She was about the same size as Summer Delvaux, Jack Delvaux's wife. He'd just blindly pulled out a bunch of stuff so Honor could choose. Thank God Summer was a neat freak, everything was clean and folded and actually arranged according to color. Matt had never seen that before and had sent up a silent blessing to his friend's wife because that color coordination meant he wasn't going to fuck up his choices. He'd picked up things in green which seemed like a color that might suit Honor.

Right on the head because she fingered the pile approvingly. There were several soft pants, tops and a couple of jackets. Socks and underwear. He'd winced picking that stuff out, intending on apologizing to Summer later, though knowing her, helping a woman in distress would absolutely meet with her approval.

Honor stood with the pile of clothes in her hands.

"You're hungry," Matt reminded her.

She nodded.

"So — " he gestured awkwardly. "I'll let you get to it. Do you think you can find your way to the breakfast nook? It's across the great hall, next to a willow tree in a big blue vase."

She nodded again, eyes huge.

"Right." Matt backed away, really really glad that she was watching his eyes and not his groin, because he had a boner that wouldn't quit. He turned and exited the door with a sigh of relief, trying to think of sad things to get his boner down.

He'd seen a lot of bad and sad things in the 'Stan. By the time he crossed the Great Hall, his wood was under control. Usually his dick was obedient. It did what he told it to do. But Dr Honor Thomas was testing the limits.

Six

The outfit was pretty and comfortable. Honor had lucked out in being rescued by someone who took her to a place where so many women kept spare clothes. She took a long, leisurely shower, donned sweat pants and a tank top and then a zippered hoodie in soft pure cotton, all in a flattering shade of green, found a pair of ballerinas in her size and was ready to go.

Honor moved slowly. In her normal life, she zipped through things. Her morning shower was really fast and breakfast was fast and she was fast. Moving slowly wasn't her style. But moving at all right now was a miracle, though she was getting better.

Right now, she didn't feel that bone-deep sensation of weakness she had the past few days, as if her muscles couldn't hold her up. She was getting stronger by the day. It was the washout of the drugs but it was also the rest and good food and lack of fear.

And being looked after by Matt Walker.

He was by her side constantly and it was impossible to feel fear when he was near. But it wasn't just a lack of something she felt in his presence. There was something else now — hot sexual desire. That kiss had sparked her back into life, her entire body coming alive in an electrifying shock to the system. Honor had had boyfriends, lovers, but nothing had ever made her feel like that — like coming into contact with life itself, a primal force, magnetic in its hold.

And addictive. Right now she needed to be in Matt Walker's presence like she needed food and water and air.

Funny how that was. Honor prided herself on not needing anyone. It was even a bone of contention with her dad, who wanted her to need him, who'd desperately wanted her to work with and for him. But that wasn't her, wasn't her nature. You couldn't become an ER doctor if you weren't independent and self-sufficient by nature.

When Matt rescued her from the river, she'd been at the lowest point of her life. She remembered with a sick feeling how weak she'd been, how close to death. How her light had almost been snuffed out. She'd have drowned if he hadn't rescued her and afterward, she'd been so frail and sickeningly disoriented, her life force almost gone.

In his presence, she borrowed some of his strength and determination. When he left the room, it flicked an off switch in her.

This wasn't her, though it was her right now. Right now, she needed Matt Walker and wasn't afraid to admit it to herself, shameful though it was.

His instructions were clear. The room door closed behind her, sliding shut automatically with a silvery whooshing sound. He'd said there was a Great Hall and there it was, right in front of her. Amazing.

A huge plaza full of glossy plants, flowering bushes, even trees. The air smelled fresh and clean and lightly perfumed, like a secret exotic garden. Pave-stoned paths criss- crossed the plaza among the plants and the way across was clear. She headed toward the other side, forcing herself to keep walking straight ahead. The place begged for a person to linger. Perspex benches lined the walkways. One was right under an amazing magnolia tree, white fleshy flowers in full bloom, smelling like heaven.

Walking past that required real discipline.

But soon the smell of muffins and freshly baked bread overwhelmed the delicate fragrance of flowers as she exited from the Great Hall and, just as Matt had said, two arches to the right after the huge willow tree was a meal nook.

He was placing two plates on an ash table but looked up as she approached.

His dark gaze was like a punch to the stomach. It took her breath away and stopped her in her tracks. She had to force her feet forward. His eyes followed her as she made her way to the table and she felt almost touched. When he looked away it was as if someone holding her tightly had let her go. She nearly stumbled.

"Here." He slid a plate in front of her and she looked down. Breakfast in her house was usually a

Danish held in her teeth while she put on her jacket, on her way out the door. No time even for coffee, which she got from the hospital vending machine.

This was almost sinfully elaborate and more than she ate in a day. When she hesitated, he put a fork in her hand. "Eat up. You don't have to be a doctor to see that you need to regain your strength."

The plate was more a platter than a plate and it had a full serving of scrambled eggs, six pieces of crisp bacon and hash browns. His steaming plate was heaped even higher with food.

A smaller plate held two bran muffins and a lemon bar. That was more like it. Matt placed a mug of piping hot coffee in front of her and she slid it toward herself with both hands, pulling in the fragrance.

"This smells delicious. About as far from hospital coffee as you can get."

He pushed a milk pitcher and sugar bowl over too. "My company solved a big problem for a gourmet coffee importer. Stock was disappearing from warehouses. We solved it and we have the most amazing coffee in perpetuity. I think this is Colombian. Some kind of rare variety."

She knew how it worked. "The beans gathered by virgins under the full moon?"

"Exactly. Now eat —"

A loud noise came from far away. His eyes met hers. That was the exact sound that had interrupted what would have been an epic second kiss.

"Sorry about that. They want to finish the work fast.

They might actually finish today."

"No problem." Honor sipped the coffee, feeling the fragrant warmth all the way down to her stomach. It was truly sterling coffee. For coffee like this, they could have a drum concerto in the Great Hall for all she cared.

She was startled by the opening bars of Born to Run. Matt pulled out a super sleek, super thin phone. Unlike any brand she'd ever seen. "Sorry again." He thumbed the screen. "My colleague who is helping oversee the rebuilding. He's coming with some news."

Matt stood up, got another mug and filled a platter with enough bacon and scrambled eggs to choke a horse, plus four muffins.

"Walker," a basso profundo voice said right behind her. She jumped, a little coffee sloshing over onto the table. She hadn't heard anything at all.

"Goddammit, Jacko." Matt wiped the table. "Make some noise when you walk, man. Gets fu—freaking creepy."

Honor turned around and stared. If Matt hadn't been there she'd have panicked and run. Standing at the table was the scariest looking man she'd ever seen and she'd grown up around stevedores. He wasn't as tall as Matt but was definitely as broad, with massive bulging biceps. He was wearing a gray sweatshirt with the sleeves ripped off and his arms looked like they'd been stuffed with basketballs.

But it wasn't the oversized and freaky muscles. It was the man's expression. He was dark, with flat expressionless eyes. He looked like he could kill you without a moment's qualm, hostility and coldness coming off him in waves.

Matt sighed. "Honor, meet my teammate in the military and now one of my co-workers, Jacko Jackman. Jacko, meet Honor Thomas. Doctor Honor Thomas."

"Ma'am," he said, his voice so deep it echoed in her diaphragm. She knew all about vocal cords and it seemed impossible that that sound emanated from a human throat.

Thank God he seemed to show no signs of wanting to shake hands. Honor needed her hands for delicate surgery, she didn't want one of them crushed. Matt's hands were large and broad and strong but this guy's hands looked like they could crush steel.

They stood awkwardly for a moment, though this Jacko showed no sign of feeling awkward. He was impossible to read. He simply stood at what she recognized as parade rest — legs braced shoulder width apart, hands folded neatly in front of his crotch.

"Sit," Matt ordered. "I fixed breakfast for you, too." He slid the platter stacked with food in front of Jacko. "Nick told me you have some things to report?"

Jacko nodded.

"And Dante's coming up?"

He nodded again. Clearly, speaking actual words hurt him.

Matt turned to her. "Dante is Jacko's father. He's ex DEA and a really good investigator. We called him in to get his input."

Honor barely heard him, having tripped in her head over the idea of Jacko having a father and not being hatched.

But something had to be said. "Ahm. Cool."

Matt nodded and Jacko picked up a fork and demolished all the food in the wink of an eye. It was astonishing to watch. Honor dropped her eyes to her plate to split up her huge bran muffin into four parts and when she looked up again, the muffins on his plate had disappeared. Not even crumbs around his mouth. He was staring fiercely at her as if she'd done something wrong. And then switched his cold gaze to Matt, as if *he'd* done something wrong. So this Jacko was an equal opportunity grouch.

Meeting his dark cold gaze was uncomfortable so she glanced around the room rather than looking at him. They were in what was clearly a breakfast nook — small, efficient kitchenette, ash table and ash chairs — open to the Great Hall.

Everything was pleasing to look at. Someone with a very good eye had decorated. The furniture was sleek, elegant, comfortable. There were a few pieces of art scattered around. A laser-etched hand in a Plexiglass cube. A hand-thrown and hand-painted enamel vase. And — my goodness!

"Wow." Honor stood up and took a few steps toward the wall where a large, exquisite watercolor was hung. Just a few brush strokes of a fall of wisteria in a ray of sunlight. Absolutely stunning. She looked over her shoulder at Matt, ignoring Jacko, who probably disdained watercolors. Or ate them for breakfast. "Is this a Lauren Dare?" She peered and, yes, saw the precise signature in the lower right hand corner of the picture. Honor had a tiny Lauren Dare, her thirtieth-birthday present from her father. Typically, he'd bought it, had it framed and delivered to her in Portland without ever leaving Los Angeles, after she'd told him she'd been to a show of Lauren Dare's works and loved them.

She'd been exasperated at her father, who hadn't come up for her birthday because of his thousandth work crisis. But she loved the tiny oil painting he gave her.

She walked back to the table. "Sorry, but I just love that artist. She's amazing."

Matt's face had an unusual expression. "Yeah," he said in a choked tone and looked at Jacko.

Honor didn't particularly want to look at him but she followed Matt's gaze and did a double take. What just happened? What was wrong with the guy? It looked like his face had melted.

He'd taken his cell out, scraped his chair to the left so he was elbow to elbow with her.

Honor didn't want to draw back because it would be rude, but having Jacko so close was unsettling. Jacko thrust his cell under her nose, big finger scrolling through shots of … Lauren Dare artwork?

How could that be?

"That series is a big favorite," he was saying, tapping hard on his cell screen. "This one, this one for instance,

I love this one."

His big finger was fixed on an image of a huge peony in pastels, creamy petals like velvet. He sighed. "It's so great, isn't it?"

Jacko turned to look her full in the face, having morphed from dark pit bull to dark Golden Labrador. He all but had his tongue hanging out, dark eyes intense but friendly now.

"And look at these." His finger started scrolling again, image after beautiful image of flowers and trees. "Her landscape series. She'd never done landscapes before but just look at them." He lifted his eyes and stared at her intently. "Right?"

Honor felt frozen in place, wondering what was happening. What had turned this fierce taciturn warrior into an oversized puppy dog?

"Lauren Dare is Jacko's wife," Matt offered, then shrugged.

It was rude, but Honor stared. *This man was married to Lauren Dare?* She'd never met the woman but at the exhibit she went to, there was a photograph on the back cover of the catalog. Lauren Dare was a delicate beauty, ethereal and almost fairy-like. And she was married to *Jacko?*

"I know what you're thinking," Jacko said and she immediately stopped thinking it. Could he read minds? Oh, God.

"Why isn't she Lauren Jackman? She kept her professional name after we married. Though Dare isn't really —" He waved a huge hand. "Never mind. And look, look here —" He simply beamed as he stared at his cell screen. He held it out to her. "Our daughter, Alice."

Lauren Dare had *mated* with Jacko. Honor tried to wrap her head around that. She wouldn't have been surprised if their offspring was purple and had tentacles. But what she saw on the screen was Lauren holding a remarkably beautiful dark-skinned child, with — thank God — Lauren's delicate features and amazing silver eyes. The little girl was absolutely stunning.

"What a lovely child," she said and Jacko's chest, already the size of a gorilla's, swelled.

"The best," he said and gave her a sappy smile.

Matt sighed, placed an elbow on the table and leaned toward her. "Now you've done it," he murmured. "There's no stopping him now."

Jacko was still scrolling, holding individual screenshots up to her. She nodded and smiled.

A pneumatic hammer started up and another man arrived. A darker older version of Jacko, like his identical twin brother born thirty years earlier, except he had Alice's silver eyes.

Honor had taken three genetics classes in med school but the effects of genes sometimes still surprised her.

"Dante." Matt reached out a hand. "Glad to see you."

The man took a seat next to Jacko, who nodded, put his cell away and morphed back into his excellent imitation of the Grim Reaper.

"Dr. Thomas, I am Dante Jimenez. I worked at the DEA for thirty years and I still have contacts there and in other government agencies." His outstretched hand was callused and huge, the grip firm but not crushing. He pushed an iPad into the center of the table. "Back at ASI we've been working on your case nonstop. Both because of Matt and Suzanne and, well, because no one at the company likes the idea of people going around abducting women. Makes us mad. So." He cricked his thick muscled neck to the left, to the right. "What I'm about to show you is footage taken off a KH-15 satellite."

"KH-15?" Honor repeated. She had trouble focusing, still fixated on Jacko and Lauren Dare.

"Keyhole Satellites. They orbit about two hundred miles in altitude. Basically orbiting cameras with a really good lens. Operated by the NRA."

"I imagine that isn't the National Rifle Association," Honor said.

"Nope."

"So it would be the National Reconnaisance Agency," she said and three pairs of eyes, two dark, one silver, turned to her. She shrugged. "I read a ton of thrillers. It's a hobby of mine."

Matt gave a faint smile.

"I also imagine any images would be confidential. Top Secret, in fact."

Silence.

Well, she didn't care. If what they were about to show her could help her recover her lost memory, she was all for it. "Show me."

Dante swiped and tapped and all of a sudden there was a black and white image filling the screen. Honor turned the tablet so she could see it better. A mountain scene, a twisting two-lane blacktop, a black SUV in the middle of the road. The image had an enormous gray arrow in the center of the screen, pointing right.

Honor tapped on the arrow and the image came to life as a video of an SUV being driven erratically, the truck crossing over the narrow road into the opposite lane often, and at every curve. Granite walls to the right, a steep cliff to the left.

The SUV made a hairpin turn, the back of the vehicle hanging over the cliff for a second, then shuddering back onto the road.

Honor studied the crazy dangerous driving, the landscape. Something about the road ... "Oh my God!" She leaned closer to the tablet. "That's me! That's me driving!"

"Watch," Dante said. He didn't need to say it, she was riveted to the screen, couldn't wrench her eyes away. She barely remembered living through what she was seeing on the screen. It was as if she were living this for the first time, only there was an echo, a déjà vu effect. She'd done this before, though she couldn't remember it. She was remembering it as she saw it.

Everyone was silent as they watched the SUV — the one she was driving — veer over the median line again and again.

"Looks like I was drunk, but I wasn't."

"You were fighting the drugs," Matt said and she nodded.

The asphalt ended and the road became a dirt track, strewn with rocks which she imagined had fallen from the cliff face. In parts, the cliff had netting to keep boulders from crashing to the road.

"Plates?" Matt asked without taking his eyes from the tablet.

"Fake," Dante answered. He, too, was riveted on the tablet. "Not stolen, which is interesting. Perfectly normal-looking plates, registered to a non-existent company."

Honor was barely listening, following the SUV's dust trail. On the unpaved road, the dust kicked up camouflaged the vehicle, but it made it very easy to follow. She winced as the vehicle came so close to the edge the dust fanned out across the canyon.

"I'm going to go off the road."

"You are. Right ... now," Dante said. Another hair-pin turn, something dark crossing the road. A deer. The vehicle missed it by a hair, dust rising from the wheels as they suddenly braked, but the vehicle couldn't hold the road.

Honor gasped as the back of the vehicle slid to the left, the driver — her — overcompensating. The SUV teetered on the edge of the cliff, then slowly slid over.

The vehicle rolled slowly, once, twice, then picked up speed as it tumbled down the cliff, bouncing over and over in clouds of dust. It was a horrible, fascinating thing to watch.

"Fuck," Jacko breathed then moved his eyes to Honor when Matt elbowed him hard, so hard it would have broken the ribs of a lesser man. "Sorry."

"I work in the ER," she said absently. "I've heard it all. And I've heard that particular word as a noun, a verb, an adverb, an adjective and an exclamation."

But she didn't take her eyes off the vehicle careening down the steep cliff until it juddered to a stop at the river bank, upside down, steam coming from under the hood.

Honor shuddered.

"Watch," Dante said. He didn't have to, everyone was riveted.

Honor saw something white and red exit from the driver's side window. The vehicle was upside down so the window was at ground level. The white and red thing moved. Though the resolution was excellent, it took Honor a moment to realize that the moving thing was a hand, then an arm. Her hand, her arm.

The red was blood.

She watched herself crawl out of the shattered window, slowly, painfully. She had no memory at all of this.

On the screen, she moved toward the river, crawling with the help of her hands and elbows. Though Honor didn't remember it, she could recognize that despite her drugged-up concussed state, she'd headed for the river because she somehow knew she had to get away from the vehicle as fast as she could and the only way to do that was to let the river carry her away. No way could she walk or run.

Steam was pouring out from under the hood, blown away by the wind. She watched herself tumble into the water, where the current simply took her away. She disappeared in a matter of seconds. It was as if she'd never been.

"Continue watching," Dante said quietly.

Honor didn't understand why until she saw another vehicle drive along the road and pull up at the top of the cliff. The satellite had moved on in its trajectory and the view was slanted, but the image was clear enough.

"We didn't get enough data from the face for facial recognition," Dante said, regret clear in his voice. "And he didn't move outside the vehicle enough to get gait recognition." A man got out of the black vehicle. The slanted image never showed his face. He took three steps to the edge of the cliff and looked down. He towered over the roof of the SUV so he must have been tall. He was dressed in black, and looked very bulky in the torso.

Honor peered more closely. "Is he wearing body armor?"

Matt touched her hand. "Yeah. Good call."

She looked at him indignantly. "He was wearing body armor to chase *me*? I wasn't armed. He must have known that."

It was Jacko who answered. "One." He held up a thick dark finger. "He can't know whether you are or aren't armed. Not for sure. It's always better to have armor and not need it than need it and not have it. That's true for more or less everything. And two," he held up another thick finger, "I'm assuming that if you escaped, he thought you might be some badass ninja chick and wasn't taking any chances."

Honor nearly smiled. "Badass ninja chick, I like that." Though of course it was so far from the truth it was ridiculous. True, she wielded a knife — scalpel — but only to do good. "I don't know how I escaped." She met each man's sober eyes. "I have no memory at all of that."

On the screen, the man was standing on the edge of the cliff, broad back to the camera, head bowed as he looked below through binoculars. He jerked back and at first Honor couldn't understand why. Then she saw red-black smoke billowing far below in the canyon. The fuel spilling from the vehicle had caught fire.

The man observing it all from the clifftop got back into his black SUV, executed a smooth K-turn on the narrow track and drove back the way he'd come. In a few seconds, the car was gone from the screen.

Honor sat back. "I was very lucky," she said. "They must think I'm dead."

The three men nodded.

"That's to our advantage," Matt added and she turned to him, grateful for the plural pronoun. He made her problem his. Theirs.

All three of the men nodded again.

"So." Dante swiped the tablet closed. "Let's deal with the obvious conclusion first."

"Obvious? There's an obvious conclusion?" If there was, it was beyond Honor's confused and muddled understanding.

"Yes." Dante watched her face. "Do you think you were kidnapped for ransom?"

"No." The answer came straight from her gut and all three men reacted. They reacted in minute ways, almost imperceptible, but she was used to reading people's body language. Often in the ER, people's bodies said the opposite of what their mouths said.

No, I haven't taken drugs.

I fell down the stairs.

My kid is hyperactive, keeps hurting herself.

"Why do you say that, Dr. Thomas?" Dante asked.

"Please. Honor."

"Okay. Why do you say that, Honor? I understand your father is a wealthy man."

She refrained from rolling her eyes. "That depends on your definition of wealthy. Some years my father is rolling in it. Some years he is up to his eyeballs in debt. This past year it's been more the latter than the former."

"You okay with your old man?" That was in Jacko's basso profundo rumble. Jacko's father, Dante, shot him a wry glance. "What?" Jacko asked. "Not be the first time someone's kidnapped and the ransom isn't paid."

This was a dead end and Honor had to make them understand it. "My father and I have had our differences, and twice we didn't speak to each other for a couple of months. The first time was when I enrolled in pre-med instead of business school. Though I've never shown the slightest interest in the shipping industry, and Quest Line Shipping in particular, my dad got it into his head that I'd take over from him. Never going to happen. I told him that over and over and over again. From the time I was a kid I knew I wanted to be a doctor. And the second time is now. Dad's had one massive heart attack, he's got three stents, he's overweight. His blood pressure hovers around 180 over 100 and he's pre-diabetic. And he refuses to slow down, refuses to even contemplate retirement. When I told him he had to take better care of himself, he reacted angrily. We haven't spoken in a month." Even talking about it, Honor could feel herself become agitated, worried sick and angry as hell, equally and at the same time.

Dante nodded. "I see."

She shook her head. "No, actually, I don't think you do. Whatever our differences, even when we're not talking to each other, I love him and he loves me. I wasn't kidnapped for ransom and held a prisoner because my father didn't pay. He would've paid immediately. No way would he have let me be held captive for six days. No matter what amount they asked, he'd have sold everything." Something in her voice must have convinced them. And she knew it from the bottom of her soul. If she'd been kidnapped for ransom, her father would have moved heaven and earth and certainly would have impoverished himself without a second thought. "So it wasn't a kidnapping for ransom. Not if I was held for almost a week."

"Do you think it might be something work-related?" Matt asked. "You crossed some drug dealer or mobster? Is that a possibility?"

Honor thought about it and sighed. "Well, we get plenty of addicts and drug dealers in the ER. And unsavory characters. I suppose it is a possibility, but I don't know how I could have become a target for anyone. I didn't hear any deathbed confessions, no one gave me anything for safekeeping. Not that I remember, anyway. I just can't think of anything that would make someone abduct me." Even just saying it made her feel ridiculous. She was a busy, tired doctor who knew no secrets and knew no bad guys. All she did was work and go home. And yet, the bruises and the scabs from the shackles were still fresh.

"Here." Matt held out a smartphone. "Call your dad. Unknown number will show on his end and no one can trace it. If it goes to voicemail, don't answer. Just hang up. I've put it on speakerphone."

"Okay." She punched her father's private line number and waited. Very few people had this particular number. He always picked up. But she got a voicemail. "Hello, this is Simon Thomas. Leave a message."

Matt shook his head and she thumbed the connection closed. "Well, that's unusual," she said, perplexed.

"How so?" Dante asked.

"It's a number very few people have. Me, his personal lawyer, I guess Marianne, this Frenchwoman he's been seeing, his CFO. Maybe a few others. But he always picks up, even just to say he's busy and he'll call back. Can you find out where he is?"

A faint smile creased Dante's face. "Yeah, we can. And we will. In the meantime, I suggest you stay here.

Matt will make sure you're safe. Right, Matt?"

Matt's face tightened. "Count on it."

Seven

Laurel Canyon
Los Angeles

"The shipowner received a call on his private line," Ivan Antonov said.

"Who cares? Here." Chamness waved one hand while pouring a twenty-year-old Macallen into two cut crystal tumblers. He handed one to Antonov and sank into a light gray designer leather armchair.

Everything about the house — mansion really — was stylish. Perched high in the hills above Laurel Canyon, with high stone walls and no neighbors with line of sight, it had perfect privacy. The mansion was huge with a large patio, an infinity pool, a professional kitchen, all marble and stainless steel.

By design, all this luxury came with no exposure. Any five-star hotel would have required documents and contact with a front desk. The opulent mansion had been booked via Airbnb. There had been no physical contact at all, just a fake credit card in a fake name with real money in the account, booked via a fake email address. Once booked, they'd been given the address, with the keys in a hidden lockbox just outside the gate. They'd been provided with the code to open the lockbox and they'd taken possession, and no one on earth knew where they were.

Antonov and his men had disabled the security cameras, the cars were kept in the underground garage, the pool was under a portico so not even drones could see them.

"Drink up," Chamness motioned with his tumbler and Ivan obediently drank. The whiskey went down very smoothly. It should. Chamness had told him with pride that the bottle sold for four hundred dollars. And yet it went down like any five dollar bottle of vodka.

Chamness had been CIA and when they'd met in Afghanistan, he'd looked like anyone caught in a dirty, dusty, endless war. He'd looked like Antonov. Filthy, bearded, grime caught in every crevice of their exhausted faces, dust-covered boots, clothes that stank of old sweat. The only clean thing their weapons.

Two soldiers from developed countries fighting Bronze-age goatherds. And losing.

It had destroyed the Soviet Union and it was destroying America.

Antonov had been undercover as a Bulgarian military contractor and had been told that Chamness was corruptible. He'd facilitated shipments of heroin, which to Antonov didn't mean corruption. You'd have to be crazy to be in Afghanistan and not be involved in drugs.

There was nothing else, just stones and goats.

So Antonov had made a proposal that was irresistible and Chamness hadn't resisted. Not for one second. He'd heard the plan and instantly embraced it.

The fact that it would lay a segment of his own country to waste didn't stop him for a minute. Good thing, too, because Antonov had had strict instructions to terminate Chamness if he refused. No one could know about the plan.

Chamness definitely hadn't refused.

No Russians were to be involved, except for Antonov and a few of his men sent for security. The bulk of the plan was to be carried out by Americans. American fingerprints all over the place.

A genius plan and perhaps the last shove necessary to push the Motherland's oldest enemy right into the abyss.

He sipped the whiskey and looked out over the stressed-wood terrace and infinity pool, out past the wooded hills dotted with outrageously expensive mansions connected by winding roads full of late model luxury cars.

A sea of lights, an inverted starry sky. More lights on the ground than up above, colorful, beautiful. In the distance, he knew, were the skyscrapers of central Los Angeles, modern monoliths, lit up like spaceships.

A very pleasing sight.

Oh yes.

Though soon — in three days, actually — everything Antonov saw would be a wasteland. Or rather,

Antonov wouldn't be seeing it in person. They had set up cameras all along the perimeter of the house and at strategic places in trees overlooking vast stretches of territory, and he would be observing the chaos and panic and destruction in the flatlands below from a distance.

They would also remotely send up cubed drones and keep track of the devastation.

From outside the country.

In a sunny climate on a white sandy beach. Though lately he'd been thinking — maybe he'd be observing it from a room in the Kremlin.

In the last couple of weeks Antonov had had a very good look at how the idle rich lived and it wasn't attractive. It was empty. He knew this was Lee Chamness's ideal life, full of luxuries, with a staff quivering with eagerness to please. Every experience a peak experience. The finest food, the finest wine, the softest chairs, the silkiest sheets …

A world of soft down instead of iron will.

To his surprise, Antonov preferred iron to down. Preferred the company of disciplined men to the pampered and manicured and massaged men of Hollywood, who depended on a vast ecosystem of luxury and services to exist.

Just before the end of his war, Antonov had spent ten days in the Hindu Kush after his helicopter crash landed, pursued by savages. He'd barely survived but he *had* survived and was the stronger for it. Hard men, men he admired, treated him with respect when he had limped into the base, emaciated and dehydrated but alive.

He belonged to a fraternity of hard men, survivors, that no amount of money could get you into. You joined that club through sweat and blood and will. You couldn't buy your way in.

So — maybe after all this was over, he'd be joining the ranks of the men organizing the new world order. An order where the iron men of Mother Russia reigned supreme and America was a vanquished country.

"Ivan."

Even Chamness's voice was weak — a languid treble. They were planning an attack that would bring the world's pre-eminent superpower down and Chamness sounded like he was at a cocktail party ordering another mojito.

Antonov turned, his face bland, the contempt he felt nowhere visible. He merely raised his eyebrows in question.

"Captain Perry just reported in." Chamness stopped to light a cigarette from a gold Cartier lighter, flipping the top closed with a light click and inhaling. Making the act of lighting a cigarette an exercise in style. The information regarding the progress of the ship was essential, but Chamness turned it into theater.

Antonov waited patiently. His patience would be rewarded. He didn't answer, simply waited for Chamness to continue. They looked at each other.

"Everything on schedule," Chamness finally said. "No problems en route."

Unsurprisingly, it had been harder to find a corruptible Navy officer than a CIA official. Antonov's partners had had any number of sailors ready and willing to do off- the-books navigating for shockingly small amounts of money, but Antonov also needed an officer. A man who could command a container ship. He'd finally found one, Lieutenant Commander (retired) Marcus Perry, who was undergoing a vicious divorce. He said his wife was making off with his house, half his pension and his balls.

He'd leaped at the opportunity to make a million dollars over the course of two weeks. He had an inkling of what the ship was carrying but had demonstrated exactly zero interest.

Half the promised amount was in his name in an overseas account and that was all he was interested in.

If the American authorities backtracked to the source of the attack, they would find the bridge of the ship covered with the fingerprints of a retired Navy Commander and his American crew. Several of them had been recruited from disgruntled and cashiered CIA agents.

An American presence was the most important thing. The blame would be cast on homegrown terrorists. It would be vastly destabilizing. Even better, homegrown terrorism with an establishment pedigree — the Navy. And the owner of a well-known boutique shipping company. Antonov was delighted that a former Navy Commander would be considered one of the authors of the most vicious attack on American soil in history. Casting the attack on Pearl Harbor in the shade. It would throw the American government into a state of crisis like no other event in their history.

Alas, Chamness would never be investigated. He made that a condition of his help with Al Rashid. Chamness was clever and understood the basics of the plan immediately. He also immediately covered his ass, as the Americans said. He would cooperate, sneak the material out from under Al Rashid's misshapen nose, help on the ground, at a cost. Fifty million dollars and Antonov's word as a gentleman that his role would never be divulged.

Antonov had had no intention of keeping his word until Chamness had said that hard evidence — video footage and voice recordings — of Russian involvement was already in the hands of a lawyer, and that if he didn't send a message to the lawyer once a week via encrypted email, the information would go straight to The Guardian, the New York Times, the Washington Post and Le Monde.

Possibly sparking off a war.

Antonov and his backers wanted America brought low, not retaliating. Reluctantly, Antonov arranged for Chamness to have safe passage and agreed never to seek him out afterward. He was certain Chamness had his own post-apocalypse plans and that he was going to live out his days in luxury in some sun-dappled paradise.

The thought was irritating.

"Are the trucks and agitators ready?" Antonov asked.

"Oh yes." Chamness's mouth lifted in a half smile. Waiting. Was he expecting praise for doing his job? The job he was being paid millions to do?

Antonov gave a brief nod and walked out of the room.

God save him from weak men.

The Grange

Everyone left. Honor's hands had started trembling, eyelids drooping. Matt had abruptly stood up and sent everyone packing.

Her memory was coming back and she had more of a sense of who she was. She knew that this weakness wasn't normal. She had images of herself working well past exhaustion, yet still completely functional. She didn't do weakness but here she was, knees trembling, almost unable to walk a straight line, as if drunk.

She stopped halfway across the Great Hall on the way to what she now considered 'her' room and swayed. Her body was almost completely out of her control.

She hated it, but was helpless to do anything about it. The exhaustion was mental and physical and there were no reserves in her. None at all.

"The hell with this," Matt said and swung her up in

his arms.

It should have been awkward but it wasn't. Her arms found themselves around his neck, forearms lying along the strong muscles of his shoulders. The instant he lifted her, her body relaxed, certain that he could carry her.

He could.

"I can walk." It came out a whisper against his corded neck. Her lips were so close to his skin she could feel the heat. Smell him. He had an amazing smell, like iron and leather, with a touch of wood smoke. There was a big fireplace with a huge burning fire in the Great Hall.

"No. You can't." He strode across the Great Hall as if she weighed nothing. "I'm surprised you stayed upright as long as you did. You gave everyone a lot to go on but you were hanging on by sheer grit. You're never going to recover if you push yourself this hard."

All she heard was that she gave his friends a lot to go on, even if she didn't really remember everything that she'd said. That was really weird. She'd managed to get through medical school just fine. Medical school was essentially one long test of memory — and an ability to see blood without feeling queasy.

This fog in her head was awful, but fighting it didn't help. It only made things worse.

Matt bent his knees, pulled back the covers with her in his arms, and lay her on the bed. She tried to sit up in bed but didn't have the strength.

"Here," he said and pulled her gently up against the pillows he stacked against her back.

Honor instinctively put her hand out, palm up. And he took it, settling into a chair he hooked with a booted foot. The contact was electric, like she'd been plugged into a socket. Strength and heat surged through her and shocked her awake, as if she'd been sleeping.

Matt settled in the chair and looked like he had no intention of getting out of it soon. His eyes were riveted on her face.

She studied him, as if seeing him for the first time. He looked so rough, sitting there, legs splayed, torso leaning slightly forward. His hair was too long and unruly, curling darkly around his face and touching his broad shoulders. He was dressed in a sweatshirt and faded jeans and hard black boots . Dressed for construction, or maybe combat, since he was a soldier. Or had been one.

Metal and Jacko treated him with easy friendliness but he kept himself a little apart. He spoke of the company, ASI, as if he were part of it, but if he was, why wasn't he going to work? When he saved her life, he'd been fishing. The day she ran away from her captors and was rescued had been a Tuesday. It was Friday now. She'd asked, because there wasn't anything up here to mark time's passing.

So what was an obviously super fit and capable man doing fishing on weekdays up in a luxury mountain retreat?

He had a tension about him which she recognized. She sometimes had the same tension, and it came from a job that pushed you to your maximum limits.

There was a story there and she wanted to know it.

Because the truth was, she was attracted to this man. Really attracted. When he touched her, it was as if she were being brought online after being shut down. It had been a long time since she'd felt this tug, she knew that. At the moment, she couldn't actually remember any of her former lovers, not in any detail.

She knew every detail of his face.

He was sitting next to her and they watched each other. It wasn't embarrassing, though with someone else it might have been. He fascinated her and she clearly interested him.

There were lines in his face that gave him character but that also looked recent. From his body and the way he moved, he was still a fairly young man, but his face looked older, as if he'd been through hard times.

Honor was used to understanding people at a glance. Everything about a person who came into the ER was potentially vital information, so besides using her instruments, she checked eyes and the movements of hands and body. Matt wasn't giving her much, though he seemed perfectly healthy. Stronger than most people, actually. But he was always so still when he wasn't doing something and he was hard to read.

He wasn't a happy man, though. That much was clear. There was some trouble there.

"Can I ask you a question?" Her eyes never left his.

"No problem." Matt's voice was deep and calm. "Ask me whatever you want."

He let go of her hand and opened his hands on the

blanket, as if catching a question. *Ask me what you want.* An invitation. He took her hand again.

Oh, God. She'd felt cold and bereft for the short time he wasn't touching her. Once her hand was safely in his again, she felt warm and safe and alive.

Her sense of well-being was now defined by physical contact with Matt Walker.

Another Matt Walker side effect was that he calmed her mind. Since gaining consciousness, Honor had tried and tried to probe the past two weeks, trying to overcome retrograde amnesia.

There were tantalizing glimpses but they came with a price. The more she concentrated, the sharper the pain in her head. At first, it was a popping sound, distracting and unpleasant. But soon it turned into a loud buzzing in her head. Painful if tolerable, at first. But the more she tried, the harder she focused, the greater the pain until there was nothing but sheer agony so intense she thought her heart would burst.

But not while Matt Walker was touching her. Crazy. With her hand in his, the piercing pain abated until it was a distant nuisance and she had a sense that maybe those lost days could be hers again. That the impenetrable wall separating herself now — broken and beaten — from the Honor of before could be breached.

The pain was bearable as long as he was touching her.

He was tough and unkempt and looked nothing like what a Guardian Angel should look like. Guardian Angels should at least shave once in a while, shouldn't they?

But there it was. Some broken bits of her soul were soothed by this rough man.

He didn't say anything, just watched her. Didn't fidget, didn't ask what she wanted. No, he was completely still and just held her hand.

"Why did Jacko ask how long you were going to sulk up here?" She'd overheard Jacko asking Matt.

The question was blurted out and Honor was mortified. She wanted to gently probe, find out more, find the answer in a roundabout way. Ask discreetly.

This was so unlike her. Or she thought it was unlike her.

"S-sorry," she mumbled, knowing her cheeks were red. Which was strange enough in itself. Honor never blushed. She'd seen it all in the ER, nothing shocked or embarrassed her.

Under the black scruff covering his face, she discerned a line running down his lean cheeks.

"Are you asking whether I'm sulking or why I'm sulking?"

It might or might not be a smile. Just to be safe, she smiled back. The dents deepened. "Both."

He gave a deep sigh. "Well, I don't like to think of it as sulking but it's true, I'm fine up here on my own, without seeing other people —" this time the smile was a full one, his lips curving upward, "— present company excepted."

She nodded.

"My separation from the Navy was … not a happy

one and I'm taking some time off just getting my head around some stuff. Don't know if that makes sense to you."

Honor nodded again, eyes never leaving his. "Makes a lot of sense to me," she whispered. And it did. Something had happened to her, too, that she had a hard time wrapping her head around. She couldn't remember exactly what it was, and trying to remember was like driving spikes into her own head, but whatever it was had been serious, and had made her deeply unhappy.

Matt's gaze sharpened. "Are you remembering something?"

Blood and tears and shattered bodies … Honor's eyes closed but she could still see terrifying scenes on the inside of her eyelids. A little girl looking up at her, blinking …

The pain was so strong she wrenched her hand out of Matt's and held her head as if her hands were the only thing keeping her head from exploding. A moan escaped her.

"Hey. Hey." Matt kept his voice low and gently pushed at her shoulders until she was leaning back fully against the pillows. "Don't push it. I was reading up on ketamine and the side effects aren't fun. You need to let time do its work and to wash it out of your system."

Honor turned her head on the pillow and looked at him. "I feel … a sense of urgency. And I also feel like if I push it, my head will explode."

He nodded. "Yeah. Exactly. So the answer is to relax and let things come to you."

Honor frowned. "That doesn't sound like me."

His eyes narrowed and he gave a small smile. "I bet. I don't imagine ER doctors to be passive delicate flowers, no. But the fact is that you were abducted, kept drugged, you were in a vehicle that rolled down a cliff and you nearly drowned. Though you and Metal both say you're not badly concussed, you bounced off rocks in the river. I saw you do it. I think you can be excused if you're feeling a little off."

She sighed, unhappy at the thought. But there was nothing she could do. There was no strength in her to shake things off and get her life back.

"I'd like to go to my apartment." She was perfectly comfortable here but her apartment was her haven, her safe place.

She watched his face morph from impassivity to concern and then alarm.

"Whoa." His dark eyes showed the whites all around. "I don't know where that thought came from but no. Not just no, but *hell* no." He stopped, some strong emotion making his jaws clench. "Sorry, I don't mean to tell you what to do and if it's a medical question, I bow to your expertise. But this —" he bent forward a little and clutched her hand a little more tightly. "This is *my* area of expertise. You have bad guys after you and you could say that's my specialty — stopping bad guys from ruining lives. I'm something of an expert and I've done it all my adult life. And let me tell you rule number one in dealing with fuckheads — sorry —"

Honor thought of everything she'd heard in the ER

and smiled. "I told you before. Believe me when I say that I've heard it all. Fuckheads sounds like the technical term for the men who abducted me."

His eyes burned dark and intense and his gaze never wavered from her face.

"Okay. Rule number one about bad guys — they never ever give up and they never go away. You don't go over them or under them or around them, you go through them. Or — in your case, you stay far away from them."

There was something about the fervor in his tone, the burning intensity of his dark eyes. This was wrenched from the deepest pit of his being. There was a story there too.

He placed his other hand over hers, encasing her hand in warm hard male strength.

"We have one huge advantage. They think you're dead so they aren't coming after you again. But if we lose that advantage and they know you're alive, then we'll have to fight. But we'd be fighting in the blind."

She stared into his eyes, wondering whether he was listening to himself. Whether he was hearing what she heard.

We.

With every word he said, Matt showed that he had made her problems completely his. Plus of course he had enrolled what looked like a formidable team to be their backup.

Honor dug deep inside herself. No memories of her confinement came welling up, but there had been strong emotions and she could access them now. One of those strong emotions had been a feeling of complete solitude. She'd been alone in her prison and at no time did she feel that someone was coming for her. Never once had she felt that all she had to do was hang in there, because someone who cared for her was coming.

There was no one. The only person that might have noticed her absence was her father and they'd been in a serious I'm-not-talking-to-you phase and had been for weeks.

She'd called her father's doctor in LA and forced him to tell her the results of her father's latest blood work, which she'd had to bully her father into doing. The findings had been bad, and when she talked to her father about them over the phone, he'd hung up on her. And that had been that.

They hadn't spoken for a month, that she knew. There were huge gaping holes in her memory, but she remembered that.

The thing is, she wouldn't have wanted her father coming for her anyway, not under those circumstances. She had a sense of the men who'd kept her a prisoner and they were cold and hard and cruel. Her seventy-year-old father, with a tricky heart and very high blood pressure, would have been no match for them.

The only thing he could have offered was money, and he'd have done that instantly, more than willingly. But apparently, no ransom had been demanded.

Her colleagues would miss her, sure. But she had a

lot of accumulated time and though it wasn't like her to disappear, they'd cover for her and not give it a thought.

She'd been so utterly alone. That was the one thing she knew. She could have died and her corpse left to rot and no one would know.

No one, really, would have cared, except her father.

But now there were people who cared. And the one who seemed to care the most was right here with her, holding her hand.

He was frowning, black eyebrows drawn together, shaggy hair partially hiding the frown lines on his forehead as he chewed his way through the problem. It wasn't a handsome face but it was a strong face and she couldn't tear her eyes away from him.

He leaned forward a little and spoke earnestly. "Do you need something from your apartment? Is that it? I could send Nick and Joe. They're both really good at infiltrating. None of your neighbors would ever know anyone had been there. They could —"

She leaned forward and pressed her mouth to his.

Honor had no idea she was going to do it until she did it. His mouth was softer than it looked and the scruff around it prickled the skin around hers. She could almost taste his surprise.

A moment after she kissed him, she realized with her head what her heart — or her hormones — had made her do and she pulled back immediately, mortified. He was frozen.

"Oh God." Her free hand covered her mouth. Had she misread that kiss they'd shared?

He kissed her back.

Simply leaned his head toward hers and pressed his mouth to hers, just like she'd done.

Only more. And better. No awkwardness at all.

He licked her lips and a bolt of electricity shot through her, unlike anything she'd ever felt before. Like touching a live wire. God, just from a kiss.

They broke apart at the exact same time, to breathe. She hadn't breathed, hadn't consider it necessary. All she'd needed was that punch of heat from the touch of his lips to hers.

One hand left hers and he curled it around her neck. She couldn't move her head back because he was clasping it. That hard hand keeping her head still.

Yeah. It wasn't necessary, though it felt good. She didn't want to move back, away from him. God, no.

Their faces were barely an inch apart, so close all she could really see was his eyes. The irises a deep brown striated with lighter brown and the pupils slightly dilated.

Which is what happens during sexual arousal. Her own pupils were probably enormous.

He pulled gently on the hand clasping her neck, bringing her head forward and his mouth covered hers again. He opened her mouth with his, tongue touching hers. Her breath shuddered, her hand clutching his forearm. His skin was so hot she could feel the heat through the sweatshirt he was wearing. The last of the cold she'd felt these past days was blasted out of her, a flush of heat pulsing through her system, head to toe.

Matt angled his head and the kiss became deeper, hotter.

Somehow Honor found herself on her back and Matt on top of her, kissing her wildly. Her body burst into flames. No other way to describe it. Searing heat, inside and out.

She almost didn't recognize herself. Almost looked around to see if it was someone else in the room experiencing searing heat at a man's touch, his kiss. But nope. Just her.

His hands slid to her waist and then ran along her ribcage, raking up her sweater, tank top and bra with it.

"Lift your arms," he said. That was command in his voice but she didn't need command. No, the thought of her naked chest against his filled her with heat. She lifted her arms and layers of clothes were tossed to the floor. Somehow while he was stripping her of her clothes, he managed to pull his own sweatshirt off and ah! Just the feel of his chest against her breasts was heaven.

He had chest hair, which was very unfashionable. She'd dated a lawyer who shaved his chest, which was not a good idea because when it started to grow back, it was prickly, like a beard. He'd been a bit prickly, too, she remembered. After a couple of dates and one night in bed, they'd parted ways.

Matt's chest, on the other hand, had a mat of wiry curly dark hair that covered his pectorals. It felt good against her skin, like a soft cushion over very hard muscle. Very hard muscle. She'd seen every iteration of the human body and this one was just superb.

But they'd tried to break it.

Honor ran her hands over his back, stopping at a puckered scar just to the side of the scapula. Her mouth was against his neck and she kissed him. "Bullet?" she whispered.

"Yeah. Stupid accident. I was swapping out body armor. Dumb move."

She wondered what it would be like to have to wear body armor all the time. Not fun. "It missed bone. That's good."

His hand ran from the bottom of her spine up her back, to tunnel in her hair. "Missed the lung, too. Lucky."

She ran her hand down his side, along the hard highly-developed muscles, so firm she couldn't make a dent in them. Near the hip was another scar, long and ragged. He stiffened. "And this?" she whispered into his shoulder.

The sigh was gusty enough to shift her hair. "Bad scene," he said, as if the other scar were a good scene. "Guy we thought was on our side. Came into command with empty hands. But he had a knife in a sheath inside his *tunbaan,* these loose pants. Wounded me, killed our terp. I was treated by a medic who did a good job but the scar is ugly. Sorry."

She shook her head and kissed his shoulder again. He had nothing to be sorry about and anyway, she was used to scars. She was only sorry that he'd gone through that. To be attacked by someone you trusted must have been awful.

Matt took her hand, brought it to his mouth, kissed her palm. "We done mapping my scars?"

She smiled against his skin. "Depends. What else do you have to show me?"

"This." He kissed her hand again and brought it down, down, over his chest, stomach, further down. He wrapped her hand around his penis and Honor was shocked and aroused. She curled her fingers around it, feeling the heat, the steely hardness yet the softness of the skin covering it.

As penises went, it was a champ. The touch of her fingers made him swell even further, blood surging through the organ. And then, to her surprise, feeling that, her vagina clenched. Instinctively, her fingers tightened, more blood surged through his penis and her vagina clenched again.

Their bodies were ... dancing. A sexual dance that had nothing to do with volition. And Honor realized in that moment that with her other sex partners, she'd sort of willed herself into it, into sexual desire. She didn't have to do this here.

Nope.

Her body didn't care what her head was doing, it was going ahead all on its own, readying itself for him.

She could feel it, feel the arousal running through her. Her vagina becoming soft and wet, her nipples, rubbing against the wiry hairs of his chest, becoming hard, her skin becoming super sensitive.

It was amazing.

"I can almost feel your head buzzing," he said, his hand cupping the back of her head. "What's running through that super smart mind of yours?"

She didn't feel super smart right now. Right now, she felt like one giant throbbing hormone. Telling him that, though — it would put a lot of power into those big strong hands. Wouldn't it?

She pulled back to look him in the eyes. He wasn't looking smug. He had heat in his eyes and there was a slight smile but there was nothing there for her to be afraid of or to distrust.

Something deep inside her unclenched, something she didn't even know was tense. That something was the wall she'd kept up all her life as a woman, keeping men out. They were allowed some small part of her, but not all. She never let down her defenses, not entirely. Even during sex, something inside her was kept tightly to herself.

It was gone. Something had cracked her wide open. Someone had cracked her wide open. This big man who'd done nothing but care for her since he'd saved her life.

"I don't think it's my head that's buzzing," she said softly, looking him straight in the eyes.

His black eyebrows rose.

"I think it's my body that's buzzing."

As if her words galvanized him, he bent his head and started kissing her wildly. She welcomed it. She welcomed everything he did to her. And he was doing it fast as if she'd unleashed something in him.

Fast was good. Honor found herself wanting fast. Wanting fast and hard and hot, because that was what was making her feel so *alive*.

His mouth caught hers, tongue licking inside her mouth, while his hands slid her soft pants and panties off under the covers. He lifted the duvet and she could hear her clothes slithering to the floor. Followed a second later by his jeans which made more noise. He had a lot of stuff in his jeans pockets and it all pinged off the floor.

Somehow — she had no idea how — he'd also managed to get his boots and socks off. They were both naked and she felt that hard, long body against hers.

It was delicious but she barely had a chance to relish it before hard hairy thighs pushed her legs apart. This was going so fast! She usually liked long lingering kisses and careful foreplay. This felt like being caught in a tornado.

And her body was with it, already open for him, already wet for him. Whatever he wanted, she wanted to give him because this feeling of power and heat was too wonderful to resist. She tried to touch him all over, everywhere her hands and mouth and legs could reach because he was a source of power, of otherworldly energy. When she touched him, it was like touching a huge life source that crackled under her fingertips.

Sometimes it felt like she dealt in death, day in day out. But not now. Now there was life in the bed with them, huge and hot and heavy and smelling of male sweat and somehow leather again and altogether heavenly.

She put her nose to his neck and simply inhaled, smiling against his skin. He smelled of sex, too. They smelled of sex even though, technically, they hadn't made love yet.

Soon, though.

Matt shifted his body until he was completely covering her, his huge penis poised at her entrance. It might hurt. She was prepared for that. He was bigger than most. But she didn't care because she was about ready to explode, on the verge of orgasm just from touching him.

This was so very unlike her. She'd had lovers who complained about how hard it was to get her to come, so she'd learned the fine feminine art of faking it. She wasn't faking anything right now. She was shaking, right on the verge of a climax, completely open to him.

He positioned himself, began slowly entering her and all her energy coiled, spiraled to that one spot where they were joined. She was shaking, so close …

Matt stopped, lifted himself up on his arms.

He was stopping?

He was *stopping?*

Right now?

Her eyes snapped open. "What?"

His horrified face was so close it was all she saw. "Condoms!"

Honor could barely think, moved her hips so she could take more of him. What was he saying? He held himself up and away from her. The beast!

"Honey, I don't have condoms! Fuck fuck fuck! Never even occurred to me that I would need them up here. What are we going to do?"

Honor pressed the back of his head down to her, until their faces were touching, their mouths almost kissing.

"We are constantly tested. And I take contraceptive shots."

His breath left his lungs in a huge whoosh.

"And you?"

"I've been tested too. No diseases. Clean as a whistle. The only thing I'm suffering from is blue balls."

He slid a little further into her and she shivered, tightened her legs around him.

"Ahhh." They were kissing and she smiled into his mouth. He lifted his mouth from hers and her smile grew larger as he moved deeply into her. "We can't have that, can we? Make love to me, Matt. Doctor's orders."

And he began moving.

Eight

Matt's face was right up against her neck. He could feel the softness of her skin against his lips, smell her skin, which smelled of that rose-scented soap all the bathrooms had. Rose-scented soap for the women and pine-scented soap for the guys. Her skin smelled of roses and a light veil of sex.

He drew in the smell. Mmm.

She'd been holding him tightly. Everything about her had been tight as she climbed that peak up to orgasm. Arms and legs tightly wound around him, muscles tight, face tight.

Then that glorious release and she turned boneless, arms flopping to her sides, legs relaxed and open.

He wasn't relaxed, particularly one part of him. That part was still tight and hard inside her.

But it didn't matter. He didn't want to draw attention to himself. Besides, just watching her come — man, that had been amazing.

"You didn't —"

He lifted his head a little. She was smiling at the

149

ceiling, eyes closed.

"No. I didn't."

She hesitated. "Do you —"

"Nope." Her eyes opened at that. Man, her eyes were something else. So light gray they were almost silver, with that dark blue band around the rim. He ran the back of his finger down her face, down that velvety skin. "Whatever you're going to say, I am absolutely fine. That was amazing."

Her face softened a little. "It was. I think this is the first time I've felt good in a long time. Maybe longer than my abduction."

His chest tightened a little at that. He knew very little about Honor Thomas, almost nothing of her background. From what Felicity uncovered, she was a dedicated and capable doctor and seemed not to have broken any laws. Other than that, what he knew was what he'd observed after he fished her out of the river. He liked everything he'd seen. He knew the basics. That she was strong and brave and uncomplaining. That she was smart.

And alone.

At no time had she mentioned a partner, not even the shadow of one. No one had come for her.

That threw him. Even this close to her, so close that his mouth brushed her skin, she was flawless. Fine features that didn't need any make up, smooth ivory skin, those gemlike cat eyes. Then there was the fact that she was super smart, funny even while in distress and was instinctively kind.

Any man who spent a couple of minutes with her and didn't fall for her didn't deserve a Y chromosome.

Matt himself had already fallen.

"I'm really glad you're feeling better." He couldn't get his fingers to detach from her skin. She was like a magnet to his hand.

Honor's lips upturned. "Orgasms release oxytocin and they lower cortisol. That's a very powerful endocrine reaction." She opened her eyes to look him fully in the face. "To all intents and purposes, Matt Walker, you drugged me."

Yep. Witty.

He moved his finger down the side of her face, outlined her lips. "Happy to oblige. Looking forward to doing it again."

Her eyes opened at that. She could tell what he meant because she could feel it.

Matt pressed inward, tightening his buttocks. Her legs were fully open, she was very wet. He slid forward easily. Pulled back. Slid forward again.

Slowly. Savoring every moment. He lowered himself more fully onto her, supporting a little of his weight on his forearms. He was heavy and he didn't want to crush her. Oh no. He wanted her to feel only pleasure. Judging by the sigh that ruffled his hair, it was working.

Matt threaded his fingers through that remarkable fiery hair until his hands cradled her head and closed his eyes. Touch and smell were more than enough.

Touch — oh my god. That silky skin. She was so soft and so firm all over. All woman, but strong. And that smell of roses and sex, it hit something deep in his brain and just switched him on.

He swelled inside her. "Wow," she whispered. "I don't know what you were thinking, but it was something else."

He'd picked up the pace, couldn't answer. Could barely talk. His entire being was concentrated on where he was joined to her, where she was so warm and wet and welcoming.

Time fractured, split, rearranged itself. He felt like he'd been in her forever because where else would he ever want to be? Inside her was softness and warmth and an excitement so fierce his heart was bouncing around inside his chest.

She curled around him again, legs twined around his, hands on his back, riding his thrusts. She was panting, moaning. Oh God, yes. Matt was going to make it good for her, keep it going, but then her fingernails bit into his ass and she arched and started convulsing around him and — he lost it.

The bed was creaking, pounding against the wall. They were both sweating, Matt more than her, bodies clinging together as he moved faster and faster ...

With a shout, he thrust inside her as hard as he could and started coming in jets so strong he thought he'd pass out. And just as he began slowing down, her sheath would clutch him and he'd swell again. Which made her cry out and hold him more tightly and clench around him in rhythmic waves. Their bodies talking to each other in a language as old as time, on and on for what seemed like an eternity.

Finally they both quieted and his heart settled to a fast beat rather than the wild gallop of before. He took in a deep breath, let it out, settled on her heavily.

He should be a gentleman, roll off her. He didn't have the strength to keep most of his weight on his forearms. Most of his weight was on her. When he could talk again he'd ask if he was crushing her.

In just a minute …

Matt drifted off to some quiet lush place where it was always sunny and warm. He had no idea how long he stayed in that place because time lost all meaning. All he knew was that he had no desire to move. He was exactly where he wanted to be — inside Honor Thomas, where it was warm and welcoming.

She drew in a big breath. Another. Ouch. That sounded like a wheeze. He was awake now but something had happened to his spine. It had disappeared. He'd lost use of his muscles, too.

Too bad. Maybe he'd just have to stay in this position forever. Worse things had happened. But when she wheezed again he was shocked into action. Or rather moved his fingers and toes.

Yup. They worked.

"I should get off you," he said.

"Mm." Her arms tightened around him briefly, but then she let him go. "Maybe, yeah. I love this but I also love breathing."

"Breathing's good. You're a doctor, you know that."

She expanded her chest to get some air. "I do like

being like this. Maybe breathing's overrated?"

He laughed, their bellies rubbing against each other. They were stuck together by their sweat and he could feel the wetness between her legs. Not romantic, but in a crazy way it was. They were as physically close as two human beings could get. He felt closer to her than he ever had to any other woman.

Usually when he noticed sweat and wet spots it was time to bug out. A quick shower and out the door. But not now. Now he was the one who was reluctant to move.

"I'm going to get up," he announced lazily.

"Any moment now," she answered.

They laughed. He lifted himself up a little. It was hard, but it also allowed him to look her in the eyes. Give a little, get a little. Man she was just so pretty after sex. Eyes shining, a glow in her cheeks. And the way she was looking at him ... *man.*

He idly rubbed his chest where his heart had suddenly given a kick.

She pulled in a breath, nostrils opening. He knew what she was smelling.

"We should shower." Her eyes half closed, lazily. "We smell."

"We do," he agreed. "It's not a bad smell, though."

"No." Her face turned serious. She reached out and cupped his cheek. "Not bad at all. Even sort of nice. In a gross way."

They both laughed again.

"You're a gentleman," she said and he nodded.

"That means I get to shower first. And I mean shower shower, not frolic under the showerhead. I saw that gleam in your eye."

"Busted," he groaned, flopping over on his back. True, he was a gentleman. Sort of. The truth was, he was too blasted to get up and shower. He needed recovery time. Even better if he got credit for gentlemanliness for it.

Honor threw back the comforter, letting cold air into their little nest. He could hear her padding to the bathroom, the shower being turned on. The shower wasn't the only thing being turned on, though. He was getting all heated up thinking of her under that shower, slowly soaping up a washcloth, wiping her breasts, down over her belly, between her legs …

The soft porn images were cut off by Honor pulling at his arm. "Your turn."

He hadn't even realized that the water had stopped running. She did everything fast, his lady.

Honor slid into the bed, eyeing his half boner bobbing in front of him as he shuffled to the bathroom, zonked with exhaustion and with hopeful lust. He glanced down at himself. Half boners were not a good look.

He made it a cold shower, so the boner would go down and so the shower would be short.

She lifted herself on one elbow and watched him as he walked back across the room. "Why does one of your boots have a knobby thing at the top?"

He stopped, trying to switch gears. "Knobby thing?"

She pointed at his right boot, lying askew on the floor. Ah. He bent, picked his boot up and slid out his Kershaw knife. It was razor sharp but didn't gleam because of the black oxide coating.

"A knife in a *boot?*"

"Damn right. Very handy. In fact, I used it to cut the fishing line when I caught you in the river. Without it, I'd have had to pull back and wait for it to be pulled out of your flesh."

She looked at it, at him. "Is that the knife you used?"

He slid the Kershaw back into the boot. "Nope. I had to leave it on the river bank. But I always have extras."

She was silent, taking it in. He let her. This was part of who he was. She nodded once, meeting his eyes.

At the bed, he smiled down at her and made a rolling gesture. "Scoot over."

She did, lifted the comforter, lying on her side so they were facing each other.

"So." She reached out, touched his face, slid her hand down to cup his shoulder. "You never really answered my question, you know. All you did was waylay me with sex. It worked, mind you. But the oxytocin is dropping and the neocortex is firing back up."

He heard one word in three because he was so fascinated by that beautiful face. "What?"

Her lips turned up. "When we started this conversation, I asked you what Jacko meant when he asked if you were done sulking up here in the mountains. Why are you up here when your job is in town at ASI?"

It felt like a bucket of cold water dashed in his face. Matt abruptly came into himself and withdrew. He was still right next to her, still touching her but he felt like he was a million miles away.

She waited, watching him.

She waited, this woman who'd been abducted, kept drugged, managed to escape only to nearly drown. Who hadn't once complained.

She wasn't pushing him for an explanation, either. No morbid curiosity in her gaze. There was simply warm acceptance, whatever he said.

Her job, probably. Her job led her to take care of people without any judgment at all. Matt was suddenly absolutely certain that she was a fantastic doctor, not only very capable but also very human.

"I'm not employed by ASI," he said. The words were wrenched out of him, coming from his mouth before he'd decided to talk.

She frowned, her grip on his shoulder tightening. "You're not? But everyone talked as if —"

"This isn't easy." Matt sighed. Evidently he was going to do this. He didn't want to but he was going to. "John and the Senior have me on the payroll but my bank has instructions not to deposit the money they keep sending me."

There was nothing on her face but acceptance. "I didn't even know you could do that at a bank."

"You can't. I had to negotiate it, because my bosses gave instructions to their bank not to accept the money coming back to them from my account. So there's now a considerable sum waiting … in limbo I guess."

"And who is the Senior?"

"We call him that because he was a Senior Chief in the Teams, which is somewhere between God and Satan, and as powerful as both. His name is Douglas Kowalski and together with John Huntington — Suzanne's husband — they own ASI. Though we are all given shares. The company is growing really fast. All of us are going to be very rich one day."

Her eyes searched his. "You don't care."

He sighed. "No, I don't. I mean I'm not stupid, but money isn't that much of a motivator for me. I need to derive meaning from what I do."

Honor nodded. "Same here."

Yeah, if her father was super rich but she refused to step into the company, he imagined that money wasn't that big a motivator for her, either.

"Don't get me wrong. I like ASI and they do good work. I like and trust my bosses and my coworkers. They do good stuff and there's no nonsense like there was —"

He looked away a moment, jaws working, the words not coming out. An anvil was sitting right on his chest, heavy iron, making it hard to breathe.

She didn't press. Didn't do anything, really, except watch him. Watch as he worked his way through it. He'd never talked about it to anyone who didn't already know, didn't already have the facts.

"Like there was in the Teams," he finished. Now the

anvil had moved up into his goddamned throat.

Her eyes searched his, back and forth, back and forth, flashes of silver.

"I imagine being a SEAL wasn't easy," she said finally. "That's what you were, right? A SEAL?"

He nodded. Something about her calm easy manner, her sympathetic unjudging eyes, made him relax a little. He pulled in some air, pushed it back out. Did it again. He could breathe.

"Yeah. Being a SEAL is a hard and dangerous job. But we train hard, too. And we all work together. So that part is great. Everyone on the Teams has each other's back. But sometimes, sometimes other aspects weren't great."

Again, he looked away, though it was hard to wrench his gaze from hers. He tried to look away but there wasn't anything to look at in the room that was better than looking at her.

"Your superiors?" she asked softly. "They had you and your guys doing things that didn't sit well with you?"

He stared. "Yeah. How did you know?"

She shrugged. "My hospital administrators regularly turn away bleeding and broken people who don't have insurance. I know all about terrible bosses."

"It wasn't my bosses, really. Our commanders were tough but they led from the front. No, it was the brass back home and some guys coming in from the outside. From a three-letter agency, mainly."

She nodded. "Who had other priorities."

Honor was making this all sound … normal. The anvil lifted away a little more.

"Yeah. Very different priorities. For a while we were tasked with liaising with an Afghan warlord in the foot-hills of the Hindu Kush. Al Rashid. Nasty mean son of a bitch, but the word was we were operating on the principle of 'my enemy's enemy is my friend'. So he was officially our friend. We were told that there were other priorities involved. He was a nasty and ignorant son of a bitch but keeping him happy seemed to be important. So I held my breath when I talked to him and did my best not to punch him in the face. Though every time he opened his mouth it was a real temptation. Our terp was embarrassed at what he had to translate."

"Do you think it was heroin? That was the priority?"

He stared at her.

Honor shrugged. "I read the news. If you're not fighting the Taliban what other priorities could there be? You don't seem to be the kind of man who would promote the heroin trade."

The anvil was gone but his chest burned.

"Fuck no." She didn't even blink at the profanity and he relaxed a little. No way could he get through this without a few f-bombs. "The man from the three-letter agency was involved in the heroin trade, I am absolutely certain. And the warlord was sitting on miles and miles of poppy fields. We had orders to keep him happy."

She grimaced. "That must have been hard."

Fuck yeah. "You have no idea."

"Actually," she said, her voice soft. "I think I do.

Go on." Her thumb was caressing the back of his hand, a smooth regular motion that somehow synched with the beat of his heart.

Her touch calmed him.

"So. There was a firefight where we had to defend the warlord and his property. From on high was the word that we were fighting the Taliban but I think it was just some poor fucks in the area who wanted to get rid of the warlord. Well, we saved the warlord's ass for about the tenth time. And I lost two of my men."

Chavez and O'Leary. Two of the finest men he'd ever met. Al Rashid hadn't been worthy of shining their combat boots.

Her hand tightened around his.

"I had to put their belongings into a box together with their tags to send to their families. Chavez had a wife and two kids. O'Leary a girlfriend he was going to ask to marry him. They'd died to save that nasty fuck's life and to make sure someone had access to the poppy fields."

"I'm so sorry," she breathed. He looked at her and saw that it was true. She was sorry, it showed in her face and eyes. It made it easier to go on.

He nodded. "So you'll understand that when I went up to his compound without an appointment to deliver some news, I wasn't in the best of moods. His head-quarters was basically a hovel of crumbling stucco walls with flea-infested rugs on the floor and a few rickety pieces of furniture. But he had brand new weapons and brand new SUVs and gold rings on every finger of his hand."

It came back to him in a rush. The heat of an unrelenting sun beating down, the sight of an emaciated villager beating some poor mangy dog, the smell of dust and untreated sewage, sullen eyes following his progress through the unpaved streets leading to the compound, then everyone disappearing all at once.

Gritting his teeth as he walked into the village because the warlord had an aura of crazy nastiness that required every ounce of self control he had.

Entering that village of beaten-down souls was like entering hell itself. He hated it, his men hated it, but they had their orders and they did what they'd been told to do. They bitched on the way there and on the way back but they were complete pros while there.

Just the memory of that place now made his heart beat faster. "The village was completely deserted by the time we came to the compound. And I could hear screams."

Her eyes widened. "Screams?"

He nodded. The sound still woke him up in his nightmares. "Screams. The screams of a child. High pitched and desperate."

She let go of his hand to cover her mouth. "Oh no," she breathed.

She understood. She was like him. The thought of children being mistreated drove him insane. He'd thought everyone was like that until he'd found out the hard way that some people liked hurting kids. But she felt the same way he did. God knew how many mistreated kids she'd seen in the ER.

"I ran, my men behind me. The screams were coming from the compound. I thought — I thought someone had finally come to assassinate the warlord, maybe a kid with an explosive vest, and I was bound to defend the fuckhead. We rushed into the courtyard and then into the main room. No one was assassinating the warlord."

"What did you see?" she whispered.

Matt's teeth clenched so hard he was surprised shards weren't shooting out his ears.

"I saw the warlord raping a little boy so hard he was screaming in pain."

"Oh God." Her voice was just a thread, eyes wide.

Matt closed his, but it didn't do any good. For the rest of his life he'd see that vicious scene over and over and feel the same things over and over. Horror and rage and disgust.

He huffed out a breath. "It's called *bacha bazi*, which basically translates as boy toys." He was looking away but slid his eyes back to her face for a moment. She was pale, horrified.

Yeah.

"We were briefed on this going in, but we were also told that it had been all but eradicated. Yeah, right. Fuckhead warlord didn't get the memo."

"What did you do?" Her voice was laced with sorrow.

It took him a second to answer. "I broke his jaw. First thing. I wanted to kill him and I would have, without a second thought, but one of my men caught me. Stopped me. He didn't pull his weapon but he said afterward he was thinking of it."

She laid a hand on his forearm and could probably feel his tension under her fingers. "I'm surprised they stopped you. But I understand why they did. I nearly attacked a 300-lb 6'4" man who came in with a little girl who was cradling a broken arm in complete silence because she was terrified of him. She froze every time he looked at her, tried to make herself as small as possible. And her stepfather would stand over her, watching every word she said. I wanted to knock him out cold. But I took an oath to heal."

"Yeah." Matt nodded. She understood. She understood completely. "I wanted to waste the fucker, but I couldn't. Had to be content with breaking his jaw. And besides that, there was a wounded little boy to look after. He was bleeding. And he was shackled to the table."

Her eyes widened.

"Yeah. Just like you. It had been badly forged and had sharp edges. The kid had nearly cut his own hand off trying to get away. Luckily, I had our corpsman with us and he was able to stop the bleeding, stitch him up." While he'd been stitching the kid up, the fuckhead on the floor had started groaning. Matt had kicked him in the head and he went back out like a light. No one said anything, anything at all. "The kid started babbling. I know Pashto. But the kid spoke some kind of dialect. I did recognize one word though. Others. He kept repeating it and he pointed to a back room."

She was watching him so intently, silvery eyes sad. She gave a little sigh, knowing what was coming. She squeezed his hand.

"Yeah. So I followed this kid down a dusty filthy corridor, down a rickety wooden staircase to a room underground. Just following that kid was the saddest thing I'd ever done. He was emaciated, in rags, bleeding from the wrists, so stressed he'd lost his hair. When he turned to point down the stairs, he was actually crying blood. I've seen a lot of shit in the military but I'd never seen that before. It took me a minute to look at what he was pointing to."

Matt stopped, jaws working.

"Bad?" she said softly.

His head hung heavy between his shoulders. "Bad."

He'd seen bad shit but never like this.

The memory was with him constantly. Often all he had to do was close his eyes and he could see those little boys in hi-def, 8K. Eleven of them, shackled to the wall like miniature Counts of Montecristo. Only they weren't men, they were boys. Tiny, emaciated, dressed in rags that stuck to filthy skin where they'd bled. Cheekbones stark in furrowed faces that somehow looked old, though they were just kids. Eight, nine maybe ten years old.

But also a thousand years old.

Matt had grown up in a stable and loving family in Santa Cruz. When he was ten, the biggest thing in his life had been baseball, Little League. He slept with his brand new catcher's mitt and neglected his homework.

His world was made up of loving parents and two sets of grandparents nearby, friendly neighbors, a crowd of baseball-crazy boys to run with. His world had been stable and safe. A million miles away from what those boys had gone through.

"There was a key hanging from a ring on the wall. I took the key and unlocked all the shackles. My men watched me without saying a word. I told the boys that it was going to be okay, though it was never going to be okay for them, ever again. But I told them I was going to take them somewhere safe. I don't think they understood me but they understood the tone. They believed I was there to help, though they had no reason to. I think it was because anywhere else would be safer than there. We had to walk out through the warlord's council room. His jaw was mangled and he couldn't talk, but he had four of his fighters behind him and they were holding AK-74s, aimed right at my chest."

For the rest of his life, Matt would remember the metallic sound of his men bringing up their weapons in perfect unison, all the muzzles pointed at the warlord's chest.

Stalemate.

Matt was not going to back down and he knew the warlord knew it. Bullies know. Matt was not going to put those boys back into that man's hands. He'd rather die.

He knew he'd reached a turning point. A line in the sand had been drawn in his head. He was not walking away from this. All the shit he'd seen and done in Iraq and Afghanistan … it stopped here.

His jaws clenched and his breathing sped up, remembering.

"Matt?" Honor laid a hand on his forearm, grounding him, bringing him back. "What happened?"

"The warlord finally broke the stalemate. He made his men lower their weapons."

"You'd have shot him." She said it as a statement, not a question.

"Damn right. It was point-blank range but we had body armor and they didn't. And I was not going back down that hillside without those boys. I was not going to leave them to that monster. So I walked out, herding those boys in front of me. I didn't dare look behind me, but I knew my men were with me, watching my six."

"He was too scared to attack you. Bullies are like that."

Matt nodded. "Once inside the troop carrier, we saw that the kids were still terrified. Not much we could do about that, but we gave them bottles of water and MREs and they relaxed a little after that. I just wanted to get them down off that damn mountain and to a UN medical station about 40 clicks from our FOB. Our Forward Operating Base."

He hesitated, memories crowding in. The heat, the dust. The terrible smell of the kids, their open pus-filled wounds. The way they attacked the water and food. They'd been so starved their systems couldn't take it and several vomited the food and water right back up. It had been an endless ride down to the base.

Honor looked down at his suddenly clenched hand. He had to focus to relax it. She traced the lines of his palm then looked up. "Please tell me this story has a happy ending."

"No, ma'am, it doesn't."

She didn't wince, her face just became sadder. As an ER physician, he imagined she was used to unhappy endings. You can't save everyone. "What happened?"

"Well, fuckhead must have radioed down because we had our CIA liaison waiting for us, fuming, when we got back from the UN camp where we left the kids. He was nearly frothing at the mouth. Got right up in my face, screaming threats."

"What kind of threats?"

"That I'd be court-martialed for stealing the property of a CIA asset, for one."

She shot up straight at that. "Stealing the property of that vile man? He called those kids *property*?"

Matt had gotten used to the story but he could see that it hit her just as hard as it had hit him. Color was in her face and her gray eyes flashed with rage.

"Yeah. He said we had to respect local customs and *bacha bazi*, using small boys as sex toys, was a longstanding custom."

Honor's eyes narrowed. "We fought a bloody civil war so that no human being would ever be considered anyone's property, ever again. We can't condone slavery overseas either. I don't care what local customs are. That's precisely why we fight."

"That's what I said, only I used more colorful

168

language."

"Well, could you report him to — to the authorities?"

Matt felt the weight of it all over again. "No, but he reported me."

Her eyes widened. "He *what*?"

"He reported me for insubordination, dereliction of duty, violence toward an American military ally and theft. And though my commanding officer vouched for me, Lee Chamness had a lot of power. It — what?" Her hand had jerked inside his. "What is it?"

"That name." her voice dropped to a whisper. She stared at him, eyes wide. "Chamness —"

"Lee Chamness. Yeah." He wasn't ever likely to forget that name. Just hearing it, even when he himself said it, made his heart race with rage. "Corrupt piece of shit." The color had drained from her face. "Hey. Do you know him?"

She looked poleaxed, but was shaking her head. "No. N-no. I've never heard that name before, yet when you said it, my heart jumped."

Matt frowned. "Do you know another Lee Chamness? I mean it's not a common name but it's not an unusual one, either."

She sat transfixed, unmoving, barely breathing. Her gaze had turned inward as if consulting herself. She gave a little shake. "No. No, it means nothing to me and yet — it does." Her face was troubled. Her hand shook in his. "How can that be?"

"I don't know." Matt ran a gentle thumb across the

deep frown lines between her brows, trying to ease her anxiety. Man, he was asking so much of her and she was still recovering. "You know, it's probably nothing. Maybe the name is similar to a name you know. Maybe some former patient."

"Maybe." She looked troubled. Shook herself as if shaking off a bad dream. "So what happened? What did he do?"

"Chewed me out in front of my commanding officer, who had no choice but to take it. Said I'd destroyed a long game. He took it all the way up the line. I was spared a court-martial only because half the Navy stepped in. But the CIA has real clout and I was kicked out. Given an Other Than Honorable Discharge. It's what they give to drug addicts or alcoholics. Or soldiers with dementia."

"Oh my God," she breathed. "That's awful!"

Matt nodded. "The brass was only able to save my ass because I had a chestful of medals and a couple of big ones in a shadowbox that civilians couldn't know about but that the DOD did. Guaranteed." He blew out a slow stress-relieving breath. "The fucker tried to wreck my life. An Other Than Honorable Discharge stops you from ever working for the government. I lost my pension. Luckily, ASI knew the whole story and they couldn't care less about the OTH. So, in the end, it's okay. I heard Chamness left the CIA."

"And the kids?"

He sighed. "The kids." He picked up her hand, played with the fingers. No rings. Thank God. "The kids didn't make it."

"Not one of them?"

"Not a one. The UN camp was running low on supplies and they didn't have much beyond antibiotics and some other meds. They did what they could but the kids were weak, malnourished. Stressed beyond imagining. There was no saving them. And that's why I am sulking on the mountain."

She laid her hand over his. "I'm so sorry. You trashed your career to save them."

He lifted a shoulder. "Well, I tried. It's all anyone can do."

"Don't I know it. We've had kids come in after getting drunk and crashing the car, we prep them for surgery, then a team of surgeons and surgical nurses will work ten hours to save them and then they just slip away. It's heartbreaking."

He watched her face as she spoke. Watched the passion and the sadness and the regret and knew that she understood, as few ever could.

Nine

The next morning, Honor woke up again, refreshed. Each time she slept she woke up feeling stronger, more like herself.

The clouds in her head wouldn't lift completely, though. Retrograde amnesia was a bitch.

Ribot's Law, governing the interaction between the medial temporal hippocampus and multiple areas in the neocortex. The stronger the trauma, the further away the lost memories could be. She'd studied it, she'd dealt with it in the ER, but she'd never experienced it. It was frightening beyond measure to lose memories of your life, of yourself. To have a black void where *you* should be.

She still had no real memories of anything after the eruption of the volcano. She had a few images, like photographs briefly flashing across her field of vision, some snatches of conversation though she couldn't identify the voices. No clue as to what was being said. Every time she thought things were coming into focus and concentrated, an almost crippling flash of pain shot through her brain, so intense tears would spring in her eyes.

She learned the hard way not to push it. The pain was so intense she thought she'd pass out.

It was horrifying to think that she might have lost those days forever.

Could Matt and maybe some of his people help her find out?

But if people started enquiring after her, would word get back to the nameless shadowy people who'd kidnapped her? Would they realize she wasn't dead after all, and come after her again?

So many questions, so few answers. Still, she was getting physically stronger. Maybe her memory would come back, too. Not ever coming back — no, that was too awful to contemplate.

There was a dent in the pillow next to her head and the blankets on Matt's side of the bed were thrown back. No sounds from the bathroom. He'd let her sleep.

She showered and changed into a pale gray sweater and soft black yoga pants, again blessing the women who'd left clothes here.

Oh man, she'd give anything to go back home. To her quiet, restful apartment. To have her things around her. This place was super luxurious and there was everything she needed, but it felt as blank as her mind. Nothing here was hers, nothing here touched her in any way.

Except, well, for Matt Walker. He touched her, big time. The sex they'd had filled her with joy and heat and life. Just his presence made her feel better. Talking to him was reassuring, made her feel a little less lost.

Honor had never needed a man to make her complete. This was entirely new. The thing was, it didn't feel backward and needy. It felt … right.

It felt right to talk to Matt holding his hand. Him heating Isabel's excellent food for her felt right, too. Walking around the Grange, hand in hand, made the place less foreign to her, more welcoming.

Truth be told, she missed him. She never missed anyone, but she missed him right now. Was that dependency?

Well, no point feeling bad about that, not when she had so much to feel bad about. His presence was one of the good things about her situation. His presence and that of his friends. They all had her back.

Imagine if she'd survived the rapids of the river, found herself beached on the river bank, in the cold, wet late afternoon. Battered and bruised, danger screeching in her mind but not knowing where the danger was.

She was strong, but she wouldn't have survived that. Where would she have gone? They were out in backcountry here. She'd have frozen to death that night, or if she'd somehow survived the night, she'd have starved to death because she had no way to get into town, back to civilization. She still didn't know exactly where they were.

The door of the room closed behind her and she walked slowly toward the Great Hall. Though there didn't seem to be any windows the area was filled with light. What time was it, anyway? The light was artificial but the air smelled fresh, maybe because of the huge plants in big enamel vases. She skirted an enormous lemon tree, taking in the slight citrusy scent with pleasure.

What would have happened without Matt? Someone would have found her bones, maybe months from now. He'd saved her.

And there he was, walking toward her. His head cocked as he studied her. It was the assessment of someone who cared. The second assessment was pure male, his gaze like hands reaching out and touching her. Heat filled her, down to her fingertips.

"Hey," he said softly. "You look —" he paused. She expected him to say she was looking good, looking rested. Instead what he said was, "You look beautiful."

The way he was looking at her, she felt beautiful.

He held his arm out at a weird angle. "Ma'am? May I escort you to your breakfast?"

It was role play but it felt … good. The men in Honor's life had never been particularly chivalrous. She'd dated mostly med students and fellow doctors and they were not romantically inclined. Presumably soldiers, too, were not romantically inclined, but though Matt was play-acting, there was something genuinely chivalrous about him. He was a protector, an old-fashioned kind of guy.

And it just so happened she needed protecting.

She fluttered her lashes, appalled to find she did it completely naturally. Without a hint of irony. Putting her hand in the crook of his elbow she smiled up at him. "Lead the way."

They set off very slowly and Honor frowned. Then realized Matt was setting his pace to slow. The kind of slow nurses were familiar with as they escorted patients down the hallway of the hospital. But Honor didn't feel slow. She felt … *strong.* Well, if not strong, then stronger.

She tugged at his arm. "Hurry up, slow poke. I'm hungry!"

"Yes, ma'am." And his stride lengthened.

He led them across the Great hall to the small kitchen and table. The table was already set. He seemed to always be cooking for her. Or at least nuking for her, he'd said his cooking skills were nonexistent. Still, it was the thought that counted.

"Ma'am." He pulled out a chair and seated her in it as if she were the Queen of the Grange, then rounded a counter to the kitchen area.

He frowned with concentration as he transferred something from a plastic bin to a plate for microwaving, like some five-star chef checking the arugula leaves were placed just so. He looked up suddenly, met her eyes. That dark intense gaze, it just took her breath away.

Heat flashed through her again, life-restoring, glorious sexual heat. For the first time she understood the phrase she'd heard hundreds of young girls use — I have the hots for him.

The hots. Yeah.

What she felt flashing through her was hot and

elemental and … healing. For the first time since he'd fished her out of the river, Honor felt like she was going to be okay. Maybe. At least her body. Maybe her mind would continue to be like Swiss cheese but she could feel strength flowing back into her, like a beloved long-lost friend.

Matt came around the kitchen island, a slight smile on his face. "Well, look at you. You're looking real good." He walked up to her, so close she had to tilt her head back to meet his eyes.

"Thanks." She tilted her head to one side. There was something about his face …

"What?" he asked.

"You're — you're smiling." Not a big smile but definitely a tilting up of his mouth. A slight dent in his cheeks which in a lesser man might be dimples. The first real smile she'd seen.

"Am not." Said with a straight face.

"Are too." She huffed out a little laugh. Her first laugh since she'd arrived.

It felt good.

Nothing had changed. She'd been abducted, had almost died escaping, she had to stay under the radar for who knew how long. But she was alive. Alive and in the company of a very vital and attractive man who made her heart beat faster. A man she'd had sex with and judging by his look and what she felt, would have sex with again. Very soon.

Not only that. They were in some kind of luxury stronghold that not even alien forces could penetrate, as safe as safe as could be.

Matt lifted his hand, stroked her cheek. His hand left warmth in its wake, a little streak of heat. "Good to see you smiling."

"Yeah." Her throat tightened. So many things she wanted to say. Thank you for risking your life to save mine. Thank you for doing so much to solve the riddle of my abduction. Thank you for all the amazing people willing to help. But the only thing that came out was, "I'm alive."

Such a stupid thing, it didn't express a billionth of what she wanted to say. But somehow it made sense to Matt. He nodded. "You surely are." He turned at the sound of the microwave dinging. "Let's keep you that way. First, food."

Yesterday it had taxed her to cross the Great Hall. She'd been tired by the time she made it across. Now it had felt normal, just a pleasant walk, made even more pleasant by her hand in the crook of his arm.

"Wow." She looked up at Matt. "You know, I don't feel exhausted. I feel pleasantly tired but not like I want to curl up on the floor, like yesterday."

"I'm really glad. You're recovering very fast." He narrowed his eyes. "Are you sure you're not a SpecOps soldier? A SEAL?"

She smiled. "Nope. I'm not a strong swimmer at all and my idea of strenuous exercise is walking to the corner coffee shop. You'd probably consider me a real wimp."

That wiped the smile off his face. He brought her

hand to his mouth, kissed the back of it. "I think any woman who managed to get away from kidnappers who'd shackled and drugged her is anything but a wimp. I think you're one of the bravest people I've ever met."

She wanted to scoff but his dark eyes were so serious. It felt like he was looking right into her and that he liked what he saw.

She blushed.

Dear sweet God. She seemed to be blushing all the time. Honor *never* blushed. She was an emergency-room physician, for heaven's sake. Her daily job was getting up to her elbows in gore and blood. She'd heard it all and she'd seen it all.

Good sex had changed her.

For some reason sex and attraction had fled from her life. A series of small steps had just whittled her life down to work and home. Her best friend at the hospital, a thoracic surgeon, had left three months ago and Honor still missed her. There wasn't anyone else she'd want to go out with on a Saturday night for a drink or two.

The men — they were as tired as she was and lately the hospital administration had hired only unattractive ones, screening them for lack of sex appeal. Or at least that was what it felt like.

It had been a long time since she'd felt that tug of desire, that flutter inside.

And so she blushed.

It wasn't anything serious. Honor knew the mechanism inside out. Matt triggered a response that caused her glands to release adrenaline in her body. In reaction, her nervous system caused the capillaries carrying blood to her skin to widen, coming closer to the surface of the skin. Making her blush.

No big deal.

She glanced up at him to see if he'd noticed but he went back to the kitchen island. Inside, she blew a breath of relief. He hadn't noticed. Good.

"So I chose the breakfast menu. Or rather brunch, since you slept in," he said as he put food on the table. It was set with a pretty pale yellow cotton tablecloth and thick brown earthenware dishes. "Eggplant parmesan, focaccia and then later homemade blueberry ice cream. But that's the last time I choose. From now on, I'll just get you the spreadsheet and you choose what you want to eat. So far I've chosen Italian because I like Italian, but there's every single cuisine here. Your choice from now on. How does that sound?"

He was looking down at her with a slight frown, as if she might possibly object.

"Sounds great."

His face cleared. "Good. Now I'll …" the microwave sounded again. "There we go. My work here is done."

He put a huge ceramic serving dish of steaming eggplant parmesan, oozing tomato sauce and melted cheese, in the middle of the table.

The smell was almost overwhelming.

"Fat and carbs," she sighed. "Two of the major food groups."

"Yep." He cut her a humongous slice. "And later we'll have sugar. All the bases covered."

She was about to protest the size of the serving he heaped on her plate, expecting her stomach to close up. But nope. It just opened wide, all but curling its virtual fingers. *Gimme gimme.*

Another ding and Matt got up to get the focaccia out of the oven. Oh man, it was almost more awesome than the eggplant parmesan. Crispy gold, with flakes of sea salt, glistening with olive oil. That wonderful smell of hot bread. Matt tore off a big piece and handed it to her. She picked it up then immediately dropped it. It was piping hot.

Matt hadn't even noticed how hot it was when handling the focaccia. Without thinking, she picked up his big hand, turning it over, palm up. His hand was covered in calluses. He sat quietly while she traced some of them with her index finger.

"What do you do to have calluses like this?" Her gaze met his and like magnets meeting, there was an extraordinary moment of connection. This was a closed man who had decided to open up to her. His entire big body was built for battle. She imagined he didn't give up control easily. But here he was — his hand in hers, eyes fixed on hers, seemingly open to any question she had.

Her hand curled around his. It was warm and large and very very strong, with raised veins on the back.

"Matt?"

He'd been staring at her eyes intently and he suddenly seemed to come back into himself. Glancing at his hand, he gave a half smile.

"Well, let's see." He traced thick calluses on the side of his fists. "Those are karate calluses."

She traced them too. Hard tissue. Calluses came about by repeated pressure or friction which caused the skin to die and reform until it created a hard, protective surface. To create calluses like these would have required repeated pressure. If it was because of karate exercises, then repeated blows. "And these?"

Her finger traced the top part of his palm.

"Basically, carrying things. We hump a lot of crap in the field. Some on our backs but weapons have to be kept close."

She nodded, then frowned. He had heavy calluses in the webbing between thumb and forefinger. She tried to imagine anything that would create friction there but couldn't. "And this?"

He sighed. "Shooting practice. We shoot maybe fifty thousand rounds a year. It breaks the sensitive skin there, the skin scabs over, it's broken again, scabs over until finally it gets really tough."

He was watching her carefully. Was he gauging her reaction?

"Repetition," she said. "The only way to learn. In medical school I spent about four hours a day every day practicing suture knots. I could do it in my sleep. Even now, under stress, my fingers twitch. I think it's the autonomous nervous system, my fingers tying knots without me realizing it."

He was looking down at her, completely serious,

unmoving.

Honor cleared her throat. Glanced at the table. He looked a second away from kissing her and man, she was up for it.

Then her stomach growled.

"Someone's hungry," he said. That intent look was gone.

Someone was.

Matt sat down opposite her, and she ate the entire huge serving of eggplant parmesan and a huge slice of focaccia.

He kept pace, and stood when she'd mopped up the last of the tomato sauce with the bread.

"Where are you going?" she called out to that broad back.

He took something out of the freezer and grabbed two small bowls. "I promised you desert."

She was full. "Oh no. I couldn't."

He placed a bowl with two scoops of blue ice cream in front of her. "Okay. But as a favor to me, just try a small spoonful of this. It's homemade."

Put like that ... Honor tried it and it was like eating fresh fruit only sweeter and creamy. God.

"This is sinful. You say you have a bunch of this stuff?"

Matt nodded. "Freezers full and several walk-in lockers. My guys believe in being prepared. Plus Isabel teaches classes up here and they freeze everything. Everything's in a computer file. All of us could live up here for years and not starve."

Honor looked around at the beautiful space. The Great Hall was lit up, no natural light, but somehow glowing. "Almost makes you long for the zombie apocalypse, doesn't it? Just … stay here with friends and eat well. But then I guess the food stocks would eventually run out."

"Maybe not." Matt stood and carried the plates to the sink. He held out a big hand for her to remain seated. "They're experimenting with hydroponics. If the zombies come, and if we're willing to go vegan, we should be okay."

Honor drained the last of her glass of wine. Excellent wine. "Maybe wine making will cease."

"Maybe." He stood next to her, a hand on her shoulder. The heavy weight of it felt good, reassuring. "I don't know. But the wine cellars are pretty extensive. Take a lot of time to drink it. Even for us. Listen, I called in a buddy. He was an Army puke but we forgive him. He's okay. Right now he's a detective in the PPD. Will you talk to him? We can Skype on the big screen."

"Sure." She looked up at him. "You trust him." It wasn't a question.

"Absolutely." He looked at her straight on, face sober. "With my life and with yours."

"That's good enough for me." They crossed the Great Hall and went into another stylish room that had a 60" flat screen on one wall. "Wait. You said he's a detective 'right now'. What does that mean?"

Matt picked up a remote and switched the big screen on and sat down. He patted the cushion next to him and she obediently sat down. He put his arm around her shoulders and she leaned into him. Leaned into that warm strength. Oh God, this feeling was almost addictive. Of being protected and safe and excited, all at once.

"His name is Luke. Luke Reynolds. Like I said, an Army puke, became a Ranger. We all cross-trained. He's not bad for being Army." Honor knew that Rangers were Special Operations soldiers like SEALs. "When he separated, he became a cop. A really good one. Medals up the wazoo, excellent recommendations, on his way up. Then he arrested the Sigma Phi Five. Cracked the case wide open."

Honor looked at Matt. The Sigma Phi Five. Sigma Phi was a fraternity at an expensive private college. A young girl had been found raped and then suffocated in a park six months ago. No clues, no leads. For a while, the rape and murder had been attributed to a homeless man who'd been camping out nearby, but there hadn't been any forensic evidence linking him to the crime.

And then five young men were arrested. The evidence against them was strong. All of them except one had very powerful fathers — two billionaire internet moguls, a Senator and a famous actor. The fifth was relatively poor, father a high school teacher. The fifth testified that the boys had met the young girl at a club, given her something to 'make her happy'. They then took her to a nearby park and brutally raped her and suffocated her. The fifth young man wept bitterly as he recounted the story and said he didn't take part in the rape. And there was no trace of his sperm.

And yet, the four rich boys got off on technicalities. During the trial, the police officer who'd made the arrests had been crucified by the most expensive lawyers in the land.

The boy without family money was serving a twenty-year sentence.

"So the cop in the case – that's your friend?"

Matt nodded, eyes sober. "Yeah. Luke is a fine cop, the best, and he was mauled to death by lawyers and the press. The police commissioner, Bud Morrison, fought tooth and nail for him and went to the mat. But the commissioner was going to lose his job, so Luke quit, effective the end of the month. Said there was no point in two good men going down."

"My God," she breathed. "That's awful. Those fathers bought their way out of a murder conviction and destroyed the life of the police officer."

She remembered how it played out, though it had been a time when the ER had been short two doctors. But she'd been fascinated and had followed as well as she could.

"Well, our bosses leaped at the opportunity to get their hands on Luke. Not only was he a Ranger but he is a fine detective and the company is getting more and more requests for jobs that require investigative skills. He's slated to begin next month, just like me."

Two fine men who'd been betrayed, she thought.

Matt checked his watch. "Five minutes." He turned to her. "I told Luke to make discreet inquiries about you." He felt her stiffen. "I swear, Luke knows what he's doing."

Her heart thumped hard in her chest. It was instinctive, primal. "My God if the men who abducted me find out I'm not dead, they'll —"

"Shh." Matt placed a finger on her mouth. He pulled her head forward until their foreheads touched. "It's okay, honey. It's okay, I promise. Luke knows what he's doing." He pulled his head away to look her in the eyes. "Would I do anything to endanger you? Would I?"

She barely heard the words. She only heard 'honey' and her heart gave another thump. A better kind of thump than the panicked thumps of before. His words played again in her head.

Would he do anything to endanger her?

Well … no. Since he'd fished her out of the water, risking his life, he'd done nothing but take care of her and protect her. He wasn't likely to put her in jeopardy.

Honor was used to taking life and death decisions, fast. She didn't like putting power over her in anyone else's hands. But this wasn't a medical emergency or even a medical issue. It was a security one and she was out of her depth. Security for her meant making sure she had a hand on her pepper spray when walking to the car at night.

She shook her head.

He held her shoulders, forcing her to look at him. "It's very important for you to stay in hiding. But it's also important to understand what we're up against.

You can't hide forever. At some point we have to be proactive, and that's what Luke's done. Will you hear him out?"

Her instincts vied with reality. Her instincts told her to tuck herself away from the world. Just go under the bed or in a closet or in a cabin somewhere and lock the door. But he was right. Nobody could stay hidden forever. And that 'we' felt so good. She wasn't alone in this. She had a team.

"Okay." It was the only possible response, but it was hard to say. She was putting her life, quite literally, in Matt's hands.

"Good girl," he said and kissed her on the forehead.

Turning to the screen he touched a button and all of a sudden a person was there on the big screen, looking straight ahead.

He was very handsome, like a Ken doll, except a Ken doll that hadn't slept in three months, hadn't shaved in weeks and hadn't had a haircut in a long while. He looked like a good-looking man who'd died and been badly embalmed.

Very fair, long blond hair that hadn't seen a comb in a while, light stubble on his face, lines and bags around light blue eyes, fine features.

Completely serious expression.

"Matt," he said in a low baritone.

"Luke." Matt nodded his head. "What do you have?"

"Did you tell Dr. Thomas what the mission parameters were?"

Honor spoke up. "I haven't been told much of anything, Mr. Reynolds."

"Luke."

"Okay, Luke. And I'm Honor."

"Honor." He nodded gravely. "I don't want you to feel we did an end run around you, Honor, but the fact is, we did."

Honor wanted to be angry. "Yeah, you did."

"If we want to hit back against the guys who took you, we need more intel." He seemingly looked straight at her, face sober.

There was no disputing that. The one thing that was terrifying about what had happened to her was that the reasons were shrouded in fog. Not only did she not know what had happened during the days she'd been in captivity, she also had no idea why she'd been abducted.

Given that, they'd had to go out to get information. She sure couldn't.

Honor gave a half shrug. "I don't like it, on several different levels, but I do understand why you had to do it. So, Luke, what did you find out?"

The man on the screen leaned forward on muscled forearms and stared straight at the screen. "I went to your place of work."

"To the *hospital?*" The hairs stood up on the back of her neck.

"Yeah. Don't worry, I didn't give anything away. My cover was that I was an old university buddy of yours and I was in town and we'd made an appointment to meet but you hadn't showed up."

"Okay. That works." It did. Was clever, even. "What did you find out?"

"First of all, that the last time anyone had seen you was June 6th."

Honor sat up straight. This was what Felicity had said. She glanced over at Matt. His body language didn't change but his face tightened.

Luke continued. "Worked a full day shift. No one noticed anything wrong."

Okay. June 6th was ten days ago. She didn't remember anything about that day. The retrograde amnesia created by the drugs was still a fog in her head.

Luke had a notebook in front of him but didn't consult it. "I spoke with three doctors. Two men and a woman. Dr Green, Dr Harvey and Dr Lin. Like I said, I told them I was an old friend of yours from college days, had moved to Connecticut, but was briefly in Portland. We had arranged to meet for coffee to catch up but you didn't show. So I went to the hospital, thinking you'd been caught up in an emergency, and was prepared to wait for you. I spoke with the nurses and all they knew was that you hadn't been in for the past ten days. They told me to speak to an administrator, an Emily Cotfield, but she'd taken personal time unexpectedly. Her daughter broke her arm at school. I was prepared to come back later or the next day but then I spoke with Dr Lin."

"Mei." Honor smiled as she suddenly remembered Mei. One of her few close friends on the job. Green and Harvey were just colleagues, not friends. Mei was a friend, and would have been a close one if they saw each other more. They rarely saw each other outside work. Mei had a husband with multiple sclerosis and rushed home after work as quickly as she could. As far as Honor knew, Mei never allowed herself even a cup of coffee with a colleague after work hours. But she was funny and hardworking and they'd struck up a friend-ship at work. Mei knew the basics of her life and she knew the basics of Mei's life.

"I have to say, I wasn't impressed by your other col-leagues. They seemed really annoyed at being asked."

"Green and Harvey." Honor clenched her jaw. "Neither of them like me that much. Green is really handsy and I told him the next time he touched me I'd report him to admin."

Matt made a weird sound. Honor turned her head to look at him. Luke's eyes widened. "Matt," he said. "Did you just *growl?*"

Matt didn't answer, just glared at Honor. At least it looked like a glare. He sure looked pissed. "That fucker harassed you?"

She wrinkled her nose. "Harass is a big word. He's a grabber. Touches my arm but manages to miss and touch my boob. When I told him if he touched me again I'd report him, he stopped. But he's the kind of man who never looks a woman in the eyes, just drops his gaze." She stopped to think it over. "Hell yeah, he harassed me. And other women too. I'm surprised he's still there. I never thought about him too much, just that he was annoying. I'm a colleague, though. He wouldn't overstep the bounds too much with me."

"If I'd known, I'd have been less polite," Luke offered.

"When this is over, remind me to punch him," Matt said.

The slightly sick feeling she had when she thought about Royce Green dissipated when she thought of Matt punching him. She smiled.

She turned to the screen. "Now Sean Harvey is just incompetent. Suzanne Huntington is grateful to me for saving her father's life but really what I did was save him from Dr. Harvey. I was going off duty when her father came in. He was having a heart attack, but Dr Harvey misdiagnosed it as a stroke and was about to give tissue plasminogen activators, which would have killed Professor Barron right away." She shrugged. "To tell you the truth, I don't think those colleagues would be worried if I didn't show up. If anything, they'd be annoyed. But Mei would worry. I'm surprised she didn't sound the alarm. Or at least contact me at home."

Luke shook his head. "She said you took personal time off. She said you sent her an email."

Whoa. "She did?"

"Yeah. Do you remember that?"

"No. I don't remember anything. What did I say in the email?"

He hesitated. She didn't know him at all but it seemed like the hesitation was out of character. She looked over at Matt but he was looking odd, too.

"Matt?"

Matt coughed into his fist. He shifted his broad shoulders against the back of the couch as if something were itching. Then he sighed. "No way around it. We hacked your friend's email. We had to. Either you sent the email or someone else did. Either way, it would contain intel. Luke couldn't ask to see it because it would have looked weird."

Honor was quiet for a moment and they let her work her way through it. She tried, but she couldn't think of a way for them to get the information without hacking. "Okay," she said finally. "Show it to me. But how did you get her email address anyway? It's Lotusblossom —"

"Lotusblossom88," Luke said. "Yeah. It's actually on her personnel file. I got it, so anyone could get it. And your email was on file, too." He stared into his camera disapprovingly. It looked exactly like he was staring at *her* disapprovingly.

Honor sighed. "Okay, okay. I'll change my email and I won't post my personal email on the hospital site. We get assigned hospital email addresses, I'll post that."

Luke nodded.

"But I asked her. Dr. Mei gave me her email address . I asked for it and she gave it to me. I said that I wanted to send her some photos of you."

"She believed that?"

Matt gave a little snort. "Luke can be very convincing. He's spent a lot of time undercover as a cop."

Luke scowled. "You doctors have the security awareness of an amoeba."

Honor didn't roll her eyes. These guys were doing their best to help her. Plus, with her newfound experience, they were absolutely right. Security awareness had played a minor role in her life. It would play a bigger role from here on out. "Okay, show me."

Luke clicked on something on his end and a page showed up on the screen. A classic gmail page, from her email address — which was boringly hthomas@gmail.com to Mei at Lotusblossom88. "I didn't look at any other emails in your friend's feed. Just the one from you. If it was from you."

Honor barely heard him. She was reading off the screen.

Hi Mei,

This will be quick. I had a personal emergency so I won't be at work tomorrow. In fact I don't know how long I might be away and I'm not sure if I'll have wifi. I have personal time and will be taking it.

I've already contacted admin.

Don't worry about me, it's just something I have to take care of. I'll get in touch soon.

Best, Honor

It read perfectly normal but it wasn't. "I didn't write that," she said.

Matt simply looked at her. Luke's gaze into the camera was unwavering.

"I won't insult your intelligence by asking—are you sure." His voice was flat.

"Thanks. And I'm sure. In emails to friends I never use a comma after the greeting, just put a dash. In emails to friends I take a less formal tone. And with Mei I sign myself 'Red'. It's an inside joke."

Matt looked at her hair. She shook her head. "It has nothing to do with my hair color. I told her once I couldn't stand to be in debt. All my life my father alternated being rich with drowning in debt. I have an allergy to personal debt. When I said I never wanted to be in the red, she laughed and said she'd call me Red. And that's how I sign myself with her. Whoever sent that email isn't me. I'm surprised she didn't notice it was odd."

"But it did the trick," Matt growled. "The hospital administration might be pissed that you disappeared but they're not worried, because they received an email, too. No one would have contacted the police."

Honor couldn't answer that. Her throat just seized up. "God." She shivered, suddenly chilled.

With each word, she had a clearer understanding of what she was up against. Not just a group of men who'd abducted her and kept her prisoner. But some kind of conspiracy. Something planned and carried out. Some kind of organization with weight and heft.

"But … but why?" she whispered. "Why me? Why any of this?"

Matt's heavy arm tightened around her shoulders. "That's what we'll find out. Right?" His eyes lifted to the screen.

It was exactly as if Luke Reynolds were in the room with them. His tired green eyes narrowed. "Better believe it," he said and the screen winked off.

Ten

There was a change in the atmosphere of the room, like a current of cold air, though the outside temperature was mild and no outside door had been opened.

Chamness knew what it was. That icy Russian had come in. Chamness had worked for the CIA for 20 years and he'd met his share of tough guys. Hard men who had aggression profiles that were off the charts.

Matt Walker had been one of those, that fucker who'd almost derailed the present operation that was going to see him set for life. Walker had unexpectedly trashed his career for a bunch of Afghan boys.

Ivan Antonov was not that kind of man. He was tough, yes, but he was also cold. Nothing moved him, unless it was some preternatural allegiance to a distant concept he called Mother Russia. Some kind of construct some of the Russians in his orbit held of a resurgent Russia, born from the ashes of the Soviet Union to rule over the world.

But even here, Antonov didn't show passion. To him, the rule of Russia over the world was a done deal, he was just putting the pieces into place.

Personally, Chamness didn't give a fuck.

He intended to be far away when the shit hit the fan and to live out his life in ease and luxury. With the kind of money he'd have and with the kind of medicine available in the Far East, he'd live forever, too. Just buy himself replacement organs from the poor until his entire system failed, far far into the future.

"Chamness." Antonov's voice, a deep bass without inflection, startled him a little. Antonov was right behind him. The man moved soundlessly and Chamness found that creepy. "Thomas's daughter escaped. She escaped four days ago. She died escaping."

Chamness turned in alarm. He was the one responsible for keeping Thomas in line and functional. It was his one duty and it was an important one.

"What?"

Antonov didn't repeat himself, just nodded.

Chamness damped down the squirt of adrenaline and bile. He wasn't responsible for the fact that Thomas's daughter had escaped but somehow it made him look bad. The men controlling her were Antonov's men but the control itself, the fact that Thomas's daughter controlled Thomas himself, was on him.

It was a complex plan that required Simon Thomas's acquiescence, something he would never give without the strongest weapon they could wield — his daughter's life.

Sweat broke out over Chamness's back, but he would rather burn himself alive than let Antonov know how stressed he was.

He took a moment, sipped his whiskey. "How did she escape? I thought you were keeping her drugged and shackled."

Antonov's jaw muscles worked as if he were chewing on something unpleasant.

Well. Yeah. They were in the endgame now and they still needed Thomas. Afterward, Thomas would have to remain alive to absorb a goodly portion of the guilt. A wealthy shipowner who was drowning in debt who used his shipping company to poison Los Angeles for money. Exactly the kind of story that made sense to a lot of people. But Thomas's daughter would be food for the fishes, as an old mafioso once said to him.

Who would believe the old man's story when he was such a convenient scapegoat? Rich men would do anything for more. Everyone knew that.

"My men there think she managed to pull the IV from her arm for the night, and was weak but awake the next morning."

"What was the drug?"

"A mixture of ketamine and diazepam."

"She should still have been disoriented, even after a twelve hour washout."

"Well, she might have been disoriented, but she managed to stick the needle in her guard's eye, grab the keys and unshackle herself and escape. She would have been weak but she managed. She stole a vehicle from the garage but crashed and burned."

Chamness was frightened of Antonov, but he schooled his face. "Why wasn't I told? I thought she was being filmed. And that the film was livestreamed to Thomas."

"Filmed, yes. But not livestreamed any more, though that's what we told him."

"What is he watching, then?"

"We have a lot of hours of his daughter, sleeping, drugged. We are looping it. He won't be able to tell anything from the short videos we are showing him."

"And nobody was manning the video cameras there? How many men are there anyway?"

"Two. And they were asleep. They were the ones to loop the recording. They were too frightened to tell us. But I found out. I'd sent one of my personal team up there and he didn't tell me, either. He's very sorry for that."

Chamness put the glass down, hand steady. Well, none of this was his fault or even in any way controlled by him. These were men Antonov had recruited. "I trust the men have been punished. That is really sloppy work."

"They are dead," Antonov said, his voice flat. "All three of them. It took them a while to die."

Chamness' heart gave a huge thump in his chest, though nothing showed on his face. "Do we know what she did?"

"She took one of the vehicles. It had a transponder.

Once they figured that out, that one of our vehicles was gone, one of the men followed the transponder."

"That's not good." Chamness allowed himself a frown. Just enough of one to show worry about the plan, given the incompetence of Antonov's men. He had nothing to do with this. "Where did she go?"

"Oddly enough, nowhere. She headed for the foothills of Mount Hood. She was driving fast. My man clocked the vehicle at 120 km an hour on bad country roads. She would have still been under the effects of the drug. She ran off the road and rolled down a steep cliff. My man got there in time to see the vehicle explode."

"So she's dead. What are you going to do now?" Chamness took another sip of his whiskey. Careful not to say 'we'.

Antonov's expression grew even icier. He understood well enough that Chamness was distancing himself from the fiasco. Good. Suddenly, Chamness was tired of all this alpha male bullshit. He'd had more than enough of that in his years at the CIA. Posturing, constantly calculating words and actions.

So tedious.

Well, in three days, when it was over and he was flying to his island near Bali via Mexico, he'd congratulate himself on keeping his cool and keeping his eye on the big prize.

Antonov stood rigidly, gazing out the big picture windows at the mansions below. Mansions that would soon be abandoned. He looked pissed, but in control. There were, however, micromuscles around his eyes and mouth that twitched.

Chamnes understood body language. At the Farm, Chamness had attended lessons by professors who had made it their life's task to study the body language of humans. He knew how to interpret Antonov's body language.

Antonov was pissed and he was tense.

He was pulling off something huge, something world-changing, so … as the youngsters would say, props for that. A lot could still go wrong, though.

Chamness, all in all, didn't really care. He had his money in the bank. In three days, whether the plan was successful or not, the bank had orders to transfer the second half of the money that would change him from a rich man to a tycoon. He had his alternative persona ready, his bug-out plan was airtight. His ass was covered. So the daughter had been sacrificed. Too bad.

"So …" He glanced at Antonov out of the corner of his eyes. "What's the plan?"

"We proceed as planned. We don't really need her any more, as long as those images control the father, we're fine."

"Good," Chamness said, and finished his whiskey.

Eleven

The Grange

"Another bite." Matt held a fork of apple-cinnamon muffin in front of her mouth. They'd been having breakfast and somehow she ended up on his lap, being fed. She didn't even remember exactly how she ended up here, on his hard thighs, back supported by his strong arm. It felt delicious but it also felt like a very un-Honor thing to do.

She couldn't actually remember the last time she'd sat on a man's lap. Maybe never. Maybe the last time had been when she sat on her Daddy's lap when she was a little girl.

Maybe not even then because she hadn't been much of a snuggler, and her Dad had always been busy.

Why, oh *why* had she not tried snuggling before? It was so amazingly delicious, being held. Feeling Matt's warm skin and hard muscles, under her, around her. She placed her palm over his chest and felt his strong, slow heartbeat.

When had she last felt a heartbeat in a non-medical setting? Not frantically looking for a beat in an accident victim who was bleeding out, but feeling the strong beat of someone she cared about, simply because she could.

"Another bite," Matt urged. "I worked really hard on these muffins."

Honor rolled her eyes but obediently opened up. Man, those muffins were good.

"You did not bake these muffins," she said.

"I nuked them." That dent appeared in his cheek. "That counts for something."

"Not much."

"I chose them. Out of a menu of ten types of muffins. Surely *that* counts?" His voice sounded aggrieved.

"Yeah, choosing these gives you points, though I suspect the others are just as delicious."

"Tomorrow is cranberry. My favorite."

Honor opened her mouth to reply and Matt's phone pinged.

Video conference now.

Honor leaned back, looking at his screen. "Who's that?"

He kissed her, eased her off his lap. "Luke. I think he has news."

And just like that, the mood shifted, the world crashed back like an anvil bearing down on them. For a moment, Honor had felt almost light-hearted. For a moment she'd forgotten that she was fighting for her life. Because as long as her abduction was shrouded in mystery, they could come for her again as soon as she showed her face.

Appear out of nowhere and take her away, with no guarantee that she'd live through it.

She had Matt, now, true. And his team. And they were formidable. But she was an emergency ward physician. No one knew better than she did that a hair separated life from death. If her shadowy enemies wanted to get her, they would, eventually. If they waited long enough, she'd make a mistake and in one second they could kill her.

Death was so easy for humans. She'd seen people die by slipping in the bathtub, choking on a piece of bread, touching an electrical outlet. One second you were full of life and then the next second you were pounds of meat that was already decaying.

Matt held her hand as they crossed the Great Hall, looking down at her occasionally, a worried expression on his face. "Luke wouldn't call unless he had news. At this stage any news is good news."

Oh God. He'd felt her mood. That sudden black depression that had fallen over her like a veil — he'd perceived it. He wasn't supposed to be sensitive. He was a tough guy. She wasn't used to being with a man who could read her moods, it was almost scary.

Matt and his friends and his company were doing their best — and it was a good best — to keep her alive. The least she could do was try to remain as serene as possible, not burden them with her black thoughts.

She sketched a smile. "I know. I wonder what he found?"

"Well, we'll find out right now." And he led her into yet another room. Large, comfortable, not intimate like the other room they'd been in. It was more like a conference room, with a long highly-polished oval table and comfortable chairs around it. Matt took a chair at the head of the table to the right and gestured for her to sit down. He entered a code on a console and pressed a button. At the other end of the room a screen flicked to life.

Honor nearly gasped. It covered the whole wall. It *was* the wall, which became a screen at the touch of a button.

Luke's grim handsome face filled the screen. "Matt. Honor." He nodded twice. It was like he was in the room with them, only blown up to giant proportions. Hidden speakers made it sound like he was sitting beside them.

Matt leaned forward, pressing another button. A thin screen shot up from the surface of the table near them and a panel retracted, showing a keyboard. The screen was on a swivel and he turned it so she could see too.

"Honor." Luke's voice was hard. There was some kind of alignment of the cameras, brilliantly done, because it looked on the screen as if he were looking right at her instead of at a camera.

His voice was somehow accusing.

"Luke?" Matt cocked his head at the tone.

Luke scowled. "Why didn't you tell me — tell us — that your father's company has an office right here in Portland?"

He made it sound as if she'd been hiding something. Her brain stalled. Her tongue stalled. Matt had swiveled his head to look right at her. A whole bunch of tough-guy disapproving male energy, directed right at her.

"I — ah …" Her mind whirred emptily. "I — I don't know. I honestly didn't think of it." Why hadn't she told them? It quite frankly hadn't even occurred to her.

"Didn't think of it?" Matt's deep voice was slow. As if he could hardly believe the words he was saying.

"I mean —" She scrambled to gather her thoughts. "It's not really an office of Quest Line Shipping. Daddy just designated it as that for tax reasons. Though it is in an office building. Quest Line ships rarely come into port in Portland. He bought the office suite basically so he'd have a place to stay when he came up to visit me — when we weren't fighting. I mean he had computers that were slaved to his office computers back in LA and there were duplicate records. But mainly he kept two rooms that were used as a bedroom and living room with kitchenette so he wouldn't have to sleep in a hotel. He said he spent way too much time in hotels as it was."

She looked at Luke's tight mouth.

"Why? What does this have to do with anything? I told you we'd been sort of fighting, because he refused to look after himself. I haven't been there in — in months."

"You went to that office on the 6th, the day you were abducted. You're on tape. The whole thing is on tape."

Honor's mouth fell open. Her chest was tight, she could barely breathe. "What?"

Luke nodded and somehow, on camera somewhere else, he switched his gaze so he was looking at Matt. "I found the office by chance because it's not called Quest Line Shipping, like normal people would call it, but Q Supply Services. Had to dig to get the ownership and it was Simon Thomas, all right."

Oh God. If she could disappear, she would. As it was she scrunched down into the chair hoping to just disappear.

"I never go there," she offered.

Luke switched his gaze to her again. "You did that day. You were definitely there."

Well that shut her up. She didn't remember anything about that day, or the days before it. "This sounds weird, but — what did I do?"

"From what we've seen, you went there, went into the office. The office itself doesn't have security cameras, but the building does. You were there for a while. We saw two men walk into the building and we watched as they carried you out, semi conscious. You were walking but not under your own steam. Someone needed to hold you upright."

She could see it in her head. The image was chilling. Matt looked at her closely, rolled his office chair close to hers and put his arm around her. She was cold and leaned into him, into all that strength and heat.

It felt like somehow she'd landed on a different planet. Working the emergency room, she knew full well the violence and danger of the world. The ER got it all — gunshot wounds, knife wounds, bones that were broken not by accident but by design. But she played no role in all of that. Her role was to patch things up afterwards, when they landed in her hospital. And to bear witness when, despite everything modern medicine could do, the victims couldn't be saved.

But this — this was personal. It was happening to *her*. Unknown, shadowy men, who came from the bowels of hell for all she knew, wanted her, wanted to punish her for no reason she could think of and were going to a great deal of trouble to do it.

"You say you didn't often go to this office?" Matt asked.

"No." The answer came spontaneously. She'd only gone a couple of times. If her father came up to Portland, they met in the city center for meals.

"So what were you doing there?" Matt kept his face expressionless. "Tell us. Don't think about it. Talk."

"He wasn't answering." Honor surprised herself. She hadn't known she was going to say the words until she said them. Matt nodded at her surprised look. "Your memory's coming back."

Was it? There was pure white static in her head between when a volcano erupted and Matt rescued her. But she'd had a flash ... a flash of something. "I was still mad at my father but I was also worried. And I wanted him to take another blood test to see if the statins I told him to take lowered his cholesterol a little. And — well, I wanted to hear his voice. He has two cocker spaniels and I wanted to hear how they were doing and ..." she sighed. "I wanted to hear his voice. I love him, even if he is the most stubborn man on earth, driving himself into an early grave."

Honor recognized a rant coming on and stopped herself.

"So you went to the office?" Luke asked.

Had she? Honor rubbed her forehead. "I think — I think I tried to contact him and he wasn't answering. He always answers, immediately, when I reach out to him. We have a little Kabuki dance and I'm always the first one to break the ice, after which he contacts me. Right away. I mean sometimes he'll contact me five minutes after I email him, as if he's been sitting at his computer, waiting." She smiled. "Which he probably is."

"But he didn't this time." Matt made it a statement not a question.

"No. Apparently he didn't. Otherwise I can't think of a reason to go to the Portland office, unless he was there." She looked at Luke, the image so very clear it was as if he were in the room with them. "Was he?"

"No. No record of him on tape."

"Well then. The only reason I'd go is to get onto his laptop. We have an email contact, a little messageboard of our own. He always answers immediately, like I said.

So if he didn't and if he wasn't answering his cell, I must have decided to go into the office and log onto his computer there. It's slaved, and it would be like using his computer in LA."

Matt let go of her to lean forward toward the computer that had magically appeared from the conference tabletop. She felt cold, and bereft, even though he was still inches away from her. But he wasn't touching her.

Since when did she need to be in physical contact with anyone?

"So think back what you did, why you were there."

Honor tried. She really did, closing her eyes to focus. All she got was a headache that made her feel dizzy. A wall of pain rose in her head. Shadowy figures were just beyond her reach behind that wall. Her head throbbed.

"It's okay, shhhh," Matt said, cupping her neck.

It was only then that she realized she was whimpering with pain. Her eyes flew open and saw only his face — rough, with that scruff of black beard, dark eyes warm and full of sympathy.

Oh man. Matt was a tough guy. The real deal. A former Navy SEAL for heaven's sakes. Those guys could probably run a marathon on a broken leg. And she was a tough guy too. She'd once worked a 36-hour stint straight through. She was tough and resilient. She did not whimper with pain because of a headache.

There was something about this situation that was breaking her down and Honor Thomas did not do breakdowns. She sat up straight, swiping her eyes — that was not a tear, that was moisture leaking out of her eye — and looked him straight in the face.

"Sorry," she said.

He shook his head. "Nothing to be sorry for. I keep telling you that. Let's try something." He took both her hands in his and oh! How good it felt to be touching him again. His large hands were so warm, heating up her own. "Now, I want you to close your eyes."

She shut her eyes.

"Good girl." His hold on her hands tightened. "Now I want you to empty your mind. Think of absolutely nothing. Shut that big brain of yours right down."

"Not that big," she murmured with a smile, eyes closed. Nope. She didn't feel supersmart at all right now.

"You've got a medical degree and a specialization right there in your head," he replied. "That's a lot more education than I have. I joined the Navy right out of high school and got a bachelor's while serving. Okay, so I want you to do this. Don't think of anything specific. But — imagine that you're worried about your dad."

"Not hard to do," she said wryly. "He was born to worry me."

"Mmm. Been a long time since anyone worried about me. I imagine that deep down, he doesn't mind."

Her mouth lifted in a half smile. With her eyes closed, she couldn't see Matt's face. That face was so tough and uncompromising. He looked like someone who didn't need anyone else. And yet, he also seemed to be at the center of a group of people who all looked after each other.

Must be nice.

"I don't think he minds, no," she answered. Her dad actually lapped it up, though he ignored her advice. "But then he doesn't do what I say. And before you think that I am bossy, I'm not." She paused for a moment. "Not too much, anyway. All I ask is that he watch his blood pressure, his cholesterol and his blood sugar." She opened her eyes and glared at him. "Is that too much to ask?"

Matt shook his head. "No. Absolutely not. Close your eyes."

Oh, right. This was some kind of exercise. "Okay."

"So, you're worried about your dad. That shouldn't be too hard to imagine, then."

She shook her head no. Not hard at all. Though this was an imaginary exercise, she felt that quick, razor-sharp pang of deathly fear that her father would be taken from her soon because he wouldn't take care of himself. He was the only family she had left in the world and she didn't have the network around her that Matt seemed to have.

"You've tried to contact him, but he's not answering," Matt said in that low, lulling voice. "That's wrong. He always answers, right? Even when you guys are mad at each other. So why isn't he answering?"

It was a hypothetical but again she felt that pang of fear. And it felt real.

"Yes. That isn't normal."

"So, let's suppose that you're really worried this time. You can't get in touch with him. You're working hard but when you have a free moment you're trying to get in touch."

"Yeah." That felt right.

"So if he's not answering you —"

He left the sentence dangling.

"I go to the Portland office." She didn't even think about it. Her eyes opened and met his. "That felt right, when I said it. That I'd go to the office."

"You're worried." Matt looked over at the screen, at Luke, then looked back at her. "Okay. Close your eyes again. And imagine going to the Portland office."

She did. And this time ... this time she could see things. Not things, really, but she had perceptions. Feelings. The sensation that she was treading on familiar ground, not hypotheticals. There was a slight taste of truth.

"So ... you want to go check up on your father but you don't have time to make it down to LA. So you go to his Portland office to contact him, right?"

"Right." Even she could hear the certainty in her voice.

"How do you get there?"

"I — what?" Honor opened her eyes in confusion.

"How do you get to your father's office? Drive? Take a cab, an Uber? Someone drive you? A bus ..."

"I drove. Drive." Clouds and confusion but for a moment there, she could feel it. The steering wheel in her hand, a rainy day, the wipers going full blast. Feeling a little annoyed, a lot worried.

"Luke," Matt said without taking his eyes from her

face.

"On it," he said. "I've got the make and the license plate and … yeah. Here we go."

On the screen was her pretty little green Prius. Parked outside her father's compound. There were parking tickets stuck under the windshield.

She recognized the street, the trees, lushly green. She'd parked across the street from the crafts shop she sometimes visited.

"Why not park inside the compound?" Matt asked, voice still low and calm.

"Where there are fixed security cams instead of having to hack into the security cams of front doors," Luke said. Unlike Matt, his voice was exasperated.

"Well, I don't — I don't know." Think Honor! she told herself. And a memory came, clear, unclouded. She opened her eyes, turned to Matt. "I keep the keys to Dad's office on my keychain. But I don't always carry the security pass for the car. That I keep at home, in the top right-hand drawer of my desk. Stopping by the office was a spur of the moment thing. It would have been really tedious calling up the security guy to open the gate for the car. There's a pedestrian gate and I have the keys to that."

Oh man, she could see it. And it was real! A real memory, not the shadow of one. It had the weight and heft of reality, not the elusive texture of something that maybe was or was not.

"That's good," he murmured. His thumbs rubbed across the backs of her hands. It was so oddly reassuring, like his voice. It said — I'm here and I'm with you. "Good detail. So you parked your car and went in through the pedestrian gate. Before telling me what you see, tell me what you're feeling."

Well, that was easy. "Fear. Fear and exasperation. Like when your child is missing and you will hug them hard when they get back home and then scream at them for being irresponsible. Both. I'd sent several messages to him, like I said. My phone calls went unanswered. That is really unusual and I was frightened that he'd received bad news from the medical tests I insisted he take. Or that —" she coughed to release a tight throat. "Or that he was dead. That occurred to me, too. As a possibility, I mean."

Her voice wobbled. Now she remembered it with an intense pang as if reliving the moment, rather than remembering it.

And she was remembering the panic that pierced her when her father didn't answer immediately, as he always did. Half scared, half angry, feverishly praying to whoever it was up there who looked after foolish old men that she'd find him deep in business negotiations, and not that he'd collapsed in the boardroom and was currently on a slab in an LA morgue.

Her breathing was picking up and Matt smoothed a hand over her hair. "Hey." He hooked the hand around her neck and gently pulled her head forward until their foreheads were touching. "It's okay. Whatever happened, you survived it and no one's touching you ever again." He leaned forward until his mouth touched her ear and whispered, so low she could barely hear it though he was speaking directly in her ear, "Except me."

Heat rushed through her in an almost painful pulse, head to toe, in a flash. It lit her head, her lungs, her heart. She turned her head slightly and met his eyes — dark, utterly serious. He meant every word. He meant that no one was going to hurt her and that he was staking his claim.

It should have felt clumsy and super macho, Neanderthal-like even. Honor didn't like macho men. She was in a profession full of alpha males who were convinced they knew more than anyone, even when they didn't.

She'd saved lives because she intervened, quietly and discreetly, when a male doctor misdiagnosed and prescribed the wrong treatment.

Just like with Suzanne Barron Huntington's father.

But Matt wasn't giving off those vibes. He wasn't smug or superior, or even swaggering. *I'll save the little lady.* It was more like placing himself and his skills at her service, just like she did with patients.

And, of course, something more. Staking a claim because he could see that she welcomed that. And she did.

What a time for romance, right in the middle of danger and mystery.

She could barely think of it, though it was there, heavy in the air, weighing down her body. Like a basso thrumming at the bottom of a piece of music.

As if realizing that he was distracting her, Matt let her go. "So, let's go forward. You didn't want to park inside the compound because you didn't have your pass, so you parked outside. Is that right?"

"Right."

Honor knew what he was doing. She did a version of this all the time with concussed or drugged-out patients. Do a question and answer, make the patient repeat or confirm what was said, to imprint it in the memory. It worked. She was getting a clearer picture of what had happened with every passing moment.

"And once in the compound, you went up to his office." He made it a statement.

"Correct. I didn't think he'd be there but I knew his computer would be and maybe there'd be some sign of what was going on. In his constant campaign to get me to take over management of the company, my father often briefed me on what was going on with the company. And I have total access to everything."

"You thought there would be some kind of clue there."

"I did. And I was hoping with all my heart to find out that he was in the middle of some important business negotiation and not that he was in the cardiology department of a hospital, or dead in the morgue."

Honor wanted that last bit to be said with exasperation but her voice wobbled and she couldn't control the tears that sprang in her eyes. She turned her face away.

When she was composed, she steadied her voice. "I

have very vague memories of going to the Portland office of Quest Line Shipping but right now I'm not pulling up anything else, and don't remember actually going up."

Matt glanced toward the screen where Luke was watching them, a sober expression on his face.

"You went up." Luke switched screens. On the screen was a fairly grainy black and white image of her walking into the side entrance of the building. It then switched to a view of her in the elevator.

Honor watched herself. She had absolutely no memory of this. She was dressed in the clothes she'd had on when Matt fished her out of the river. The time stamp on the video said June 6, 4.17 pm, so she'd been in those clothes for six days. Clothes that had been cut off her and presumably thrown away. She'd been fond of that sweater. And those were her favorite pants.

Stalling in her head. It still made her sick to think of being abducted by unknown men.

She was standing straight and still, holding her briefcase with both hands. The briefcase.

She leaned forward. "Wait. What happened to my briefcase?"

"We found it under the desk in your father's office. Whoever took you didn't find it. They were probably intent on getting you out of there as fast as possible."

That sick feeling again, that unremembered yet potent image of unknown men, drugging her, taking her. Wiping days of her life from her memory. The sense of violation went deep.

"We'll get them." This from Matt. That deep voice sounded so sure. As if not getting them were unthinkable.

"Shit, yeah," Luke chimed from the screen. "They are going down."

"But who are they?" Honor's voice wobbled again, the fear she thought she'd beaten down rising sharply again. She hated that. In emergencies she always made sure her voice was strong and decisive. She was responsible for saving lives and tone of voice and body language were almost as important as actual medical knowledge in reassuring the broken and wounded men, women and children on gurneys who came into the emergency ward close to death.

Her voice never wobbled. Until now.

"Here's who they are." Luke switched screens again. Two men, in a grainy black and white photograph. "They wiped the tapes where they appeared but they missed a couple of seconds." He gave a wintry smile. "Felicity caught it, this fragment."

Matt's smile was wolfish. "Never mess with Felicity."

"Nossir," Luke said. He leaned forward, clicking again on an unseen keyboard.

"The images aren't sharp but Felicity done good."

The two men, tall, broad-shouldered, wearing track suits, had faint boxes around their faces. The faces were out of focus, features barely visible. How could anyone recognize anything from those photos? But then another keystroke and two clearer faces showed up, magnified. Followed by two mug shots. Data scrolled underneath them.

"Bless you, Felicity. You saved our bacon," Matt said. He glanced at her. "Felicity does what you do. Saves lives."

She did indeed.

Honor frowned as she read the data under the photos. She reared back in shock.

"They're — they're Russian!"

"Mm." Matt said. His eyes tracked the data.

Honor was almost incapable of reading and taking in the data. Her mind snagged on that one fact. The men who'd taken her were Russian. Why on earth had *Russians* abducted her, drugged her, kept her prisoner? Her head swam. Nothing made any sense.

Matt and Luke looked unfazed. They were used to this kind of thing. Maybe if the men had turned out to be three-headed Martians they'd have been surprised, but not this.

"So what's the Russian connection?" Luke asked, voice hard. As if she'd been keeping something back.

Matt made a low sound in his throat. Honor put a hand on his forearm. It felt like warm steel.

She turned back to the huge screen. "I don't know, Luke. As far as I know I don't have a Russian connection. I know I don't have any Russian blood. We're Scotch Irish all the way, both sides of the family. I've never been to Russia. My father's been twice, for business, but briefly. I don't have any Russian friends and there isn't a big Russian community in Portland. I know two words in Russian. Da and dasvidanya." She lifted her shoulders helplessly. "I just — it doesn't make any sense."

"Look at the faces," Matt urged. "Do either of them look familiar?"

Obediently, Honor turned back to the screen and scrutinized the brutish faces up there.

Igor Bugayev and Yuri Gribkov. The names meant nothing to her. The faces meant nothing to her.

She was so out of her depth in this world. Like stumbling on ice covering dark depths. This was not her world, this world where things unraveled.

Honor was specialized in putting things back together, putting them right. Her thing was using all her skills and hundreds of years of medical research to make things right again, make people whole and healthy again.

Though that wasn't quite true. Even in her world, things were unraveling way beyond her ability to heal. Two school shootings in one week had shattered her faith in the world being essentially whole and she and her colleagues were on the front lines, making sure everything held.

Sometimes things didn't hold ...

"Honor?"

She shook herself. No point in dwelling on past hells when there was a current hell to deal with. "Sorry."

Matt squeezed her hand gently. "Nothing to be sorry about. How many times do I have to say it? So Luke and I want you to look at those faces, see if there's anything familiar about them."

She did her best. Matt and Luke gave her time, not pushing her.

Showing no impatience at all, though it must be frustrating waiting for the fog in a person's head to lift.

It didn't lift. She stared and stared until her eyes burned. A sigh of frustration. It was hard to disappoint these two men who were working so hard to help her. "I'm afraid —"

Honor stopped. Cocked her head to the right, to the left. She didn't speak while she chased an elusive thought.

"I —" she stopped again.

Matt was watching her carefully, not saying a word. Not pushing her in any way.

Honor stared some more at the images. "Show me the original images of them. The full body ones."

Luke didn't answer but the screen immediately showed the men. They were similarly built, she could see that now. Tall, broad-shouldered. They were maybe six feet tall.

Their faces weren't in any way familiar, but there was something about them …

Honor held up a hand, held her breath. Matt and Luke were completely still, waiting.

She knew something, she knew she knew something, but it was almost impossible to put her finger on it. Staring at the photo so hard the figures seemed to shimmer, there was something …

One of the men kept his elbows out as he walked. The other had a swagger, chest out, shoulders back.

223

Honor suddenly knew this. But how could she know it if their faces meant nothing to her?

And yet it was as if she could see the two of them walking down that corridor, elbows akimbo, chest puffed out. How could she …

"They wore masks," she said. Almost surprised at the words coming out of her mouth. "But I remember how they moved."

Matt nodded. "Makes sense. They thought they eliminated the video footage. They put on masks later, when they abducted you. They didn't want you seeing their faces. I don't think they expected you to recognize how they walked."

"Gait." Honor switched her gaze between Matt and Luke. "I've attended several medical conferences on gait. It's as important a diagnostic tool as blood pressure. You can tell a lot about a person by their gait."

Matt nodded. "Anything else? Do you have even the slightest memory of the abduction itself?"

Honor wanted to say *no*, but she hesitated. The fog in her head was so frustrating. It ebbed and billowed, parting at the oddest moments.

"Let's run through it as if you could remember," Luke suggested. "I mean we know the basics. You were in your father's office. Presumably you were sending him a message on the office computer, right?"

Honor nodded. That sounded right. She didn't want to talk, didn't want to hear her own voice in her head because it disturbed the vague images, mere wisps, that were forming.

Sitting down at her father's desk. He had a super expensive office chair that practically held you up on air and all but made you coffee. She lusted after a chair like that and always refrained from telling her father because he'd have bought her ten of them.

Sitting down, firing up the computer. Logging in …

"They — they came in to the outer office as I was logging on to my father's computer. The outside of the building is sound-proofed but you can hear what's happening in the outer office. My dad didn't use that office much, as I said, so sound proofing wasn't an issue. I could hear —"

She tilted her head, trying to jump start her memory, as if it were a tape she could replay.

"I could hear them in the outside room. I —" she pushed her thumbs against her forehead. If she could, she would have pushed through the bone of the cranium and grabbed her own brain and shaken it. "I switched on the video cameras and looked at what was in the outer room. I saw —" she squeezed her eyes shut and all of a sudden the clouds parted and she could *see* it, feel it, as if it were happening all over again. A flood of memories that was both welcome and terrifying. "I saw two men, but couldn't see their faces because they already had masks on. If they'd managed to break into the outer room they wouldn't have any difficulties in breaking into the office. There was a note on the screen from my father. He said he was having problems with his new sleeping partner, Lee Chamness —"

Matt sat up as if poked by a cattle prod. Luke, too,

suddenly looked like he'd been given an electric shock.

"What?" Matt said.

"Lee Chamness." Honor frowned. "That name is familiar. You talked about him, right? That horrible story of the CIA officer and the young boys."

"That was him all right." Matt's face was cold, grim, dark eyes icy. It would have been scary if that expression were aimed at her but it wasn't. "Nastiest fuck on earth. What does he have to do with your father?"

"Like I said, he'd been having some financial difficulties. Two ships caught fire. Nobody knew how. But in the meantime, Dad lost two ships and two shipments and he had huge insurance problems. This guy came to him, wanted to be an investor but would leave everything in Dad's hands. My dad had him researched and he seemed solid. High-up government bureaucrat who'd inherited some money."

"High up CIA fuckhead," Matt said grimly. "And that money no doubt came from drug trafficking."

A huge painful jolt of anxiety shot through her. Honor's voice was sharp. "My Dad wouldn't have known about any of that. Nothing at all. He's a totally honorable man and would never ever do anything criminal. Ever." She gripped Matt's arm tightly. "You must believe me."

"Oh, I do." Matt covered her hand with his. Warm strength seemed to flow from him to her. "I'm sure your father is innocent in all this. But I also think he's somehow involved. So we have what? Lee Chamness investing in your father's company. Am I correct?"

Honor scrunched up her nose. It was all so nebulous. "I — I think. Dad was very expansive when things were going well but he closed up when things weren't. Which was why we were fighting because he took even worse care of himself than usual. I was worried about his health, really worried. The business was secondary. I didn't pay that much attention to what was going on with the company, I was paying attention to the effect it had on my father's health."

Matt repeated what he'd said. "So Chamness was part owner of your father's business." He made it a statement.

"I'm not sure." Honor shook her head when Matt opened his mouth to speak. "No, really. I'm not certain he became an actual owner. I think there was a complicated private contract between the two whereby he gave my father an infusion of capital and was guaranteed a big cut of the profits for a specified period of time. My father explained it to me but I was more interested in the fact that he started sleeping again after this arrangement was agreed to. I think he was just relieved that the ownership of Quest Line Shipping remained his." Matt and Luke somehow exchanged glances though they were thirty miles apart. "What?"

"Nothing, honey." Matt shrugged. "Just a theory. Let's get back to when you were in his office and you saw two masked men outside in the outer office. What were you doing when you noticed them?"

What difference does it make? Honor wanted to say, but bit the words back. Matt was trying to piece together an overall picture on the basis of her scanty information. She couldn't find any kind of rational link because what she was remembering was so episodic. And there was still a lot buried inside her head.

"I was —" she closed her eyes, dived into herself. She couldn't afford distraction, certainly couldn't afford to look at Matt, who seemed to be a black hole soaking up all her attention. "I was reading something."

Something her father had left her. Yes!

"Dad had left me a message on our secret message board. I'd forgotten all about it until now. I logged on out of exasperation and worry, thinking I was chasing clouds but then there was a message from him." Her eyes opened. She met Matt's gaze, held it. "He said Lee Chamness was dangerous. He said to find you, Matt Walker. And he gave me coordinates. His desk was empty, there was nothing to write on, the men were opening up the office door."

Matt nodded once. "So you wrote my name and the coordinates of the Grange on your arm in ink."

"Yes. I just had the time to pull the sleeve down over it and they walked in." She breathed heavily, as if suddenly all the oxygen in the world had disappeared. Her heart started beating a frantic tattoo. "They were so big and they had masks on. They were terrifying. One had a piece of cloth in his hand. By the time I thought to try to fight back, the other man had grabbed me and they put the cloth over my face. I recognized the smell of chloroform. And that was it. I blacked out."

Matt's face was even grimmer than when he'd found

her, half dead and terrified.

There was utter silence. Matt picked her hand up and brought it to his mouth. Her hand was chilled. *She* was chilled, remembering how terrified she'd been. How she'd understood that she was no match at all for two strong men. They'd been masked and she knew they meant to harm her. In those few seconds of terror as the chloroform-soaked cloth was rising to her mouth, she thought she was living the last moments of her life. The horror and despair had risen in her like a black cloud and she shivered at the memory, though the room was warm.

As was Matt's hand and his mouth. Again, it was as if he were giving her an infusion of heat and strength. Of life.

She looked at his hand. So strong. Raised veins on the back, the sinews clearly visible. Strong like that other hand, only —

"He had a tattoo," she said suddenly. Matt's eyes narrowed, as did Luke's.

"What kind?" Luke asked and she looked at him gratefully. Neither of them asked *what?* Or *are you sure?*

She was sure. Now that the image was back in her memory, she'd never forget that hand. The image was burned into her mind forever.

"Yes. On his fingers. On the proximal interphalangeal joint."

Silence.

She pointed to her own fingers. "Four letters. Or at least they looked like letters. Symbols, maybe. Right

229

here between the knuckles and the first finger joint. On the —" She closed her eyes. "On the right hand."

"Can you draw the letters or symbols?" Matt asked.

"Nope. Sorry. It was a fleeting glimpse."

Luke had vanished from the screen but she could hear his deep voice murmuring in the darkness. He reappeared.

"Got it," he said. "Matt, you're not going to like this."

"I already don't like this," Matt growled. "Anything about it."

"I contacted Felicity and had her focus on the guys' hands. She just magnified the faces before. This is what she got."

Luke disappeared and an image showed on the huge screen. A blow up of a hand.

Four letters on the index, middle, ring and little fingers.

круг

"Fuck," Matt breathed.

"Yeah," Luke answered.

They both had tight faces.

"What?" she said. "What's that?"

Matt turned to her. "That's a symbol of the Bratski Krug. Circle of Brothers."

"Never heard of it before. What is it?"

"Russian mafia," Matt said. "An international mob based in Russia. Specialized in drug trafficking."

"Oh." Thoughts swirled in her head, none of them good. "Well, fuck."

"My thoughts exactly." Matt looked angry.

None of it made sense. "What would a Russian mobster be doing in my father's office in Portland? And abducting me?"

"We need to find your father. Right now. He's clearly a key to what's going on."

"Without those Russian fuckheads realizing Honor's alive," Matt added, turning to Luke. "But her dad's in LA. Who do we have in LA right now?"

"No one." Luke shook his head. "We've got operations going on in Canada and in Jordan. And cold weather training in Alaska. We're really shorthanded."

Honor noticed that Luke, too, spoke of ASI in terms of 'us'. From what she understood, he was still officially with the Portland Police Department. Clearly his loyalties had already shifted.

"Uh, guys?" Felicity's light voice floated into the room.

Matt and Luke almost came to point. "Felicity?" Matt asked. "You okay?"

"Fine. Fantastic, in fact. Ginger did the trick. Thanks, Honor."

Honor smiled. She'd left word to Felicity through Metal to eat slices of raw ginger for the nausea. It was probably passing into the second trimester that did the trick, but ginger definitely helped. "Glad it worked."

"Dante's in Los Angeles. There's some kind of DEA reunion going on. I took the liberty of contacting him. He's already checking on Honor's father."

"Great." The tension in Matt's face lifted a little.

"And Jacko and Joe are in San Diego. They're on their way to LA."

Luke blew out a breath in relief. It was good to have his exhausted face up on that huge screen rather than those frightening men, larger than life.

Matt put his arm around her. "Looks like your father's in trouble. I'll have a couple of guys come up and keep you safe and I'll go down to LA."

"I'll go, too," Luke said from the screen and Matt nodded.

"If this mess has anything to do with my father and he's in LA, I'm coming too," Honor said.

Matt stiffened, his entire body giving off *oh no you're not* vibes. "Oh no you're not," he said.

"No." That came from Luke who looked just as disapproving and forbidding.

Honor had long and hard experience in doing what strong-willed men didn't want her to do. Her whole life had been that, in fact. She wasn't intimidated and she wasn't scared and she wasn't backing down.

She looked at Matt then at Luke, knowing what they saw on her face. Utter determination. "Oh, yes," she said quietly. "I am."

Twelve

Antonov stood on the Walk of Fame on Hollywood Boulevard. Brass stars inset into the cracked sidewalk stretched away as far as the eye could see, on both sides of the street. Names on all of the stars. Famous names and names that Antonov had never heard of before.

No matter.

They all bore testimony to the American talent of entertaining the world. Many of the names on those stars were known in Ulan Bator and Vladivostok and Novgorod. Youngsters knew them where they'd never heard of Peter the Great or Pushkin.

This stretch of road was one of the most famous roads in the world. In one of the most famous cities in the world.

Hollywood. Part of Los Angeles. In the remotest corners of the world, on black and white TVs with rabbit ears, on screens made of sheets strung up in alleys,

233

those iconic views of a low-slung car with the top down driving along streets flanked by tall palm trees, the skies an almost insane blue overhead, were the stuff dreams were made of.

Russia had famous artists, too, but no one knew their names. The most famous dancers were men who had defected—Nureyev and Baryshnikov. Russia had the finest dancers, the best musicians and composers, the most exquisite artists and yet their fame never made it outside the confines of the country unless they were exiled like Solzhenitsyn.

Russia had no place in the world's imagination.

That was going to change.

Antonov started walking slowly down the Boulevard, drinking in the sights and sounds. He was dressed in faded jeans and a plaid shirt. He wore Frye boots, a wide-brimmed cowboy hat, wraparound sunglasses and a wig of long black hair.

He was fairly sure that he would never be recognized in the footage of the security cameras he could see everywhere. And after, of course, the cameras would be lost.

It was a small risk he was taking but it was worth it. Because, just as some could see the skull beneath the face, Antonov could see the After beneath the shiny surface of Hollywood Boulevard.

Right now, Hollywood Boulevard was teeming with people. Tourists. Los Angelenos would never be caught here, in the tourist traps. If he listened, he could hear Spanish, French, Italian, Japanese, every regional variation of English and even Russian, at times.

When he heard his native language spoken, he'd look sharply at those compatriots from behind his dark sunglasses.

Traitors.

Sunburned, bags full of cheap trinkets, grinning like fools. Antonov wanted to scream at them to go home. *Idi domoy!* Back where men and women led serious sober lives, not this foolish *dermo*.

All the shops were full of childish crap, toys essentially, for adults. Even the food was for children. Overly sweet and soft, as if even the act of chewing were too adult.

Ivanov crossed the street. There was one star he had to see and he found it easily, in front of another souvenir store.

There it was. He stood over it, a name with the symbol of a movie camera. Meaning he was a movie actor. A second-rate one. But a man who'd become President of the United States.

Ronald Reagan. Ivanov stood over it, heart pulsing with hatred. He'd been a very young soldier in Afghanistan and hadn't heard the news. But when Reagan stood in Berlin and said *"Mr. Gorbachov, tear down this wall!"* that traitor Gorbachov listened. Two years later, the Wall was down. The Soviet Army was retreating in defeat from Afghanistan. And on Christmas Day, two years after that, the Soviet Union collapsed.

Enough of the past. Ivanov stopped for a moment,

moving to the side of the walkway with the brassy stars so he wouldn't impede the flow of people, and opened up his mind to what the future would bring.

In a moment, he could see it, feel it, smell it.

Utter devastation, that's what he could see. The buildings abandoned, left to the animals that would creep back from where they'd been banished up in the hills. The coyotes and wolves and rats wouldn't know about radioactivity. For the first months, they'd feast on all the food left lying around, until it rotted.

But soon plants would overgrow everything.

Antonov had been to Chernobyl, expecting devastation and desolation. What he found was thriving plants, mainly soy and flax. Green and dense, a lush carpet overlaying everything. Scientists even came to study how the plants had adapted. The latest theory was that they'd had to adapt to higher levels of natural radioactivity hundreds of thousands of years earlier, and what was dormant in their cells had reawakened.

The landscape would be pristine, the radioactivity having killed off molds and pests. Just glossy plants, doing just fine.

The same could not be said of man. This entire basin would be abandoned.

Americans were risk averse. No one would live even within hundreds of miles of Los Angeles. They would scramble to get out and never come back. It would be gone — all of it. The entire conglomeration would be empty, the freeways glittering ribbons of metal since cars would have been abandoned on the roads when they ran out of gas. It was entirely likely that there would be sun-bleached bones — too many bodies to recover.

This was a city that had an outsized hold on the imagination of Americans, of the entire world. Who hadn't watched a film set here? Los Angeles was the second largest city in the United States but it was also the beating heart of California, the richest state. A state richer than many countries. Would Americans abandon California, too? Maybe.

It would be delicious if they did, but Antonov couldn't count on it. He could count, however, on years of chaos and panic. Count on at least a twenty-percent drop in GDP. New alliances. Maybe the United States would disintegrate, the suffering western states hiving off to form their own country, shunned by the rest.

Massive economic damage, political upheaval when social media started leaking — slowly at first then faster and faster — that this was homegrown terrorism.

It would give a resurgent *Rodina* time to stretch its wings, gather its fallen children, become an empire once again. Buildings full of internet trolls working around the clock would sow discord, ripping society apart. Fingers pointing, poison seeping into politics, hatred spreading — all while California burned.

America's largest port — gone.

Much of its aerospace industry — gone.

Silicon Valley — they wouldn't want to stay only a couple hundred miles from radioactive terrain — gone.

The second largest airport in the country — gone

The nation's provider of fresh fruit and vegetables — gone.

Its wine industry — gone.

The Hollywood sign in the hills with missing letters, like a broken-toothed mouth.

Above all, the dream factory — wrecked. It was America's stranglehold on the world's imagination that was even more powerful than its missiles and aircraft carriers. African children in the veldt, old women in Nepal, roadside vendors in the mountains of Peru — they all knew Ironman and The Godfather and X-Men. Hollywood told the world's stories and was the purveyor of its dreams.

That would be gone, too.

One thousand square miles of devastation.

Los Angeles, the city of dreams would become Los Angeles, the cemetery of dreams.

The Grange

"Look."

Matt's voice was reasonable but there was a drop of sweat falling down the side of his face. Which was amazing if you thought about it. As a former SEAL, he'd gone into battle countless times. Been shot at. Been *shot*, actually. She remembered those puckered scars on his back, corresponding to the puckered scars on his chest.

He was sweaty and anxious because of her.

"We don't know where your father is." He tried to make his voice reasonable but he sounded hoarse, like he'd been screaming. He hadn't. He was speaking softly. "We don't know for sure if he's even in LA ."

"True." Honor put down the tea she was drinking. There were thermoses of tea and coffee on a sideboard and she'd gotten up to pour tea and coffee for them before Matt's head exploded.

Matt was a bundle of tension Honor could feel, sitting so close to him. It was like he agitated the molecules in the air. He was ignoring his big earthenware mug of coffee. "I'm assuming Dante will be able to find out if Dad is in Los Angeles, one way or another?" she asked.

"Yeah." Matt cleared his throat. "He's pretty good at investigating and he's got an unofficial network of retired DEA agents that are good at undercover work. We'll know something by morning." He looked down at the steaming mug in front of him, turning it around and around with his big hands.

"He's there," Honor said softly. "And he's in trouble."

He looked up sharply. "And you know this how?"

She hesitated. "I just know it," she said. It was too insubstantial a thing to talk about but she and her father had always shared a bond. It was why she was so adamant he take better care of himself because she could *feel* that he was in bad shape, risking serious health issues. Here, too. It was like she put out feelers that were telling her that something was wrong.

In any other instance, she'd be on the phone with him, maybe even booking a flight down to LA. Imagining him collapsed on the floor or in bed, unable to get up. She'd have sent one of the employees of Quest Line to see how he was.

But of course she couldn't get in contact with anyone. Whatever her abductors wanted from her they'd surely be watching her dad. True, they thought she was dead, but her safety depended on that.

And — the thought was painful, like shards of broken glass inside her head — it was entirely possible that all of this — whatever this was — involved her father. He had a shipping company and all sorts of —

Honor gasped. "Oh my God!"

Matt's head swiveled and so did Luke's, on the big screen. "What?" Matt said.

Honor's hand covered her mouth as she worked through it. Her mind wasn't as sharp as it usually was, otherwise she'd have made the connections sooner. But the big elements here were pretty clear.

"We have this Lee Chamness and my dad and you. Somehow connected, though I don't see the connections clearly. But Chamness is definitely connected with my father. And you said that he was protecting this warlord in Afghanistan."

Matt nodded. "'Our guy', he called him."

"And 'our guy' was sitting right in the middle of a

field of poppies."

Matt's eyes narrowed. "Go on."

"My father's shipping line has a B-43 exemption."

Both Matt and Luke frowned.

"It's a little-known exemption for transporters, particularly for shipping lines. A sort of a relic from before the days of terrorists, but some shipping lines still have the certificate."

"Which is?" Luke asked.

"Except for security measures like retinal scans that are carried out by the government in the shipping line head office and other minor security measures, some shipments can enter the United States on an expedited basis."

"Meaning?" Matt asked.

"Without inspection."

Dead silence.

"The ships just … land?" Luke asked.

Honor nodded. "Selected shipments that are time sensitive, say. They land and are offloaded without any kind of inspection. My grandfather obtained a B-43 exemption and the company still has it. I don't think my father uses it often, but if he does, no one will question the shipment."

More dead silence.

Luke seemed to turn his eyes to Matt. "How much could we be talking about?"

Matt's eyes looked up, to the left. Calculating. "The total production of heroin and opium in Afghanistan is about ten thousand metric tons a year. It could be any fraction of that. Half would be five thousand metric tons. One tenth of that, which Al Rashid definitely produces, would be half a million kilograms. The biggest problem is always shipment. If they found a way to ship most of a yearly production in one go, safely … God."

"How much per kilogram?" Honor asked. Her lips felt numb, her hands felt icy while shivers of horror went up her spine. It was like looking at pure evil. She saw, daily, what heroin addiction did.

"About forty thousand dollars," Matt said grimly. "On the streets. And that's uncut. More if they cut it. How much cargo can one of your father's ships carry?"

"His ships are on the small side, he's a specialty carrier. About two hundred thousand tons. Which is —" she tried to do the calculations in her head and gave up. "More than enough. Half a million kilograms would fill just one section of the cargo bay. If a shipment of half a million kilograms is coming, that would be —" She blew out a breath, feeling the air in her lungs heavy as stones. Did the math. "That's roughly twenty billion dollars. In one go. Not only that."

She turned to Matt, placed her hand on his forearm. The muscles there were rock hard with tension. She knew exactly how he felt. It was all theory but it had the feel of truth, like when she had to make a diagnosis on insufficient data but the input she got from the sight and sounds and even smell of a patient told her she was on the right track.

She had a sixth sense for bad things.

"It gets worse?" Matt asked.

She nodded. "Yeah. Some of my dad's ships are Ro-Ro. That means the ship's cargo rolls on and rolls off, either in trucks or sometimes in railroad cars. Those kilos of heroin could be in trucks already packed in the ship's hold. They could drive right off the docks, and right into …"

Her throat seized up.

"Right into the country. It would be the worst wave of heroin hitting the streets ever. A normal tractor-trailer truck can carry about 45,000 pounds of cargo. Twenty trucks would do it." Luke's voice was low and grim. "It would be a disaster."

"And a public health nightmare." Honor shuddered. "We already get several drug overdoses a week. We'd have thousands coming in. It doesn't bear thinking about."

Matt looked at her and then toward the screen. "I'm not in law enforcement and I'm not an emergency room physician but I can see what destruction it would cause. With so much heroin they could afford to hook people cheaply. Hell, give away doses for free for months. Then step on it. Make literally billions. The people involved wouldn't have to enter a life of crime. Just sell it to pushers in a one-time deal. This is like one spectacular heist and you retire because you won't need money, ever again."

"Whoever's involved, it's not my father." Honor set her jaw. "Apart from the fact that he is an honorable man, he is totally anti-drugs. It's true he is a child of the sixties and probably smoked a lot of weed when he was young, but I tell him stories from the emergency room. He'd never ever be a party to this."

"If this is what it is," Luke said slowly, "I believe you when you say your father is not involved. But he happens to control the perfect smuggling route."

"But he'd have to be controlled." Matt cocked his head while looking at her. "Forced to do their bidding. To okay the shipment, to sign the documents, to have his iris scanned, whatever the security arrangements are. And the best way to control him is to control you."

An electric charge went through her as it all came together. The ease with which they subdued her, because they were men accustomed to violence. But — she'd seen violence used against women. She'd treated women with shattered jaws, who'd suffered punches to the belly so hard they'd lost their spleen, whose arms had been broken. She knew what uncontrolled violence looked like and they hadn't used anything like that on her. They'd subdued her and abducted her not to hurt her, though they easily could have. It had all been to use her against her father.

"It's why I was kept sedated," she whispered aloud, more to herself than to Matt or Luke.

"Exactly." Luke nodded sharply in the big screen on the wall. "They probably took photographs with time stamps on them to show your father."

"Or videos," Matt added, watching her carefully.

Of course. Honor felt sick at the thought, but it made sense. She hadn't been harmed. Certainly nothing that could be seen. She was held shackled in place and drugged. Extremely vulnerable. If that's what her father saw he would do anything to keep her safe, anything. Whether photos or video, Honor would have been like a living breathing warning.

We can do anything we want, at any time.

The old Mafia warning. *Nice daughter you got there. Be a shame if anything happened to her.*

A wave of nausea rolled up her gullet which she had to swallow down.

Matt frowned. "You okay?"

She thought about uttering the usual — *Yes, I'm fine.* But she wasn't. "No." She set her jaw. "If what we're thinking is right, I was used in the most appalling way. Laid out on a bed, shackled and unconscious to torment my father. God only knows how he suffered."

Honor looked long and hard at Matt first then Luke. Rage was pulsing through her, in every cell of her body. She'd never felt anything like it, didn't even know she was capable of this intensity of rage. She'd been white hot with anger before but not like this. Nothing like this. It felt almost like a superpower.

"I want them. Whoever is behind this — that CIA man, or anyone else — I want them. I want to find them and kill them but I can't. But I want to see them behind bars forever. If there were a penal colony on the dark side of the moon, I'd want them incarcerated there in a cage for the rest of their miserable lives." She narrowed her eyes at the big screen on the wall. "Do you hear me, Luke? Right now you represent law enforcement. If these men have abducted my father and forced him to do something he would never ever do by turning his love for me against him, if they are planning to flood the streets of the West Coast with heroin, I want them brought to justice, I want an airtight case, and I want to sit every single fucking day at the trial."

Luke's eyelids flickered briefly when she said *fucking*. Clearly they hadn't spent much time in the emergency room in hospitals.

He nodded.

"Whoa, Joan of Arc." Matt held up his hands. "A bloodthirsty doctor, that's a scary thought. We'll get them. Do we have a date for the next ship to land?"

Honor shook her head. "If I were in my father's office I could check, because it would be an internal system. But I don't know how to check from outside, certainly not without attracting attention. I don't deal with any of the day-to-day business aspects of Quest Line Shipping."

Luke disappeared from the screen and they heard his low voice, murmuring. After a few moments, he came back online. He read off a screen to the side.

"Next landing of a Quest Line ship is the 19th, day after tomorrow. At the Port of Los Angeles. The *Maria Cristina*. Among the declared merchandise — antique pottery, elements of a triptych to be assembled for an exhibit at the Getty Museum, a shipment of one thousand antique rugs."

Honor felt her jaw drop, just a little. She closed her mouth with a snap.

"How'd you do that?" Matt demanded.

Luke smiled faintly, the first smile she'd seen on his face. "Magic," he said.

"I heard that." A light voice floated in the air.

Luke sighed. "Okay okay. To be more precise, our own magic fairy. Felicity."

"Wow." Honor's eyes widened. "I think — I think you just hacked into Quest Line Shipping's servers, Felicity. Did you? Because if you did, hats off. Dad just spent a ton of money getting this fancy computer security company to make his system unhackable."

"What company?" Felicity's voice was still disembodied.

"Ah —" she wracked her brain. "A weird name. *Akzo*."

Felicity made a noise that was both funny and disparaging at the same time. Not an easy thing to do. "Amateurs. And besides, I have a ton of time on my hands now that I'm not barfing my insides out."

Honor wisely kept quiet. Felicity had hacked into her father's super secure system in the past fifteen minutes. Which her father would have said was impossible. But thanks to Felicity, they might save her father.

"Thanks a lot, Felicity," Honor said quietly.

Luke disappeared and Felicity's face filled the big screen. She was smiling. "Hey, doc. Nice to finally meet you in person, virtually."

"Hey." Honor smiled back. "You're looking good. Happy to see it."

"Mmm. I'd forgotten how great it is not to upchuck all the time. I have you to thank for it."

"Not really, but I'll take the credit because you have to promise me something in return."

"Anything." Felicity's smile widened.

"I want you to take some B6 vitamin supplements."

"Consider it done."

"And if you start vomiting again on an industrial scale like before, I want you to promise me that you'll go to the hospital for IV infusion of liquids and electrolytes. For both you and the children."

"Hm." Felicity's pretty face tightened.

"Done." A deep voice in the background. A very large hand appeared on Felicity's shoulder. "Promise. She promises, too." Metal's big hand tightened on her shoulder. "Doesn't she?"

Felicity lost the slight pout and sighed. "Okay, promise."

"I don't think it'll be necessary. I think your hyperemesis gravidarum is probably over. While you were, um, in the system, did you find out anything about my father?"

"No." Felicity's face turned sober. "Or rather, he's been giving orders, been carrying out business, but no one has actually seen him. He might — he might be going into the offices at night."

Honor blinked, trying to process this. "At night?"

Felicity nodded.

"He's an early morning person. Unless there's an emergency, Dad always leaves the office by six. But he might be in the office the next morning at six. Why do you say that?"

"At night there's movement. Secure doors opening, using your father's card. But no recording."

Honor took a big breath, sat back. Was grateful for the presence of Matt right by her side. Scenarios were running through her head but it felt like they were in fast forward, and nothing slowed long enough for her to grasp it. "So, just to be clear, you think he is coming into the office at night?"

Luke appeared on the screen. "Either it's your father or someone using his card."

"Some of the doors require a retina scan," Honor said. "And a thumbprint."

If it wasn't her father … she couldn't go there.

"But no one's *seen* him?" That was something she could grasp onto, something she could understand.

"No. No face to face meetings that I could see, and I took a pretty thorough tour of his schedule."

Honor looked at Matt, miserable.

"Okay." Matt slapped his knees. "We've got a working hypothesis here. That maybe a Quest Line ship is carrying a cargo of heroin and will be docking in two days' time at the port of Los Angeles. Dante is in LA and like I said, he has a bunch of DEA contacts and a ton of experience. We have to be careful with probable cause here but at least the shipment can be tracked once it's off-loaded. We can get sniffer dogs down to the port. We're also operating under the assumption that Honor's dad is somehow under their control. That's what we think we know."

Honor's heart jumped when he talked about her father being in those monsters' hands. It had the horrible ring of truth to it. Like the stage 4 cancer diagnosis of someone who's been feeling unwell and doesn't want to face it.

It was horrible to be sick with worry, but completely unable to do anything about it.

This was so far outside her wheelhouse, she could barely cope.

Honor considered herself a pretty capable woman and she knew she was really good at her job. She couldn't save everyone who entered the emergency ward — that would be impossible and she'd understood it on her first day of medical school. But she did her damndest and a lot of people were still alive because she knew what she was doing.

The same with most life challenges. She hadn't married the wrong guy, she navigated her way through a mortgage, she had excellent credit ratings, she kept herself healthy.

This — this was just impossible for her to deal with. There were no parameters, nothing she could cling to.

Except Matt. Matt and his team of men and women who did seem to know how to deal with this situation.

She leaned into him, into all that heat and strength. Closed her eyes. "Thanks," she whispered.

Thanks for everything, she wanted to say. She'd have listed the things she wanted to thank him for but he picked up the remote, switched off the screen, and kissed her.

Thirteen

It was dark outside though it was late morning. Another rainy Portland morning, but there was an extra heaviness and darkness to the air. She could still feel the horror of that other morning, one week ago. Twenty one high schoolers, all with gunshot wounds. Scared kids, some of them dying.

The team springing into action, more grievously wounded kids than medical staff.

She had to triage.

Three bloody hours later, six kids were dead, four were in surgery, the rest stabilized.

The doctors and nurses milled around, exhausted and heartsick.

This was a day like that one. Dark and ominous.

Garrick Smith turned to her and she gasped, took a step back. His face was bloody, teeth caved in, deep lacerations. White cheekbone showed. He grinned, mouth bloody. "Good day for our job, eh?"

Honor took another step back, wanting to turn and run. His expression was feral, like he'd just come in from the wars. Not an ounce of compassion or human feeling.

"What?"

His grin broke open the laceration on his cheek, which widened. She could see teeth through the cheek. "Don't be a fool. It's starting. Right now. Nothing can stop it."

There was no air to breathe, the day grew darker still. This wasn't the Garrick she knew, who was smart and compassionate. This was a wicked stranger, a man who had no business in a hospital. He licked his bloody lips with a bloody tongue and smiled again.

"It's starting." He looked around, humming the funeral march hoarsely. There was something wrong with his voice. When he turned his head, Honor saw that his Adam's apple was crushed.

He shouldn't be able to talk.

He shouldn't be able to breathe.

He shouldn't be alive.

He wasn't.

Garrick Smith had died in a horrific car crash the year before.

Her skin prickled but before she could say anything, ambulance sirens filled the air. Many sirens. It sounded — it sounded like last week, when medics were finally able to get the victims of the Washington High School shooting out of the building and into ambulances. Many ambulances, many broken kids.

This couldn't be a repeat of that. Could it?

"Oh yes." Garrick's skeleton smile grew broad. "It can. It is."

No! Honor wanted to scream but suddenly the ambulances started arriving, tires slewing on the asphalt, doors slamming as the medics hurried around to lift out the gurneys. One, two, three ambulances. A fourth braked, a fifth and sixth queued up. More could be seen racing up the driveway.

It was going to be bad.

"Very bad," Garrick said, nodding. A bubble of blood from his mouth broke, speckling his ruined face with blood. "Horrible, in fact." He smiled again. "Fun."

But she wasn't listening as she ran to the door, together with the two other doctors and five nurses on duty, and met the patients being rushed in. They looked small on the gurneys, occupying half the normal space. They were children, she saw with horror. Just — just babies.

And the parade of horror started. Heads blown apart, one little boy with half his torso shot away, another with his entire shoulder demolished. They were pale little waxworks, already dead. Honor counted the kids coming in, her heart swollen and breaking.

Dead. Dead. Dead. Dead.

She walked down the line when — yes! A little girl with long shiny brown hair and brown eyes, looking up at her. The little girl held out her hand and Honor took it. The little girl's eyes closed, then opened, latched onto her face. "I don't want to die," she whispered. "Please don't let me die."

At any other time Honor would barely hear her, she'd be snapping out orders, prioritizing care, stabilizing, prepping.

No stabilizing, no prepping here. It was a miracle the little girl was still alive. Her body from the waist down was mostly missing. But somehow, the little girl was still alive, barely.

Beneath what must have been beautiful copper skin, she was ash gray, her pretty mouth was turning blue.

"Don't let me die," she begged again.

"No." Tears were running down Honor's cheeks. Mayhem

reigned in the emergency department as kids kept arriving – little kids, grade school kids, lives cut short, blasted apart by bullets. Everyone was rushed off their feet trying to deal with three, four, five emergencies at once, but Honor was frozen, holding the little girl's cold hand.

The little girl blinked once, long lush lashes sweeping down, then up, then down. They stayed down.

She was gone.

Honor stood by the gurney, still holding the small rapidly cooling hand, weeping.

Garrick shuffled to the other side of the gurney, picking up the little girl's other hand. He tugged at it, smiling that bloody smile. "Come on, honey," he said, cackling. "You're mine now, you're coming with me."

They were in a little bubble, while controlled chaos swirled around them. A mass shooting engenders a lot of noise. Shouted orders, the screams of the wounded, the whomp! of the paddles.

Garrick was pulling what was left of the little girl off the gurney. Soon she would slide down to the blood-covered floor.

"No!" Honor screamed, tears streaming down her face. The little girl couldn't go with the wrecked monster that was what was left of Garrick. The thought was too horrible for words. She needed to stay here so her parents could come and say goodbye to their little girl. Not taken to some monstrous netherworld.

Honor could barely talk through the tears. Garrick looked up at her and she could see how ruined his face was. It had been a closed casket funeral and now she could see why. As she watched him, the left side of his face caved in, an eyeball popped out of its socket, hanging by the ocular nerve. He was reverting to his real state.

And he wanted to take the little girl with him.

He'd have to kill Honor first. When he reached out a bloody hand, she batted it away and when he tried to embrace her she fought with all her strength, with her arms and legs, screaming and crying.

"Honor! Honor honey! Stop, it's me!"

The battle was unequal. Somehow Garrick had acquired iron strength in death he'd never had in life and she couldn't move him. She couldn't move at all.

Her screams wouldn't come out of her throat, they were all trapped inside. All she could do was flail and weep, because she was not going to let that little girl be carted away.

The arms holding her tightened. Not painfully but they stopped her from flailing. And Garrick was suddenly large, capable of enfolding her, bending his head above hers.

Protecting her?

She stilled, weeping.

"Honor. Sweetheart, wake up." That voice. So deep, so familiar. Speaking right into her ear.

She couldn't remember the last time someone was so physically close to her that he could speak right into her ear, the voice conducted through bone. "You're having a nightmare, honey. Wake up."

The words made no sense, but his body did. Big, strong, calm. She could feel a steady heartbeat against Garrick's chest. How could she do that? Garrick was dead.

It made no sense. Nothing made sense. The world had gone mad. Someone had shot little kids. How could anyone do that?

A sob escaped her chest, another. She bowed her head, forehead touching warm, hard muscle.

She opened her eyes, still weeping. Lips kissed her forehead, her cheek, her mouth. "Shhh, sweetheart. It's okay."

Honor was awake now and it wasn't Garrick there, it was Matt. His chest was wet with her tears. "No," she croaked. "It's not okay. It will never be okay again."

"You had a nightmare," he said matter of factly. Somehow a tissue was in his hand, and he wiped her eyes, her face.

Honor sometimes hid deep emotion behind sarcasm. Ordinarily, she'd have answered something like – *no shit, Sherlock*. But her grief was real and his comfort was real. There was no shame in her grief.

There was silence in the room, the deep silence of the night. Now that she was awake she managed to wrestle her emotions into a semblance of control. It was what she'd been doing since the shootings. There was no counting the nights she'd awoken from a nightmare to find her face covered in tears.

This time there was someone else, and all he wanted to do was help.

"Do you want to tell me about it?" Her ear was against his chest and she could feel the vibrations of his voice rather than hear it. "It must have been nasty."

Honor sighed. Yes. Nasty. And recurring. And something that would follow her the rest of her life.

Matt eased her away from his chest and she instantly missed the connection with all that heat and strength. But he hadn't pulled away emotionally. Looking up, she saw his face, focused on her, dark eyes warm and full of sympathy.

He'd been a warrior. He would have nightmares of his own.

All of a sudden, Honor had a sudden vision of all the people in the world trying to fix what was wrong, all of them failing, all of them with nightmares. Trying to hold back the tide of evil and hatred and greed. And failing.

"Honor?" Matt's quiet voice was patient. He searched her eyes.

Her hands were against his sides, holding on to his incredibly broad chest. Like holding on to a wall, only warm. Something solid and real.

Honor opened her mouth, closed it. Tried to get words out of her too tight throat. Matt waited patiently, as if he had experience with trying to talk about trauma. He probably did.

Finally, the horror of the nightmare lost some of its grip. Not all of it, of course. Because most of it wasn't nightmare, it was reality. She found her voice.

"I caught both school shootings," she said simply and saw his reaction to her words.

He sighed, a long release of breath. His eyes turned sad. "Ah, honey."

Yeah.

Tears stung her eyes and she turned her head sharply away. Though of course there was no hiding from Matt. His eyes were locked on her face.

He reached out and pushed a lock of her hair behind her ear. "Do you want to talk about it?"

"No. Yes." He nodded, as if that made perfect sense. "You know the basics. Two school shootings in one week."

Matt nodded again. His mouth had turned down, but other than that he didn't say anything.

Portland, this nice rainy city where everyone was polite and everyone recycled, had the terrible distinction of having had two school shootings in one week. One in a high school and the other in a grade school. The city was still reeling.

"On that Monday, the police department called, told us that there'd been a school shooting and we were the closest hospital. So we were waiting when the ambulances came. My God, Matt. It was carnage. Do you have any idea what a bullet from an assault rifle does to the human body?"

She stopped, closed her eyes. Of course he knew.

"I'm sorry. We were — we were overwhelmed. We're used to seeing bullet wounds, even bullet wounds in kids, but — there were just so many of them."

"Twenty one," he said quietly. "I followed the news. Trying to understand how anyone could do that."

"Six dead. Of the survivors, four lost a limb, one will have a colostomy bag the rest of her life and two will never walk again. When everyone had been processed, we looked around and — it looked like a war zone. The hospital ordered us all to have counselling. It had been so horrible. Those kids — they were terrified. One minute they were studying math and Mark Twain and the next they were cowering under their desks, hoping to avoid a bullet. Every part of the ER was overwhelmed. Triage, treatment —" she swallowed. "Resuscitation. I think TV has given people the idea that the emergency department is basically an area under siege but that's not true. We deal with emergencies, true, but we are a good team, hardly anyone ever waits. But that day we — we were just overwhelmed."

Honor bent her head forward until her forehead touched his chest. Her hand went up, splayed against his pectorals and just touching him made her feel better. It was like a transfer of energy.

Matt nudged her with his shoulder. "And then Friday."

Honor started shaking. "Yeah. And then Friday. We were still dealing with the emotional trauma of the high school shooting when a nurse came in to say that there'd been *another* school shooting and that ambulances were on the way. We could hardly believe it. And then she said that the shooting was at an elementary school."

Honor's heart beat heavily, dull thuds that sounded in her ears, that she felt in her fingertips. She knew the heart and how it worked. A complex muscle operating on electrical impulses. The heart was something else, too. The human heart is also a barometer and when it sickens, it means there is something sick around it.

"I think all of us knew it would be bad. I don't think any of us knew just *how* bad it could be. Those bullets just ... *chewed* the kids up. They didn't just blow away limbs but blew away half their little bodies. I don't think we'd ever seen carnage like that before."

"Because some fucking incel couldn't get laid and was rejected by one of the teachers."

Everything in her chest was cold, like ice water had been poured into her. "Yeah. She was the first to be killed. She never made it to the emergency department, was killed instantly."

"He pumped half a magazine into her," Matt said. His mouth was tightly drawn, long lines bracketing it.

Sam Tirrell. The man who'd been rejected by pretty grade school teacher Floriana Noces. She'd been the first person shot. Then he'd turned his assault rifle on the kids, going from school room to school room, methodically, like doing an arithmetic lesson. One, two, three, four …

"So we — we went to work because that's what we do. Right? We repair broken humans. We put them back together again. Only — it felt like we weren't given the right pieces, enough pieces, to put those kids back together again. Too much of them was missing."

The tears were pouring down her face now. She barely felt them. Tears sprang out whenever she thought of those martyred little bodies and out of self preservation, she forced herself to think of them as little as possible. At least in public.

Honor had never spoken to anyone about this except the hospital shrink. She worked too hard, too long hours, to have many friends, and who could possibly understand? She hadn't been able to tell her father. He'd been out of the country and it hadn't occurred to him that she'd caught the school shootings. When he got back from his business trip to China, he'd called up and asked how were things and she'd been completely unable to answer. Simply couldn't talk. After a long moment she'd mumbled something about someone being at the door and had hung up.

No one could possibly understand.

Except, maybe, Matt.

She was completely bound up in his embrace now, plastered against him, wetting his chest with her tears. He was holding her tightly, cheek resting against the top of her head. There was comfort in his touch. Maybe she should have spoken about it before, with someone. Though there really hadn't been anyone, until now.

They sat on the bed, Honor leaning heavily against him, holding on to him as tightly as he was holding on to her, for a long time. Time lost all meaning. She finally cried herself out. Stopped crying because her body just stopped making tears. Maybe she was dehydrated. Who knew? All she knew was that she was warmly wrapped in a strong body that was somehow providing strength and comfort.

Her breathing evened out. At some point, their heartbeats synched. She could hear his heart beating solidly inside his chest, strong and slow and steady. It calmed her, and her own heart slowed down.

She sighed, the breath leaving her body in one long slow slide and with it went the sharpest part of the pain she'd been carrying around since the shootings.

She could go on.

"We worked like crazy for hours, but in the end we were only able to save three of the little kids and even they are going to be crippled for life. The rest —" her hand on his chest started to tremble and he covered it with his own, flattening it against him. "The rest were lost. Like the week before, the off-duty emergency physicians came in to help. In the end, almost the entire staff was there. When it was over, we all sat, staring at the floor, some sitting on the floor, slumped and — and lost. Like the other shooting, it looked like a war zone, bloody gauzes and syringes scattered around. No one spoke for a long time and we were all crying. Most of the doctors and nurses — I'd never seen them cry. We're a tough lot." She glanced up at him, tried to smile. "Maybe not SEAL-tough, but still. Pretty tough."

His mouth curved. "I bet."

Honor leaned her head against him again. It felt good. She felt good, like she'd lanced a putrid boil, let the infection out. Nothing would ever make her feel whole again, not after seeing the lives of high school kids and grade school kids cut short so savagely by madmen. But just talking about it with Matt, who totally understood, helped.

Matt lay back, keeping her close by his side. They lay there quietly. Nothing had changed, both of them had demons, terrible things were happening, but for now they were in a little bubble of calm and ... love?

Was this love?

God, what would she know? Honor hadn't really

ever been in love. Infatuated, yes, briefly. She'd been more in love with medicine and her job than with any one man. There'd been a number of affairs, and she'd felt excitement, fleetingly, but not much more than that.

Matt had saved her life, so sure, she was grateful. They'd had sex and it had been the most exciting sex ever. Was that because she'd had a brush with death? There were all sorts of biological reasons why she felt so close to this man. His testosterone and her estrogen seemed to just click. There was danger and it was ongoing and adrenaline played a big part, too.

Danger was linked to physiological arousal which was very close to sexual arousal. Lots of things in common. Danger gives an adrenaline rush — the brain signals the adrenal gland which then secretes adrenaline, epinephrine and norepinephrine, which cause the heart to beat stronger and faster.

Just like seeing Matt unexpectedly did.

Then of course there was the fact that he was … hmmm. Built. In every sense of the term. And of course women were primed to respond to beefcake. In danger, in life or death situations, humans were reduced to animals and she might be responding to Matt in the basest possible way. Acute survival instinct leading her to find the biggest strongest man she could.

Plus, he was protecting her. Those were big points.

Thoughts jostled in her head as she lay on his chest, ear right over his strong steady heart as she tried to figure out why she responded so strongly to this man.

Her head was a jumble, but her heart wasn't. Her

heart was sure. He was the one. The one she'd been looking for all along, though she didn't know she'd been looking. All those dinner dates, all those coffee dates, the occasional lovers — no wonder they hadn't worked, hadn't moved her.

She'd been waiting for Matt, all along. Waiting for this feeling of certainty, of two hearts melding.

Even lying on him felt familiar and exciting all at once. She knew his smell by now. Musk and leather, though where the leather came from she had no idea. He wasn't soft anywhere but he made a fabulous pillow. She nestled her head a little, somehow finding an Honor-shaped hollow where his shoulder met his neck. His arms tightened around her. She was surrounded by hard, warm male. It was wonderful.

He was erect. She could feel him, hot and hard, against her thigh. And though she wanted sex, she didn't want it right now. No energy. All she wanted to do was lie half on, half off him, listening to his breathing, feeling his heart beating against her ear, feeling him somehow becoming a part of her.

He wasn't pushing her for sex. Matt could tell that though she was in favor of sex with him, generally speaking, now wasn't the moment.

The sex would come later. Though somehow this was sex too. It sure felt more intimate than the sex she'd ever had before, even if their bodies weren't joined.

Their hearts were, though.

She'd purged part of the pain of the school shooting. It would never be gone, but the sharp edges of it had dulled. Talking to him, having him understand completely, had helped.

Honor hadn't slept a full night since the second shooting but she thought maybe, now, she could. Tonight. She'd sleep tonight.

A small digital clock showed that it was six thirty in the morning. Soon it would be time to get up. He'd feed her. The food would be delicious. Then they'd talk, as they got ready to go to LA. Because Honor was adamant. She was going with them. No question.

In the meantime, ASI would be doing their thing. This complex piece of machinery that was ASI would be working ceaselessly to figure out what was going on. They'd find her father. They'd stop the heroin shipment.

Justice would prevail, as it so seldom did.

"It's so hard when they're kids," Matt rumbled.

Honor stiffened a little. "Yes."

"Mine died, too. All of them. Those poor, shivering, bald little sacks of bones. They broke my heart."

Her breath was heavy in her chest and she didn't have the strength to speak. Just nodded, her hair catching in the scruff on his chin.

They lay there in each other's arms, Honor thinking of her ordeal and his. At least some of 'her' kids survived. Matt said that all of the kids he'd rescued died. How had he described them? *Bald little sacks of bones.*

She shuddered, thinking of the terrible stress that caused alopecia in all of them.

Though ...

"Wait." Honor sat up, looking into Matt's startled eyes. "Did your kids have skin burns?"

He frowned but answered. "Yeah. Like all of them had been burned but not by a hot instrument. More like they'd been held too close to a fire."

"And you say they were bald?"

Matt nodded, face sad. "They'd lost their hair due to stress. All of them."

"Matt, do you have any photos of those kids?"

"Sure." He reached over to his phone. "It's not a pretty sight, though."

"Understood." She did. She was used to human suffering. It was never a pretty sight.

Matt picked up his phone. "Here's the boy who was being abused. His name was Ahmed, that's all I could get out of him. He was just terrified." Matt scrolled through his phone and was now holding out the screen. On it was a boy in bright sunlight, squinting. In the background was a tall tan mountain, with scrub and a rocky scree. The boy was standing next to a military vehicle with a canvas top, one small thin hand against the fender.

He looked scrawny, as if only his hand was holding him up. Ahmed was thin, dressed in rags, face pale beneath the dusky skin. Hairless. Even without eyebrows. He looked too small for puberty but if he had achieved puberty, Honor suspected that he would have lost his pubic hair too. She scrolled through five pictures of Ahmed. In one, the tunic covering the arm holding onto the vehicle had fallen back and Honor could see reddish burns, plus the purple bands where he'd been shackled. Some of the skin had started to slough off.

It must have been excruciatingly painful, she thought sadly, but the boy's stoic face showed nothing. It was entirely possible that all he'd ever known in his short life was pain.

Scrolling, she came across a group photo of the liberated boys. All bald, all with reddish burns, all with the sick hollow look Ahmed had.

All doomed. But not only because they'd been mistreated.

"Matt." He'd been looking at the photos too, sadness in his face, but his gaze shot to her face at her tone. "These boys didn't die of stress or malnutrition. What I'm looking at is radiation sickness. At some point in the recent past they'd received massive doses of radiation."

"Jesus." Matt's eyes widened.

"You know what?" Her mind was connecting all the dots, now. "I don't think that ship is carrying heroin. I think someone is trying to smuggle radioactive material into the United States in one of my father's ships."

Fourteen

Fuck.

Matt thought he'd seen it all, heard it all. He thought he'd plumbed the depths of Chamness's perfidy but this — this was worse than his worst nightmare. A ship's cargo of tons of heroin was bad enough. That was a cargo of shattered lives and broken souls. But if what they were dealing with was a shipload of radioactive material …

"Get dressed, honey," he said, gently lifting Honor away from him. She moved immediately. Matt loved that about her. She never made a fuss about minor things. He knew lots of women who would bristle at being told what to do. Matt wasn't ordering her around. She needed to get dressed, now, because they had to spring into action and Honor showed that she understood that, fully.

In a moment, she was dressed in a dark blue sweater, gray sweat pants and soft boots. Ready for anything. He was dressed, too. The only thing missing was a weapon and he wasn't going to leave the Grange without one.

It didn't even occur to him to question her reading of the photographs. He could tell by the instant recognition inside himself that she was right. Maybe if his head had been in a better place, Matt would have recognized what Ahmed and the others were suffering from. As it was, seeing the kid violently abused, seeing the emaciated boys shackled to the wall, it had seemed obvious to him what they were suffering from.

The cruelty of the world.

Instead, they'd not only been exposed to the cruelty of the world but they'd also been exposed to radiation.

Honor was moving quickly, taking her cues from him. "Where could radioactive material have been held? Why wasn't everyone in the village sick?"

Good question. Matt pulled a thin wool sweater over his tee shirt, pulled on his jeans. Socks, boots. From the top drawer of the bedside table he pulled out his P226 Sig Sauer and pancake holster. Honor watched, wide-eyed, but didn't say anything.

Yeah. This was gun time.

Matt put a hand to her back and hurried them across the Great Hall to the conference center. His legs were longer than hers and when he had to, he could move fast. But she kept up. No flies on this woman, no sir.

He held the door open for her and she made right for the place where the remote was kept in a recessed slot in the conference table.

They sat and Matt picked up the remote.

"It's early," she murmured. She glanced up at the big clocks on the wall showing time across all parts of the globe. "Barely seven."

"He'll be up," Matt promised. "And even if he's not, he won't mind being woken up for this. He's made it clear that if it's important, we can call 24/7."

Matt tapped a number on his cell that connected with Midnight's cell, then turned on the wall screen.

John Huntington's face appeared. His hair was mussed and he was unshaven but his eyes were clear and he was alert. "Matt. What's up?"

Assuming Matt wouldn't call unless he had to.

John's eyes shifted slightly. The flat screen's camera caught both Matt and Honor seated at the table. They were in a small screen in the lower right-hand corner.

"Dr. Thomas." Midnight gave a solemn nod. "I never got a chance to thank you for what you did for Suzanne's father." He gave a wintry smile. "Old geezer's really nice and I'm fond of him, even though he loves French novels."

Matt kept an eye on Honor. Midnight could be really intimidating even when making small talk. But she just nodded. "Mr. Huntington."

Midnight winced a little. "John will do."

Which was actually a big deal. Midnight didn't let too many people call him by his first name. Only those inside his circle.

He shifted his gaze back to Matt and sipped from a black mug. "Okay Matt, what is this about? Do you have new intel on who tried to grab Dr. Thomas?"

"Honor," she said.

"Honor." Midnight sipped again. "Are you closer to figuring out what's going on? Luke told me there was some new intel but he didn't say what. Said he'd be giving a full report later this morning."

"Yeah. Turns out Simon Thomas, Honor's father, might be involved."

John wasn't much for double takes or big expressions of surprise, but his eyes narrowed. "In what way?"

This part was Honor's story to tell. Matt nodded at her.

"I was given a drug which wiped out my memory but I am starting to remember some events before I was abducted. My father keeps an office here in Portland. He hadn't been answering his phone so I went there to see if I could get in touch with him through the company computer. While there I was abducted by two men who were wearing ski masks, so I couldn't identify them. They also destroyed the security footage except for a couple of frames Felicity managed to isolate."

"Felicity." A genuine smile crossed Midnight's austere features. Women tended to react to those rare smiles, which made him seem human and less forbidding. But Honor's expression didn't change. "She always comes through."

"Yes, sir."

"John."

"John. The frames she isolated showed a tattoo. A tattoo that Matt identified as a Russian tattoo."

"A Bratski Krug symbol," he explained and John

Huntington nodded.

"It turns out that an old nemesis of Matt, a former CIA officer, seems to be involved. A Lee Chamness. He lent my father money and I think my father was afraid of him."

At hearing the name John came to a point, like a hunting dog, even more alert and frankly, even scarier.

"Lee Chamness," he said, a very slight southern accent in there.

"Yessir. John." Honor was certain that all of this was intimately connected to this man, who apparently spread misery and pain wherever he went. "He's mixed up in something nefarious and I think he's trying or will be trying to pin it on my father." She drew in a deep indignant breath. "Which is *insane*. My father is the most honorable man on the face of the earth and would never —"

John Huntington held up a huge hand and she cut herself off.

"I have no doubt about that, Honor. And I know what Lee Chamness is like. We all do. He is the scum of the earth and would stop at nothing for money. So I understand that your father is the owner of a small shipping line."

Honor nodded.

John's gaze shifted slightly to Matt. "I guess we're talking about a big shipment of heroin."

"That's what we thought, sir. But no." Matt turned to Honor.

"It's what would make sense. Matt told me that

Chamness had an arrangement with an Afghan warlord — the one with a taste for little boys — and that he was in prime poppy country, so we all just assumed heroin. But then Matt said something about the boys he'd rescued being bald. And, well, though extreme stress can of course cause alopecia, it would be highly unusual for twelve boys to all suffer from it."

John nodded his head, unsure where she was going with this.

"Then I asked Matt if he had photos of the boys and he did. And all of them had the same signs. Alopecia, burns on the skin, the skin sloughing off, emaciation. Matt told me that they also suffered from vomiting and bled from the eyes."

"Poor kids threw up all the way to Kabul," Matt said. "We thought they'd been given spoiled food."

"And they died, all of them."

"In the space of a week." Matt's mouth tightened. "Nothing the doctors could do. I could barely follow what was going on because I was in the brig, awaiting court-martial."

John's jaws moved as if he were chewing on something really nasty.

Honor leaned forward. "But that's not natural. However badly treated they'd been, it is unlikely all the kids would have died, all around the same time. No, it was something else."

John frowned. "What?"

"I think they were suffering from radiation sickness. They were poisoned by radiation. Once you see the photos, it can't be anything else. Those kids were exposed to a strong source of radioactive material. I would bet anything on it."

John's face became tight, almost frightening. "So you think —"

"I think that someone — probably this man Lee Chamness — is using one of my father's ships to land radioactive material at the port of Los Angeles. My father's ships have a special exemption that he rarely invokes. A B-43 exemption, which means the ships can basically land without any customs inspections. And a lot of his ships have a Ro-Ro function. The goods are stowed in big trucks that are lashed down and when the ship lands, they simply drive the trucks off. Mr. Huntington — John. I feel — we feel — that there might be a radioactive shipment, or a dirty bomb, coming into the United States."

John's face turned to stone. "God. We're going to have to notify NEST."

Matt turned to her. "NEST is the agency that deals with radioactive material. Nuclear Emergency Special Team. Though we'd have to be sure that we're talking about radioactivity. We can't be calling NEST out for what might turn out to be a heroin shipment."

"Do you have any men or equipment in the Hindu Kush, John?" Honor asked.

He paused a moment and shook his head. "No. We had a team providing close protection to a WHO team last month, but right now ..." he stopped, clearly running through files in his head. Finally he shook his head.

"Nope. By the time we get people there, it'll be too late."

Matt spoke up. "John, a friend of mine works for Jacob Black. They're working right in that area. Maybe they could send a sniffer drone. If there is a source of strong radioactivity, it would have to be in the caves. That's where the kids would have been exposed. I don't know what could be there, but it would be in a cave, not out in the open."

"Okay. Good call. I'm calling Jake right now. Stand by."

John Huntington winked off.

Wow. He was calling Jacob Black. The founder and owner of one of the largest security companies in the world, Black Inc. The company had iconic black towers in many American cities and in capitals around the world, instantly recognizable. They operated mainly abroad and though they worked mostly under cover, they'd been responsible for some major hostage rescues.

The screen came to life and there he was.

Honor had only seen newspaper photos, which didn't show the vitality and intelligence. Even through a screen and thousands of miles away, he was a formidable presence. In the background was a dusty street of dun-colored buildings, a deep blue cloudless sky and mountains in the far distance.

Jacob Black himself was dressed in black, with a black baseball cap, long black hair held back at the nape. He had a long narrow face with sharp features, black eyes, black eyebrows and a scruffy black beard. Not a hipster beard, but the kind you get from not shaving for days.

He'd been walking down a crowded street as he switched on but stopped, ducking into a doorway. Behind him, Honor could see two guys stop when he stopped. They positioned themselves with their backs to him, facing outward.

Bodyguards.

"Matt," Jacob Black said.

Honor was intimidated but Matt definitely wasn't. He didn't bother apologizing for disturbing him. "Jake. We have a situation."

"A minute." Jacob Black murmured something to his bodyguards and a tank-like vehicle rolled up. Nothing was visible of the inside through the dark-tinted windows. The vehicle had three doors in the side. Black got into the back door, the two bodyguards got into the vehicle via the middle door. When Black pulled his door closed all noises of the outside world disappeared. It was like he'd stepped into a bunker.

The image was no longer coming from a cellphone but from some camera or screen that was somehow affixed at face level.

"Okay. We're secure. Shoot."

Matt put his arm around Honor, squeezed lightly. Which she understood was both a claim and a character reference. "Jake, meet Honor Thomas. Dr. Honor Thomas. She's an emergency physician here in a hospital in Portland."

If Jacob Black was curious as to why Matt initiated a

call from halfway around the world to introduce her, he gave no signs. He gave a courteous nod. "Doctor."

"Honor's father runs Quest Line Shipping," Matt said.

"Okay." Black's gaze grew a little sharper.

Matt looked down at her. "Honey ..."

He wanted her to take it from there. Okay. Honor was used to making reports to powerful men. And Jacob Black seemed as friendly as such a rich and powerful man could be, not hostile in any way. She'd briefed plenty of hostile men, particularly from insurance companies.

"My father has not been seen in public for over two weeks. Twelve days ago I was abducted from an office Quest Line Shipping has in Portland. I was drugged and kept unconscious, so I have few memories. But I was kept captive for six days. I suspect this has to do with a new partner of my father's, Lee Chamness." Black gave a minute response. "You know him?"

"Yeah. And all of us in the SpecOps community know what he did to Matt. If he's involved in something bad, I'm not surprised."

"We suspect — we suspected that Chamness and others abducted my father so he could facilitate a big shipment of heroin. My father's shipping line has a B-43 exemption."

"No inspections," Black murmured.

"That's right. And there's Lee Chamness's connection to Al Rashid, whose compound is right in the middle of poppy fields. It was a reasonable assumption to make."

Honor took a breath, looked to Matt. She didn't need his support but she had it anyway. Everything in him — from his body language to his expression — spoke of unwavering support. And something else.

She settled more closely against his shoulder and looked back at the screen image of Jacob Black on the wall. She never thought she'd ever be speaking with Jacob Black, but there he was, intently listening to her.

"Matt told me that all the children he rescued died soon after. And he mentioned that they'd all gone bald. Baldness can be some people's reaction to extreme stress — the horror of being shackled playthings for a brutal overlord, for example — but not all of them would lose their hair. When I saw photographs of the kids, they showed clear signs of radiation poisoning. Alopecia, burns. All of them."

Black's face tightened noticeably when she said 'radiation'. Anyone would be frightened at the term. But soldiers knew what the consequences would be because they'd trained for it. Something they'd thought about in depth.

"That's bad." Black looked down at something in his hand, off screen. "Thoughts, Matt?"

"I remember rumors from operators who'd been around in the 80s that the Soviets had been planning some kind of last ditch operation in Afghanistan. Some thought that maybe they'd use a nuke but what is there to nuke there?"

"Not necessarily a nuclear bomb," Honor said. She

was thinking it through as she spoke. "I have no idea what the Soviet Union was planning, they pulled out of Afghanistan when I was two years old. But in general, one could use radioactivity in ways other than a bomb. Or even a dirty bomb. If you were really vindictive, you could use radioactive salts to salt the earth, make it completely uninhabitable for generations. Or poison waterways or wells."

"The Soviet Union was already crumbling." Matt was nodding his head slowly. "There'd have been plenty of radioactive material out of Chernobyl, which was three years earlier, in 1986. They could have driven the radioactive material into Afghanistan and stowed it in caves."

"The karez," Black said. "They've been digging tunnels in the mountains since the days of Alexander the Great. They could have hidden the radioactive material in the caves. Bin Laden was in the caves for years."

"He wouldn't have found the radioactive material." Matt leaned forward, taking her with him. "If he had, New York would be a wasteland."

"It must have been the kids who found the material." Honor could see it. Kids, clambering in and out of caves and tunnels, doing what kids have done since time began. Only they explored the wrong cave.

"And then Chamness." Matt's hand tightened almost painfully on her shoulder. "Chamness found it and found a reason to placate a barbarian warlord."

She could hardly believe it. "And bring it to the States. I can barely wrap my head around that. But it's the only thing that makes sense." She turned to the screen. "Mr. Black, I believe you're in the area, is there a way you can test for radioactivity?"

"I was thinking the same thing." He glanced again downward, either at a cell or a laptop. "But there are thousands of caves in that area. I don't have that kind of manpower and I don't have permission to deploy a platoon of operators."

"How about drones?" Matt suggested. "Send in a fleet of drones. I think the DOD mapped the entrances to the caves in that area. You'd have all the coordinates. How many sniffer drones do you have?"

"I've got plenty of drones and even sniffer drones, but they're programmed to detect explosives and drugs. We have a special contract with the DEA. But not radioactivity."

Both men were silent for a moment.

"Are you near a hospital complex?" Honor asked. "Or a clinic?"

Black nodded. "There's a UN hospital complex thirty clicks away."

"They are bound to have an X-ray department and radiology. And they will have plenty of dosimeters. Grab as many dosimeters as you can and attach them to your drones. It's a crude solution, but I think it would work. Hospitals have hundreds of dosimeters."

"By yesterday would be good," Matt added. "We can't call NEST until we have actionable intel and the first ship that could be a contender is due to land tomorrow."

"On it," Jacob Black said and the screen went dark.

"So," Honor said, turning to Matt. "When do we leave for LA?"

"*I'm* leaving for LA in an hour. *You're* staying here," he said, starting to get up.

Honor grabbed his sweater, making him sit down again. "Wrong. I'm coming too."

He looked appalled. "I thought we were in agreement." He shook his head. "No way."

Honor stood up. "Way."

Fifteen

In a Cessna Citation, en route to Los Angeles

There was an impromptu strategy session at the airfield and it was late afternoon before they could take off for Los Angeles.

Matt still didn't understand how it happened that Honor was with him in the ASI jet. She simply didn't take no for an answer. He'd even made arrangements for Joe Harris and Jack Delvaux to take turns keeping watch over her at the Grange and Isabel, Joe's wife, had offered to come up and keep her company.

It was all arranged. And then the arrangements went to shit.

He'd argued while she packed a small bag of Isabel's clothes, after asking her permission. He'd argued while they made their way up to the surface. He'd started ranting while they were on the helo pad waiting for the helo to take them to a small military airfield, and he'd started foaming at the mouth when they got to the airfield and the Citation was waiting for them.

The idea of her in Los Angeles made him a little crazy. Okay, a lot crazy.

He'd listed, over and over again, why this was a bad idea and she seemed to take his arguments in serious consideration, then rejected them.

Turned out that you didn't get through medical school and then work in the ER by being a pushover.

My dad is in danger. I want to be close by in case something happens to him. She kept saying that, over and over, and well, shit. Matt could understand.

So while they argued as she packed and went topside with him and got into the helo and then the plane, deep down Matt knew it was a losing battle.

They were sitting in the Citation's very comfortable leather seats, next to each other and he was holding her hand. While he was touching her, she was safe so he made sure he kept touching her.

"I want you to stay in the safe house," he repeated for the billionth time.

"Absolutely." Honor was the voice of reason. "I will stay in the safe house until you find my dad and stop whatever it is that madman Chamness is doing. But I'll be close by if my dad needs help."

"Not a madman." Matt was clear on that point. "He's not crazy, he's just bad. He knows exactly what he's doing and he'll have it all organized. And whether it is heroin or radioactive materials, he will have a solid plan in place and it's guaranteed to earn him a shitload of money. Probably retiring-forever-to-Bali money."

"Bali's overrated," she said pensively, then looked

up at him and winked.

Oh God, he couldn't lose this woman, he simply couldn't. He'd just found her. How could he have possibly known that he kept it light with other women not because he wasn't made for settling down but because they weren't Honor Thomas?

She was everything he never even knew he wanted. Needed. Smart and kind and unfussy. Bossy, when it came to health issues. Certainly, she gave her father grief about his unhealthy habits, which she did because she obviously loved him. So far she hadn't given Matt any grief because he sort of already had a healthy lifestyle. Except she hadn't seen him when he was immersed in a job and then it was a diet of cheeseburgers and fries and pizza. Man, when she found that out …

"What are you smiling about?" she asked.

Start like you mean to go on, he thought. Make it a habit to tell the truth.

He gave an exaggerated sigh. "I was thinking you're going to give me a hard time when you realize I don't always eat the way you've seen me eat up at the Grange. Healthy eating there is easy. It's the only kind of food on tap. But on the job, I mostly eat junk food. I'm just saying this in the interest of full disclosure."

"Yeah?" That pretty face scrunched up in thought. "Well, that's going to change, but you already know that."

"I exercise," he said, in self defense. It was true. He was so used to keeping fit in the military that he just carried that over into civilian life. All the ASI guys did.

She punched him lightly in the biceps. "I noticed."

"Want me to make a muscle for you?" Maybe that would earn him points.

"Nah. I've felt your muscles. Remember?"

He met her eyes, so filled with light. Oh yeah, he remembered. He remembered everything. Every touch and every sigh. He remembered touching her, everywhere. Her touching him, everywhere. Touching and kissing and making love.

Something of what he was thinking must have showed on his face because she blushed lightly. Or at least her cheeks filled with color. It was good to know that he could make this tough woman blush. But above all, he liked seeing color in her face because he could all too vividly conjure up the vision of her face so close to death, skin gray and icy-white, lips blue with cold, the veins in her eyelids visible.

Now that he knew who she was, now that she was so precious to him, the memory made him shudder.

"Well, since we're doing full disclosure …" She smiled at him and he smiled back. She wasn't dead. She was right here, vividly alive. And all his. She cocked her head to one side, a mischievous light in her eyes. "Three, two, one … I can't cook."

Matt kept a perfectly straight face. "At all?"

"At all. I can boil eggs if I use a timer and I can slice and wash salad. I try not to eat processed foods so basically at home I eat salads and boiled eggs and slices of cheese and fruit. Which is not that bad a diet. There's an organic food section in the hospital cafeteria. I'm hoping you can cook."

"Nope," he said cheerfully. "Told you that. I can do even less than you do. I can order in, and nuke whatever Isabel and her interns cook. I have a very big freezer."

"What a couple we are."

He stilled, looked at her suddenly unsmiling. Her eyes widened as she realized what she'd said.

"Are we?" Matt asked softly. "A couple?"

It was a question with weight. He'd saved her life and he was going to do his damndest to find her father. They'd had sex. In his world, that wasn't a recipe for coupledom. He and his teammates had rescued hostages five times, and there'd been women among the hostages. He hadn't once pursued any of the women. They were jobs. But he'd had sex, with a lot of women.

Honor wasn't a job. Honor was his heart. He'd found a woman who turned him on in all senses. He found it hard to keep his hands off her, he enjoyed being around her, he liked the way her mind worked. And — besides the wild attraction — she was a kindred soul. She too didn't like how the world worked and in her way she kept trying to put broken pieces together. Not with a gun like he and his teammates did, but with the healing power of medicine. Her moral compass ran true, just like his.

Are we a couple?

Matt's question hung there in the air.

Honor ran a hand down his arm, finishing by linking her fingers with his.

"Yeah," she said pensively. "I guess we are. If you want us to be."

"I want that." Matt met her eyes. Such beautiful eyes. Light gray, perceptive. She held his gaze steadily. "I want that ... a lot."

"Even though I can't cook." There was a slight question in the statement. One he was happy to answer.

"Even though you can't cook. God invented microwaves for a reason."

"Even though I will bug you about your health."

It had been a long time since anyone worried about what Matt ate. "Yeah. I'm a tough guy. I can take it."

"Even though —"

The pilot interrupted. "We're landing, guys. Strap in."

Whatever she was going to say was interrupted by light turbulence that had her clutching his hand.

So she was a nervous flyer.

Matt wasn't. He'd flown thousands and thousands of miles strapped to a bulkhead webbing seat on C-130s. And if your time had come, there was nothing you could do about it. But he was perfectly willing to calm her nerves. He held her hand tightly as they approached the small landing field, which was lit up. The lights illuminated a grove of orange trees shuddering in the high winds.

They came down slightly sideways, touched, bounced, touched again and rolled down the runway. A bumpier landing than usual.

Honor's hand in his was damp, trembling. Once the

plane was rolling on terra firma, Honor pulled away slightly, sat up, rubbed her palms on her pants. "Thanks."

Matt was planning the next steps in his head but hit pause. "For what?"

"For not making fun of me. I don't like flying in general. That was something. I am not ashamed to say I was scared shitless. I'm sure you were laughing at me."

That pulled him right out of himself. "God no." He leaned forward, kissed her cheek. "I wouldn't make fun of you. Smaller planes experience turbulence more than larger planes. We weigh about a hundred times less than a Boeing 757. But no planes have ever gone down because of turbulence. The worst turbulence might make the nose go down maybe 20 feet, not more."

She looked at him. "Felt like a thousand feet to me."

"Yeah. But it wasn't."

"I was imagining the pilot and co-pilot, sweaty hands on the — steering wheel?"

He knew better than to smile. "Yoke. And no, their hands wouldn't have been sweaty. They were probably deciding where to have dinner this evening."

"Oh." She tucked a lock of hair behind her ear. "Okay. That's good to know."

A ping sounded in the air and the fasten seat belt sign winked off.

"Here we go." Matt reached over, unbuckled her belt, helped her get up. If she'd really had a fright, her legs would feel unsteady. Her adrenaline would have spiked and she'd now be in post-adrenaline shock.

No problem. He had his arm around her waist. He'd keep her steady and he'd make sure to have a nice meal sent to her in the safe house. After a moment, she blew out a breath and he could feel strength flowing back into her.

Matt was picking up their bags when the pilot appeared in the doorway of the cockpit. "Mr. Walker?"

"Just Matt is fine."

The pilot nodded, held out a cell. "Call for you, Matt. They said they tried your cell but it was off."

Matt fished his cell out of his pocket. Dead. He'd turned it off automatically, didn't even remember doing it. He took the cell from the pilot's hands, nodding his thanks to the pilot. "Walker," he said into the phone.

"Matt." He stiffened when he recognized Jacob Black's voice. The man was a former soldier and a brother. But he was also a brother who was worth a billion dollars. Jake was an equal but as the book said, some were more equal than others. "You guys called it. I sent forty drones over the cliffsides and we hit the jackpot on the tenth cave. Not a jackpot anyone wants to hit, though. We went very deep into the cave and maxed out the dosimeters. In the meantime we found mini Geiger counters and put those on a couple of bigger drones and had readings of over seven hundred sieverts."

"Fuck," Matt breathed. Seven hundred sieverts was death in thirty days. It topped the peak radiation levels at Fukushima and Chernobyl.

"What?" Honor picked up immediately that someone was wrong. "Who is it?"

"Hold on," Matt told Jake. "It's Jacob Black. He sent his drones like you said. Found readings as high as seven hundred sieverts. That's —"

"That's Chernobyl territory," she said and he nodded. "So — what's the theory? Your kids played in those caves? Put Mr. Black on speakerphone."

He did. "Is that your take, too, Jake ? That those kids somehow infiltrated the wrong cave and got massive radiation poisoning?"

"Yeah. My guys sent those drones deep into the caves and they were equipped with lights. Deep inside the caves the radiation was at that figure, tapering off at the entrance. The kids must have gone exploring. Maybe went back day after day. Got exposed."

"Was there anything visible in the caves?" Matt asked. Was the source of radiation still there?

"Negative. But something had been there, very definitely. There were truck tracks down to the first curve in the cave walls, then tracks of what must have been electric carts. Deep inside there'd been something stored there — there were round imprints in the dust where the dust wasn't disturbed. Those round imprints went way way back into almost the heart of the mountain. Canisters, Matt. A lot of them. All gone now. One of my operators talked to the chieftain of a neighboring tribe and he said a convoy of trucks went by three weeks ago."

Matt breathed out slowly. "On their way here, I'll bet you anything."

"Wouldn't bet against you, Matt. I've got four operators on their way up to you from San Diego in a helo. With hazmat suits for you guys. They'll be in touch soon."

He felt something ease a little in his chest. Dante was here and so was Luke. The ASI guys were almost here. The Black Inc operators were on their way.

"We'll wait here for them."

"Roger that. ETA forty mikes."

"Copy that," Matt said and closed the connection.

Inside an hour, a formidable team would be here.

But shit happens and shit happened.

He'd turned his cell on and it pinged. Felicity. He put it on speakerphone so Honor could hear.

"Matt!" Felicity sounded winded, unusually agitated.

"Hey. You okay?" Honor turned the cellphone towards her. Felicity's agitated face appeared on the screen. "Everything okay with the twins?"

"Great. Listen, bad news. I did a routine check of ports and the *Maria Cristina* landed an hour ago at Long Beach instead of its scheduled arrival tomorrow at the Port of Los Angeles. Hold on." Honor turned a terrified face to Matt. The ship had already landed! "I grabbed some security cam footage. Honor, your father is there. You can see him at one minute forty-five seconds into the video I'm sending now."

Matt was horrified. Radiological material — no one knew how much but Jake seemed to think it was a lot — had just landed on US soil.

The cell's screen showed video footage. It must

have been about an hour ago, at nautical twilight. The sodium-vapor lights along the waterfront were already lit enough to see a medium-sized modern cargo ship with the hold doors open and trucks rolling down the ramp and onto the pier.

Truck after truck.

They landed on the pier and turned right. Standing there, watching, were four men. Three had on either baseball caps or boonie hats and sunglasses, though it was nearly dark. They kept their faces down. The fourth man raised his face to the sky twice, after the man next to him bent to talk into his ear.

Honor gasped. "Dad! That's Dad!" As if to banish any possibility of mistake, her finger tapped on the screen right over the pale face that lifted to the sky. "Oh, my God. He's there with them!"

She sounded heartsick.

Matt bent down until his lips touched her ear. "They told him to look up, honey. The other men have caps on and they're keeping their faces down, but they told him to look up so he could be identified. He's being framed."

She looked up at him, angry tears in her eyes.

And another truck rolled out.

Port of Long Beach

Ivan Antonov watched the trucks roll off the boat and onto the pier, easy as anything. The sky was dark blue edging toward black, with the lights of Los Angeles a glow on the horizon.

Soon those lights would be switched off and where there had been light would become darkness.

He smiled. Such poetic thoughts, though he thought of himself as a very pragmatic man. You don't change the course of history with poetry but with planning and foresight.

Still. The thought of Los Angeles and the surrounding area switched off forever gave him a great deal of pleasure. The moment he and his men dumped the canisters of liquidized cesium-137 salts into the water supply and helicopters dispersed radioactive liquid over the city would be a major cut-off point, after which nothing would ever be the same. Like the attacks on Pearl Harbor, like the assassination of Prince Ferdinand, like the fall of the Berlin Wall.

Everything changed forever.

It pleased him so much to think of the panic. Americans became upset when their burgers weren't cooked as they liked. There were stories of Americans calling their emergency number, 911, when a fast-food place ran out of ketchup. Any minor inconvenience was cause for panic. They didn't have the iron discipline of Russians. No discipline at all, in fact. They would never have withstood the three-year siege of Stalingrad, as his countrymen had. Three years of starvation, of eating rats and sleeping in rubble during freezing cold winters, all the while resisting. No, Americans would have surrendered after day two of a siege.

They were so risk averse. This would be a no man's land forever.

"Sir?" Antonov turned to see one of the truck drivers, a young man from Novosibirsk. Siberians were born and bred tough and Antonov had made sure to recruit from the north. These men knew exactly what they were carrying and were being paid accordingly.

However each and every one of them carried American ID and they were dressed in clothes bought at Old Navy and Target. If they died, there would be nothing to identify them as Russians. Not even military tattoos. Antonov had recruited men whose bodies were sterile.

They were also brave.

It would have been far too risky to have men driving trucks in hazmat suits. The exposure had been carefully calculated. It was a different team of men from those who had driven those trucks onto the ship. The ship's crew was mainly American, the captain American and they hadn't been told anything. These drivers, who had been waiting in a comfortable safe house in Los Angeles for weeks, would be very amply compensated for a short period of exposure. The canisters were encased in lead containers. They would reach a warehouse not too far from the major water pumping station. They would don hazmat suits and mix the salts in water to make a liquid. The liquid would be loaded onto tanker trucks and four helicopters whose cargo bays had been equipped with tanks.

Most of the radioactive liquid would be dumped into the pumping station, while the helicopters would criss-cross Los Angeles, dumping radioactive water. Helicopters flew all the time, they wouldn't be stopped. By the time authorities noticed that massive amounts of radioactive material had been dumped in the Los Angeles water basin, and all over the city, the trucks and helicopters and the men would all be long gone. The men would disappear forever, millions of dollars richer.

Antonov looked over at Simon Thomas. Thomas, on the other hand, would be immediately suspected of organizing the attack. People who knew him might protest his innocence, but who would believe them? There would be documents attesting to Quest Line Shipping's massive debts. He'd facilitated the shipment every step of the way. His fingerprints — quite literally — would be all over the attack.

Antonov had on a baseball cap and was dressed in American clothes. There was absolutely nothing to distinguish him, in terms of appearance, from an American. The same with the crew. He never looked up, but told Thomas to look up every few minutes until darkness fell. The security cameras would have captured his pale worried face many times.

Lee Chamness was waiting for them at the staging area. They'd be operating in the dark, everyone equipped with night vision goggles. The security cameras all along the route had been disabled.

In and out, leaving devastation behind.

The last truck rolled off the ship. Ten trucks, each carrying two hundred canisters. An even ton of radioactive material. Enough for a very small Armageddon. Certainly enough to lay waste to the City of Angels.

Excellent, for a night's work.

Sixteen

Small airfield, Los Angeles

Jacko and Joe Harris, who had been teaching combat firearm techniques to the San Diego SWAT team and had rushed up, arrived two minutes later on a helicopter. Matt called it a helo. There was a large black SUV already parked on the tarmac.

Jacko and Joe descended from the helicopter with two heavy bags that clanked. Matt unloaded a heavy bag from the back of their business jet that clanked, too.

She was not loaded for bear. She wasn't loaded for anything and she didn't want to be. All she wanted was to be near her father. Or at least in the same city. Just in case.

They were fitted with what Matt called 'comms'. A tiny bud in the ear that transmitted surprisingly clearly. You switched it on and off by tapping the tragus.

And now their well-organized plan had been shot to shit.

"Fuck!" Matt looked like he wanted to punch

something. "Felicity! Someone needs to call NEST headquarters now! These fuckers are rolling!"

"Negative, Matt." Felicity's voice was super clear. Not agitated. Sad. "Someone already has. Turns out budget cuts have decimated NEST. They only have three active teams and two have been called out."

"Fuck." That was Jacko's basso profundo. "False calls. What about the third one?"

"In Maryland. They're in the air but it will take them eight hours to get here."

Silence on the line.

"Up to us, then." Matt. "Felicity, can we follow those trucks?"

"Yeah. I just hacked into their GPS. Let's see. Two stops. One at 12304 Lawrence Street, which seems to be a warehouse in an industrial district. Then 11805 Vanowen, which is …" The sound of tapping. Then silence. Then … "Oh fuck," on a whisper.

Matt, Jacko and Joe looked at each other, startled. Honor knew they didn't startle easily. It probably meant that Felicity didn't let the f-bomb drop often. Even though it was definitely an *oh fuck* kind of world.

"Guys, 11805 Vanowen is the PowerNorth Hollywood Pump Station, in North Hollywood. Where most of Los Angeles gets its water. They are going to irradiate the Los Angeles water supply …"

Joe tapped his ear. "Felicity, is there a staging area near the warehouse?"

"Looking." The three men stood stock still.

"Yeah." Felicity came online. "There's what looks

like an empty lot next to the warehouse. I took pictures off a satellite that passed over three days ago, so I can't guarantee that nothing's changed. I know you guys have a couple of drones in your kit. Give me the serial numbers and I'll program them for you remotely and you can send them to those coordinates. The drones have IR capability. At least you'll know what the situation is on the ground before you get there. But guys — hurry. I have a bad feeling."

"We all do," Matt said, shouldering that big heavy bag. He looked around. "What are we going to do with Honor?"

Honor stiffened. "What do you mean what are you going to do with me? I'm not a package."

Joe and Jacko gave each other a look and backed away. Matt turned to her indignantly. "Honey, we have no idea what we're walking into. A firefight, a nuclear disaster, a showdown. Your guess is as good as mine. I can't have you there, it's too dangerous and it would just distract me. Us."

Honor set her teeth because she was going to have to convince Matt of something she had her own doubts about.

"Look." She put on her serious reasonable look, when inside she was screaming *Don't take me with you! Take me with you! No, stash me somewhere safe, are you crazy? But I need to be with you! GOOD GOD I WANT TO HIDE IN A CORNER AND COVER MY EYES!*

But she was used to hiding what she felt so she knew her face was bland and gave nothing away.

Matt crossed his arms, his entire body screaming *I don't care what you have to say the answer is no.*

"Look, my father is being held by terrorists. What happens if he is wounded and I could have saved him but I wasn't there?" She looked over at Joe and Jacko who were busy stowing their bags in the helicopter, pretending not to hear. "What happens if Joe or Jacko are wounded and I could have saved them but I wasn't there? Or *you.*"

Her voice wobbled. The idea of losing Matt after finding him was almost impossible to bear.

"We were trained to deal with wounds," he said. How he managed to get those words out through a tightly clenched jaw was a miracle of anatomy.

She just looked at him. No medic training could possibly equal her training. She'd dealt with gunshot wounds. Lots of them. More than they had, that was for sure. But she didn't say that. No use pulling rank. Reason was needed here.

"And where would I go?" Honor swept her arm at the almost-deserted air field. Like most very small airports it basically shut down after dark. Though there were probably people in the admin offices about a mile away, there was no living being in sight. Not even jackrabbits. "I don't dare call someone from my father's office to come pick me up. We have no idea if there are people infiltrated into the company or whether they are bugging phones. I don't know anyone who lives around here or who could make it here under a couple of hours. Calling a taxi would be insane. I don't —"

"Matt." Jacko's deep voice cut through her litany. "We're wasting time."

Matt rounded on him. "Fuck that, Jacko! Would you let Lauren come with you into a potential firefight? With possible radiation as a side dish? How about you, Joe? You be willing to let Isabel walk into this?"

"No," both men said at once.

"So — what? What would you do?" Both men shrugged, looking tense and uncomfortable.

"Don't ask them, ask *me*," Honor said, angry and scared at the same time. "I'm the one you should be talking to. And I'm the one who'd rather be with you, walking into a situation where my father could be at risk and where I could help, than cowering out here waiting for someone to pick me up."

It was true. She did not want to go into the show-down, what they would think of as their mission. It was insane. She was unequipped in every way. She'd never held a gun in her hand, never hit anyone in anger. She was singularly unsuited to go along with them. But she was also unsuited to stay here, out on the open tarmac, all alone. She might be safer but then she'd have a heart attack or a stroke or an embolism, worried about her father and about Matt.

And besides, Matt made her feel safe.

"I need to come with you," she insisted, forcibly removing the tension from her voice. She sounded calm and authoritative, the way she did in the ER, even when she had someone bleeding out and stroking out at the same time.

"Look," she said, the very voice and picture of reason. "Let me stay in the vehicle. Wherever you go, I'll just hide behind the seats or anywhere you put me and I swear to God I will not move an inch until you come to get me. Just don't —" her voice faltered. She closed her eyes and saw herself, out here on the tarmac that felt like being abandoned in a warm Siberia, the only human in a thousand miles, "Don't leave me here alone. Please."

Honor met his eyes and put everything she felt into her gaze. Fear. Trust. Terror.

Matt made a sound in his throat, looked up at the sky which evidently was not providing much help, and held out his hand to her.

Yesss!

One hand holding a big rifle and the clanking bag, the other holding her hand, he stalked off to the SUV. She scrambled to keep up with his long strides.

"You do what I say," he said, face grim.

"Absolutely." God yes.

"You wear body armor and a helmet at all times."

"Ah … yeah. Okay."

The big black SUV had the trunk door open.

"Here." Matt reached in and handed to her what looked like a metal half-barrel and a huge helmet. Matt handed his rifle to Joe, who was standing by, already in his own body armor. Which fit him.

"Hold up your arms." It was amazing how clearly she could hear Matt over the tiny bud in her ear. Like he was talking right into her ear.

She held her arms up as if this were an old-style western and he was the bad guy saying *reach for the sky*. She reached for the sky.

Matt dropped an iron lung on her. It was rigid and heavy and hung halfway down her thighs. She staggered and staggered again when he dropped a heavy helmet into her hand. The helmet would either stop a bullet or break her neck. One or the other. He glared at her, daring her to complain.

No way. She smiled at him and held out a hand to be helped up into the SUV. Matt grabbed her by the waist and hoisted her up. The armor was so heavy she would never have made it on her own. She sat down in the rear passenger seat and Matt rounded the back and sat behind the driver, Jacko.

Matt's movements were those of an angry man, jerky and exaggerated. He slammed her door shut and then his.

Honor was not comfortable. The body armor ate into the tops of her thighs and chafed her around the neck and arms but she'd rather be whipped than complain.

"Dickhead," Jacko said to Matt, turning around, again the deep voice surprisingly clear in the comms unit in her ear. These guys had serious gear.

Matt turned his glare from her to Jacko, who gave it right back.

Honor tried to get into a position that was not actually painful. Matt settled into the seat next to her and put a heavy arm around her, which made the body armor eat into her thighs even more.

Damn right Matt was a dickhead. But he was *her* dickhead so she wasn't about to say anything.

Seventeen

They were part of a convoy. Simon was riding shotgun in a black SUV. Riding shotgun was ironic because the man sitting in the rear passenger seat was holding some kind of weapon on his lap. A real shotgun. He'd made sure that Simon saw it and that Simon understood that he could blow a hole in Simon's spine at any moment.

If he thought there was any hope at all of stopping this — whatever this was —Simon might have made a move. But even making this vehicle crash would do nothing to stop the ten trucks that had rolled off his ship.

He now understood, viscerally, how privileged he was and how respected Quest Line Shipping was. His credentials were more than enough to enter the port of Long Beach, get to where the *Maria Cristina* moored, and wait for ten trucks to roll off. Nobody stopped them, nobody questioned them, it went smooth as silk.

Of course Simon's fingerprints were everywhere — the ID used to secure entrance, the retinal and handprint scan to access the inner port, the landing of the *Maria Cristina* authorized by him. He'd even authorized the switch of port from Los Angeles to Long Beach.

Whatever those trucks were carrying, and he was sure it was either drugs or material for some kind of terrorist attack, it would look like he'd planned it all.

Which meant they were going to kill him. Just as they had probably killed Honor.

A familiar sharp pain shot through his chest at the thought. Instinctively he tried to bring his palm to his chest. His wrists were bound by plasticuffs. He couldn't mitigate the pain in his chest.

He couldn't go anywhere and he couldn't do anything. He was a helpless passenger along for the ride to nowhere good.

What was it? Were the trucks full of explosives? He knew just two trucks full of explosives in the 1990s almost brought down the twin towers.

As head of a shipping line he knew all the terrible things that could be shipped and cause horrible damage. Explosives, drugs, vials of deadly disease. Though vials were usually small, could be carried in a briefcase, because viruses replicated themselves. Whatever was in the truck beds was big, heavy and dangerous. Simon had seen the point of origin of the cargo. Afghanistan, via the port of Karachi. His best guess was drugs. A shipload of drugs would be worth millions and millions of dollars at the street level.

So these vile Russians had kidnapped him, possibly murdered Honor, all to smuggle drugs into the country via his shipping company.

Only the wild hope that Honor might still be alive kept him from trying to attack the big Russian driving the SUV. Even handcuffed, Simon could perhaps make him drive off the road, crash into a railing, topple over. If Honor was gone, Simon didn't want to live.

But if she was alive?

Then he'd live to see them all behind bars. Particularly Chamness.

The Russian checked the navigator briefly then slowed down and took a sharp left.

They were in a part of LA Simon barely knew. They were on the decaying outskirts of Frogtown along the LA River basin bike trail. He'd biked it once, thirty years ago.

The Russian turned right then left again, entering a warren of abandoned warehouses. What the hell were they doing here? Finally, the Russian braked gently to a halt and through the side rear-view mirror Simon could see that the trucks had halted too.

They were here, wherever here was.

The Russian lifted the lid on the console between the seats and took out a remote control. He clicked it. None of the street lamps in the area was working and there was a new moon so there was very little light except for the headlights, which showed a rusty steel gate.

But the gate slid open surprisingly easily and looking more closely, Simon could see that the gate wasn't rusted or broken. Just unpainted. And rolling in, he saw an apron that was clean, with no cracked concrete. A huge hangar-like warehouse was a dark blot against the dark sky.

What the hell were they doing here? Offloading?

And then his darkest imaginings proved true. The double doors into the hangar started sliding open on tracks revealing a huge lit area. Two men walked toward the opening doorway and Simon's heart started pounding when he saw what they were wearing.

Hazmat suits.

Damn.

For an instant, Matt longed for Afghanistan. He'd give his left nut to be in a convoy heading out to yet another fucking dusty village full of crazy Talibans embedded in the population, ready to fire at him at any moment. Travelling along a rutted road with IEDs ready to blow at any time. Sweating in 120° heat in full body armor, in the back of a carrier vehicle with twelve other hot sweaty men who hadn't showered in a week.

Piece of cake.

Certainly compared to walking into fuck-knows-what with a woman he loved sitting right beside him. It messed with his head and you do not walk into danger with a messed-up head. You walk into danger with icy nerves and total focus and knowing that you are in a pack of men who are locked and loaded and as well trained as you are.

Not with a slender woman who is drowning in body armor that doesn't fit and whose delicate hands are designed for sutures not shooting.

Gah.

He tightened his hand around her shoulders and sat there, glowering and angry. The only thing that made this in any way acceptable was that she was with him and he was going to keep her safe no matter what. And, well, Joe and Jacko were pretty good wingmen and would do anything to keep her safe too.

The shittiest thing about this was that she was right. Where could he have put her? They were in a race against time and he couldn't have just left her on the tarmac back at the airfield. There was no time to call someone and even if there had been, who? Couldn't just summon up a fucking uber, to take her to a hotel. He had no idea how far reaching the conspiracy was.

Hard place, meet rock.

"You're going to stay in the vehicle," he said. He'd said it before. Often.

"Of course." Her voice was soft and cool in his earpiece. Joe and Jacko were dialed into the comms system but he didn't care if he was repeating himself and coming off as crazy.

He knew for a fact that if there was any danger to Lauren, Jacko would go apeshit and so would Joe if there was anything threatening Isabel besides sharp kitchen knives and boiling oil.

They didn't react in any way, faces stolidly turned

forward as Jacko drove them straight into the heart of danger.

"No matter what you hear, you don't get out of this vehicle. It's armored." It was a miracle words were coming out of his mouth, his teeth were clenched so hard.

"No." Then a beat later, "What? You think I'm crazy?"

No, he was the crazy one. Getting crazier by the second. "I don't —"

"Cut the drama," Jacko growled. "Two mikes out."

Two minutes. A hell of a lot could be accomplished in two minutes. Matt could fieldstrip his rifle. He could check all his gear and check a teammate's gear, while doing a thorough comms check.

He didn't do any of that. He just sat and hyperventilated.

"Yo, Matt," Joe said without turning around. "Get your head out of your ass. Right. Fucking. Now."

Honor turned a startled face up at him. Did she expect him to push back? He couldn't because his head *was* up his ass. They were about to go into a hostile and dangerous situation, against an enemy whose numbers and positioning they didn't know, with radioactive material in the mix. Not a good time to be messed in the head. Going into battle was never a good time to be messed in the head. And this time, not only he could die. Honor could die, too.

She could die, anyway, if it all went south. They might be totally outgunned inside the warehouse. There might be a fucking army in there.

"What do the birds say?" They'd launched two drones to the place as soon as Felicity programmed them.

Joe's head dipped forward as he looked at the tablet on the dashboard. "The ten trucks are entering the gates." He tapped on an icon. "Each truck has a driver, no passenger. Just one heat signature in IR. That's funny…"

"What?" Jacko's head didn't turn but you could feel his attention switching briefly from the road. In any situation, Jacko did the driving. He was a superb combat driver, probably because of some special freakish spatial thing in his head, the same thing that made him an extraordinary sniper.

"I don't have any image of the back of the trucks. Nada. Zip."

"Ahm." Honor sounded tentative. "That might be because the back of the trucks could be lined with lead. If there is radioactive material, it would be shielded. Even if some of my father's cargos can land without inspection, there could be random radioactivity checks."

"Jesus." Joe stopped tapping on the screen. "Yeah. Okay. The trucks and an SUV have rolled into the compound and the gates are closing. And we have —" he mentally counted. "We have four men coming out of the warehouse and four men still inside. Huh. The four men coming outside look … weird. They're walking funny."

Honor leaned forward and looked over his shoulder.

"Those are hazmat suits they are wearing." She looked at Matt. "Do you guys have hazmat suits?"

"No." Jacko answered. "The Black Inc guys were supposed to bring them up. They're still en route." Jacko was the one responsible for gear. That same freakish lobe also made him good with gear. He could list everything in their bags, everything in the back of the vehicle, how many rounds of ammo they had.

"The NEST guys will definitely have them," Joe offered.

"When will they be arriving?" Honor looked hopeful.

Matt turned his head to her. "Tomorrow, honey."

Honor's face turned to stone. She scooted forward until her face was between Jacko and Joe.

"Okay." She pointed at the tablet which had switched from drone mode to GPS mode. The white arrow that was their vehicle was almost at the point of arrival. "I don't know what kind of radioactive material is in those trucks. I don't know if any of you have seen a case of radiation poisoning. Matt has, though he didn't recognize it. But trust me when I say you do not want to be exposed. So I would advise you to get in there fast and get out fast. As long as there is containment — Jacko, can a bullet shoot through lead?"

"Our bullets are full metal jackets," he said. "The lead lining can't be too thick because otherwise the trucks would be too heavy to move. So, yeah, our bullets could probably penetrate the lining."

"Not good news." Honor tapped them both on the

arm. "Shoot at people, not at the truck cargo areas."

Jacko cut the engine and rolled to a stop, smoothly and silently. They were alongside the wall surrounding the compound. The drones had mapped the system of security cameras and cones of vision and had even mapped them a route without security cams to a position along the wall that was a dead zone.

The system had also measured the height of the wall. Ten feet.

Doable.

Joe and Jacko got out, quietly. Jacko had cut the lights so they didn't come on when the doors opened.

Matt exchanged glances with Honor, not knowing what to say. He was conflicted, something he'd never experienced when going into battle. He was always one with the mission, except for now.

Honor lay her hand on his, pressed her cheek against his and whispered, so lightly it couldn't have been heard from a foot away. "Go make this right. Save my father."

He pulled back. Her face with taut with tension but no trace of anything but strong purpose. He nodded, she nodded back, and with that his head was back in the game.

He was where he was comfortable being. Getting ready to stop something awful, with the best guys in the world by his side. If it could be done, they'd do it.

Outside, with all the street lights along the road killed, it was pitch black. In one coordinated movement, Matt, Joe and Jacko pulled down the night vision eyepiece affixed to their helmets and the world lit up in a soupy green.

Without a word exchanged, they lined up against the wall. Jacko pulled back the sleeve of his jacket and showed them the small wearable, flexible computer that was more advanced than the ones that had just rolled out in the SpecOps community. With a tap, it showed the bird's eye view from the drones in that flat green watery light of night vision.

The ten trucks and the SUV pulled into the warehouse and the big doors closed. They could hear the faint clank of the doors closing. There was no one outside the building, everyone was inside.

Joe and Matt looked at Jacko and without a word exchanged, he tapped an icon and the screen showing the drone feed switched from night vision to infrared. Emptiness outside the warehouse, heat signatures inside. The back of the trucks showed as utterly black. One half of the warehouse showed as utterly black. Probably lead-lined.

An opening in the wall separating the two parts of the warehouse appeared. The trucks drove single file into the black back part of the warehouse and the opening disappeared. The drivers didn't come back out.

Matt pointed at his eyes then at the small screen. *Cameras?*

The drones were able to discern videocameras in the vicinity via RF detectors. On the screen, there were four security cams, all outward looking, two in front, two in back. Not good security, but then they obviously thought they didn't need it. The cameras' footprints were well away from where they were and where their SUV was.

Okay, there was nobody on the other side of the wall. Now was the time.

Matt allowed himself one brief look at the SUV, knowing Honor was in there, but not knowing if he'd ever see her again … a hard punch to his shoulder and he looked back at Jacko's pissed-off face and one squinting eye.

He held his hands up — *okay, okay. Head back in the game.*

Joe had the mini grappling hook out from his backpack and tossed it up to the top of the wall. It held. He tugged and started climbing immediately. In a second, he'd disappeared over the top. If there had been any problems on the other side, he'd have tapped the comms unit twice. But there was silence.

Matt went up next, rolled over the top and dropped easily on the other side. Jacko dropped silently next to him. For a heavy guy, Jacko could be eerily quiet. His wife, Lauren, complained often about that. She'd turn around and there he'd be. Right next to her and she hadn't heard a thing.

Jacko lifted his forearm and they looked at the flexible screen with the non-reflective surface. Okay, so the ten trucks had been driven into the back section of the warehouse that was dark to them. The four men in hazmat suits had disappeared into the back of the warehouse, too. When the internal doors closed, it was as if they had gone into another dimension. Disappeared.

Seven men milled around in the unshielded section of the warehouse. The others had all gone into the shielded and hidden portion.

Matt had no idea what was being done in the hidden part of the warehouse, but it couldn't be anything good.

He pulled a small device from his backpack and, crouching to make the smallest target possible, made it to the side of the warehouse. The unshielded half. The device had a small suction cup and he attached it to the wall. One click and they were in. It was a sound amplifier. Matt programmed it to broadcast to the three of them. If it all went to shit he didn't want Honor to know. She had to stay put, no matter what.

If he, Jacko and Joe died, there was still help on the way and they would find Honor, hunkered down but safe and alive, in their vehicle.

One voice was giving orders in Russian. All three of them had basic Russian, and anyway what was being said wasn't a lesson in philosophy. The man was giving orders to prepare for when 'the mixing' was done.

The mixing?

He looked at Joe and Jacko. Both shrugged.

"Speak English, damn it," another voice said and every cell in Matt's body surged in loathing. The voice of the man he hated most in the world. Lee Chamness.

Joe and Jacko noticed his change in body language. "Chamness," he whispered and both nodded. Everything was being recorded. Excellent. From this moment on, Lee Chamness was royally *fucked*. They might all three die, but there would be forensic evidence that Chamness had had a hand in smuggling radioactive material into the United States, was cooperating with Russian agents, was conspiring against the United States.

Was a fucking traitor and a terrorist.

Not matter what, Matt won. He might lose his life but Chamness would never draw a free breath again.

A strong hot surge of strength swelled through him. He realized in one lightning bolt of awareness how much Chamness had cost him. How much the Other Than Honorable discharge had cost him. It had cost him his honor, but more than that, it had cost Matt his faith in how the world worked.

The world was fucked up, no one knew that better than Matt. But in the end, justice prevailed because it *had* to prevail, like the second part of a fucking equation. The second part of that equation had been missing, but here it was.

Chamness and whoever he was working with were going *down.*

He sent Felicity a text. *This is Lee Chamness.* She'd understand. He opened a satellite link between their comms and HQ. From now on everything was going to be recorded centrally, too.

They might die. He might die. But justice would move forward.

It was all he'd ever wanted. That his life serve for something good. Of course it was ironic that he was walking into a situation where if a bullet didn't catch him, radiation might, just as he'd found the woman of his dreams.

Shitty luck. But it was what it was.

So, Chamness said, *read this out.* On the screen, a figure limned in red with trailing wisps when it moved handed something to another figure limned in red. The red was the heat they gave off.

One of the red figures bowed his head. "I, Simon Thomas, owner and CEO of Quest Line Shippin —"

Holy shit! That was Honor's father! He was being forced to read out something.

Thomas lowered whatever he was holding in his hand. "I'm not reading this crap. No way."

"Remember we have your daughter, Thomas. Lovely woman. As they say, be a shame if anything happened to her."

Thomas threw something that fluttered to the floor. It lost the heat from his hand as it fell to the ground and disappeared from the screen. "My daughter is dead and you know it! There's no way —"

"Chamness." One of the red figures standing against the wall stepped forward. He was tall, taller even than Lee Chamness, who was as tall as Matt himself. "They are ready with the agitators."

Matt looked at Joe and Jacko. *The agitators?*

"Proceed." They heard a buzz and Chamness picked up a cell. "Yeah. Yeah? Let me see." He looked at what was in his hand, stared at it. "Excellent. Perfect. Bring it in."

Eighteen

Don't break comms silence, Matt had said, and Joe and Jacko had nodded. Military speak for don't interrupt us, don't say anything at all. Made sense. They had to operate with split-second timing if they were to prevail and any kind of distraction could mean the difference between life or death.

So Honor kept her hand well away from her ear, didn't tap on anything, just waited. It was awful, exactly like when the team at the hospital was waiting for the victims of the school shootings to arrive. Knowing something horrible was coming but there was nothing you could do about it until it arrived.

This was just like that. Matt and Joe and Jacko knew what they were doing but she had no idea how many men were in the warehouse. What kind of enemy forces they were facing. And the men in the warehouse were all surely armed, and surely ready for violence. Never a good combo.

The vehicle was a cozy cocoon, completely sound-proofed. She could have been on a comfortable desert

319

island for all she knew about what was happening in the outside world.

God, waiting and hoping for the best was just not in her nature. She was designed by nature to *act*. To help. And she'd worked long and hard to have the tools and the knowledge to do it. But how could she help those brave men? Just climbing up that wall was daunting. She couldn't even see the thin rope they had used, though she knew it was there.

She'd watched as they'd climbed up that rope as easily as you walk up a slight incline. Right there, that was something she didn't know if she could do. And even if she made it to the top, with a lot of grunting and groaning, she couldn't do what they'd done. They'd just easily rolled over the top and disappeared. God. What did they do — jump? That wall was *high*. If she tried to jump it, it was entirely possible she'd sprain or break an ankle and then where would they be?

No. Much as she'd like to help, much as she *longed* to help, this wasn't her wheelhouse, these weren't her skills. Though she hoped with all her heart that her particular skills wouldn't be needed. It would mean that one of them, or all of them, were broken.

God, she was so tired of fixing broken people. Patching wounds, preparing broken limbs for surgery, tying off tourniquets. And those were the good cases. The ones that were caused by life, though a lot of accidents were results of sheer stupidity.

The emergency room was filled with contenders for the Darwin Awards. The man who'd driven a golf cart right onto the interstate, on a drunken bet. The bungee jumper who hadn't checked the bungee cord. The kid who'd drunk bleach to make his teeth whiter.

Those were bad but bearable.

It was the other cases — the drug overdoses, the victims of abuse, the suicide attempts ... those were just sad and hopeless and broke her heart, over and over again.

She'd become a doctor to save lives and she did, every day. But more and more she was thinking that she'd like to save lives upstream, not at the very last minute. Keep people alive and healthy rather than catch them when they were broken and almost dead.

She'd been asked a number of times if she wanted to join a family practice with colleagues she liked and respected. She'd been to the small-scale clinic a number of times and loved the calm, friendly, healing atmosphere there. Very tempting ...

She shot to attention. What was that? A shadow moving in the shadows ...

Suddenly, there was a pop on the SUV's bodywork, right beside her, the door was wrenched open and before she could fall to the ground a big hand grabbed her by the throat and pulled her out of the vehicle. Her legs tangled over the high threshold, cracking her ankle and knee painfully. She thrashed, trying to hit out at the dark form that loomed in the night, but she didn't even reach him. He loosened the straps of her helmet and then the Velcro tabs of the body armor.

There were two of them. In desperation, she tried to

reach the comms unit in her ear, but the other man saw what she was aiming for. Digging into her ear with a gloved forefinger, he pulled out the unit, inspected it, then tossed it to the ground where he stomped on it with his boot heel.

Honor was on her own with two armed men, no body armor and no way to contact Matt.

Ten mikes out, a voice said and Matt looked at his teammates in relief.

God. The cavalry, ten minutes out. Metal and someone from Black Inc were coordinating. Though there wasn't a NEST team coming, the FBI HRT out of the LA office, the LAPD Special Operations Support Division and a SWAT team would be here in ten minutes. They would surround the building and negotiate a surrender.

Whatever else he was, Lee Chamness wasn't a wild-eyed crazy terrorist. Matt knew that Chamness was cool and greedy. He wasn't about to lose his life in a hail of gunfire. He'd lawyer up and try to weasel his way out of it.

Maybe he could get away with life.

Matt didn't give a fuck what happened to him as long as he got put away. And as long as Honor's father lived through this. They'd try to use him as a bargaining chip so they wouldn't smoke the guy. He hoped.

"Remember we've got a civilian in there. We're sending you a photo so you don't shoot him. Everyone else is fair game," he whispered, nodding at Jacko to send a photo of Honor's dad.

"Roger that," said a dry voice, the sound of the whap-whap of a helo rotor in the background. "But we try not to get anyone dead. We try to get the bad guys into court, not into the ground."

Eight minutes.

"Roger, out." Matt switched comms from the link with the FBI and LAPD to the link with the sound amplifier.

The Russian dude was giving orders to hurry something along and Chamness was trying to get Honor's father to read out a confession.

Oh, man, it was going to be fun watching the FBI arrest Chamness. Smuggling radioactive material with an intent to poison the water system of Los Angeles was about as big a federal crime as there was. None bigger. You'd probably have to kill a Senator to match it. And people didn't love Senators the way they loved Hollywood.

And when the FBI agents discovered that Chamness was former CIA ... there was no love lost between the two agencies. They'd handle Chamness worse than the head of a drug cartel. They would throw the book at him and they wouldn't be gentle.

That warmed Matt's heart. That would be something to celebrate.

Oh fuck yeah. Honor was going to want to make sure her dad was okay, and there would be a lot of depositions to give, and it would take all day but afterward, tomorrow night — no tonight, since it was already tomorrow — he was going to book them both into the Chateau Marmont and they were going to have a romantic dinner and then —

And then Matt's evening went to shit.

"See, Simon," Chamness said. "Your daughter's not dead, after all. But she will be if you don't read that confession into the camera."

"Daddy?" Honor said, her voice shaking.

Honor reached her hand out to her father, but the iron hand clamping down on her shoulder stopped her from moving an inch.

"Honor!" Simon Thomas's voice quavered. He'd aged twenty years since she'd last seen him. His face was paper white, the skin falling off his jowls, eyes red-rimmed and hollow. "Baby girl! Are you all right?"

If she could have, she'd have smiled. Her father hadn't called her baby girl for twenty years.

She nodded. No, of course she wasn't all right, but she was alive, and so was he, and that was something.

She looked around. They were in a hangar of some kind, one wall completely blocked off. There was highly radioactive material behind that wall.

A cold metal circle touched her temple. Another strong male hand clamping her shoulder. This one belonged to Lee Chamness, her father's erstwhile partner. He bent down to nuzzle her cheek in a horrible parody of affection.

"She's not dead, Simon, as you can see. But she will be if you don't finish reading that confession into the camera. And sell it, because it takes four pounds of pressure to pull this trigger. Less than it takes to pop open a beer can. And we're in a little bit of a time crunch, here."

Her father was sitting on a stool, looking dazed. A small camera on a tripod was situated

Her father bent slowly to pick up a piece of paper from the floor and scanned it. The paper shook in his hands.

Honor couldn't tell if he was faking the whole body tremors or not. It didn't matter because he was buying them time.

Where was Matt? Matt and Joe and Jacko?

Lee Chamness lifted the gun from her head and pointed it downwards. Honor glanced up and saw the man as he really was. A monster. Cold and cruel, not the affable businessman her father had described. The skin was stretched tautly over his cheekbones and his voice when he spoke was icy and emotionless.

"Simon, I'm not going to ask again. And I won't kill Honor right away. I will shoot her in the knee and then I will shoot her hand off. She's a doctor. She can't function as a one-handed cripple. But if you make me shoot her in the knee and shoot her hand off, the next bullet will end her life. Not without her suffering a great deal. We can manage without your confession, but it would make our life easier. So you have five seconds to decide whether to end your daughter's life. Five … four … three …"

Honor knew exactly what a blown-out knee looked like. What it would be like to have a bullet take off her hand. She was shaking and sweating and terrified.

Her father was shaking and sweating and terrified, too, only he had a bad heart.

"Don't shoot!" He lifted his trembling hand, the other with the sheet of paper. "I'll read it out!"

Where the *hell* was Matt? Lee Chamness wasn't as cool as he appeared. So close to him, she could smell the stress sweat coming off him. His shirt was damp, dark circles under his arms. Sweat trickled down his temples and his mouth had white brackets around it. The fingers holding the gun were white-knuckled.

Jesus. Four pounds of pressure and she'd never walk again. The gun was inches from her knee. That close, it would just blow out the structure of the knee. They'd have to amputate. Then her hand, then her head …

Oh God. Chamness was looking crazy enough to do it, too. His finger on the trigger tightened …

There was an enormous explosion at the door, metal buckling like petals, and the entire world disappeared in a flash of light and a clap of thunder so loud it brought her to her knees. She crouched, dazed, hands over ears, eyes half blinded.

Matt, Jacko and Joe poured into the room in precise movements, taking small careful steps, shooting.

Honor had dealt with a lot of bullet wounds but she'd never actually heard or seen shooting outside movie theaters. It was loud and it was terrifying and chaotic. The shooting stopped suddenly, as if choreographed, and she lifted a little from her terrified crouch.

The tall man and the goons were down, but Lee Chamness had rushed to her father's side and was crouched down behind him. The son of a bitch! Taking refuge behind a sick old man, knowing Matt, Jacko and Joe would never shoot him.

He rose, taking her father with him, the gun that had been aimed at her now against her father's head.

"Guns down!" he shouted. "Put your weapons down!"

Honor looked around and to her horror saw Joe and Jacko standing, tossing their weapons on the floor. And Matt … she sucked in a terrified breath. Matt was on the ground! Groaning, trying to lift himself up on an elbow and failing.

She rushed to his side, kneeling on the floor, and started wailing. "*Matt!*" she screamed. "Oh my God, no! You're shot!" Sobbing loudly, running her hands over his body.

Matt stopped one of her hands with his. "Honey," he wheezed, voice barely above a whisper. "I'm okay. The vest —"

"I know," she whispered fiercely. "Shut up."

He shut up.

She continued sobbing and wailing, slipping his boot knife out of its sheath and rose, still weeping, heartbroken. She managed to dredge up some tears as she staggered over to her father, still making a lot of noise.

"Daddy!" She laid her head on his shoulder, crying madly, inching around to position herself between him and Chamness.

Honor ran through it in her head. She usually did this to heal. Ran quickly through which steps to take and in which order to save a life. Now she had only one step to take and she did it, fast and mercilessly and precisely.

In one whipping stroke, she ran Matt's razor sharp knife down Lee Chamness's brachial artery. It was the hand holding the gun.

For a moment, he simply stood there, his body registering the shock before his mind could. The weight of the gun brought his hand down and he let the gun drop to the floor. The thud was loud in the cavernous room.

Honor placed her father carefully behind her then stepped up and got right into Chamness's face.

"I just severed your brachial artery," she said. "I also just severed your median nerve so your hand can no longer grasp anything. But that's the least of your problems. Because you are rapidly losing blood and are becoming ischemic."

His face had lost all color and he looked down in surprise at his arm. It was red. Blood had started dripping down to the floor from his hand. He opened his mouth, then closed it.

She stepped even closer to him. To this man who wanted to poison an entire city. Who had kidnapped and threatened her father. Who had kidnapped her.

Who had ruined Matt's life.

"Our heart pumps blood at several liters a minute. We have about five liters of blood in our body and yours is pumping your blood out just as fast as your heart can manage it. In fact, your heart is racing now. It doesn't know that an artery is severed. It just knows that blood is missing and is trying to pump out more."

She looked him straight in the eyes. They were blue. Arctic blue. Cold and unfeeling and right now, very scared.

She put her face right up next to his and whispered in his ear. "You're dying," she whispered. "You're already dead. It's just taking you a moment to realize it."

"You — you can't —" he stammered.

"Oh yes. Yes, I can. You were planning on destroying a great city. You threatened my father and you were going to incriminate him for a monstrous crime. You ruined Matt Walker's life. If I could I'd kill you twice."

His mouth opened and closed and the hemorrhaging continued. Beyond the point of no return. Even if she wanted to, she couldn't bring him back.

And she didn't want to. For the first and — she hoped — last time in her life, she was violating the oath she'd taken to save lives.

This was a monster of a man and he deserved to die. His mouth twisted as he collapsed in a heap like a broken puppet with cut strings. She watched as he twitched, then was still.

"But once will be enough." She hauled back and kicked him. For her father, for herself, for Matt, for the citizens of Los Angeles.

"That's enough, Captain Marvel," Matt's deep voice behind her said. He pried the knife from her fingers. She opened her hand and it clattered to the ground as she turned and threw her arms around him.

"Easy!" he winced and she pulled back.

"You probably have some broken ribs." She fingered two bullet holes in his vest. "But you're alive!"

"I am, thanks to you. He would have shot your father and then us."

They both turned their heads as the SWAT team erupted into the premises, bristling with weaponry, fanning out. One of the insectoid-looking men shouted through the barrier dividing the big warehouse and a moment later, the men in hazmat suits shuffled out with their hands up. Ten men in hazmat suits, the good guys, rushed forward into the shielded area and closed the door behind them.

A member of the SWAT team, who'd been speaking into his microphone, came over. "You Matt Walker?"

Matt straightened and nodded. The man held out a gloved hand. "Ted Hanson, LAPD SWAT. You guys did good work." He held up a hand and cocked his head, eyes opening slightly, listening to someone talking into his ear. Which Honor took for SWAT-guy body language for total astonishment. "You know what they were doing in there?"

Matt and Honor shook their heads.

"My guys, who know their stuff, say that there are hundreds of canisters of cesium-137 in there, in the form of salts. They were mixing the salts with water to make a radioactive slurry."

"They were headed to the North Hollywood Pump Station on Vanowen," Matt said and Hanson winced. He opened his mouth but someone shouted, "Yo, Hanson! Over here!" He gave them both a two-fingered salute off his helmet and walked away.

"Jesus." Matt folded her in his arms, holding on to her tightly. She held on just as tightly to him. "That was close."

Her shaken father shuffled toward them, swaying slightly.

"Daddy." She stepped back from Matt and kissed her father on the cheek and hugged him tightly. "Daddy this is Matt Walker, the man who —"

Wincing, Matt turned, stuck out his hand. "The man who loves your kickass daughter, sir. Nice to meet you."

Epilogue

The Grange
Two months later

"John Huntington! Put that back!" Honor's voice rang out, loud and clear as a bell. "You know better than that!"

John Huntington, a warrior who struck terror in the hearts of his enemies, hunched his shoulders. There was sudden silence in the Great Hall as he slunk back to the carving station and put back the slices of tagliata beef he'd heaped on his plate. He'd been found to have high cholesterol and had been put on a diet.

His wife watched what he ate very carefully but she was at the other end of the table, chatting with Lauren and Isabel.

Everyone snickered. Most of the guys had been on the receiving end of Honor's lectures. Senior, aka Doug Kowalski, had passed by the meat carving station entirely, not without a wince.

It was Felicity and Metal's wedding and the place

looked like a fairyland, plants and candles everywhere. The long table had a white linen tablecloth with tiny white rosebuds twined around some kind of green plants. White candles all along the length of the table.

Isabel had outdone herself with amazing food that was also healthy. It was so good that the guys weren't complaining.

Felicity was beautiful, as all brides were supposed to be. But she had an extra glow. The pregnancy was proceeding well and she had a rosy glow and a cute little bump and looked like happiness itself.

Metal looked stunned. As well he should. He was getting a smart and beautiful wife whom he loved and who loved him and they were expecting twin sons. An instant family, for a man who'd lost his when the Twin Towers fell.

Honor sat back in the circle of Matt's arm. She'd quit the hospital and joined a small family practice not far from ASI headquarters. She was also on retainer from the company as their company physician.

She took it seriously and had stated her intention of making sure every single member of the company, and spouses, lived to be a hundred. She was dedicated to them all and was always available.

Two weeks before, she'd got a panicked call from Jacko and Lauren. Their tiny daughter Alice had a high fever and difficulty breathing and Honor came over right away, even though it was 2 am. She got Alice to the hospital, insisted on an IV of antibiotics and stayed with her for a day and a night until the fever went down. It had been a lung infection and not meningitis, but Honor had definitely saved Alice's life.

Jacko now would shoot on sight anyone who looked cross-eyed at Honor.

Honor had kept her apartment but she now slept over at Matt's place. He was conducting a clever campaign to have her move in permanently. He'd started with having her leave her toothbrush, and now she had half his closet and most of the drawers were filled with her stuff.

He was thrilled.

He wanted more.

"To Felicity and Metal!" Joe stood with a glass of champagne in his hand. "Another good man bites the dust!"

He looked at Honor. She smiled up at him and his heart skipped a beat. Oh, man.

Sweat broke out over his body. But now was the time to man up. He was a former SEAL, after all. They ate danger for breakfast and caught bullets with their teeth.

He was also a former SEAL with an honorable discharge. There'd been a clamor to have the Other Than Honorable discharge expunged from his record, particularly since it had been Lee Chamness who had had pushed for him to be court-martialed. Matt was glad that his buddies felt so strongly about it, but he had everything he wanted in life. A woman he loved and a job he loved and teammates he loved.

Though he was only going to ask one of them to

marry him.

He stood and raised his glass. The entire table quieted and fifty faces turned to him. A couple of the guys knew what was coming and they were smirking at him.

Oh God.

He cleared his throat. He'd actually prepared a speech but when he dug into his pants pocket he discovered that it wasn't there. Bad news, because his brain had just shorted on him.

"Marriage is, ah, a good thing. Everyone says so. I say so." Honor looked at him with a frown. "When two people love each other, they ah …" Fuck. They got married. Didn't they?

A couple of the women were now looking at him strangely.

Metal, who knew, was sitting back in his chair, arm around the woman he loved, grinning widely. Enjoying Matt's embarrassment.

Matt's throat tightened. There were so many things to say but he didn't know how to say them. That he loved Honor, liked her, respected her. Had fun with her, but knew she understood the darkness he'd seen because she'd seen her own darkness. She got him, completely. She was the woman he'd been waiting for.

Honor's father was looking at him now, too. Simon Thomas had sold his company to a Canadian consortium and had bought a small apartment in the center of Portland and saw them often. He'd privately begged Matt to give him grandkids. Once he'd pulled out the big guns and asked for grandkids before he died, putting a quaver in his voice, which Matt thought was playing dirty.

He was doing the best he could. They'd tossed out contraception and he was doing his very best to create another generation of Walkers. Honor was happy with the idea of kids. A little reticent when it came to marriage.

But Matt discovered with a shock that he was old-fashioned. He wanted kids *and* marriage. Both. If possible, marriage first.

Now everyone was staring at him and no words were coming. None at all. White static in his head.

"Fuck it," he muttered, pulled a box from his jacket pocket and held it out to her. "Honor Thomas, will you marry me?"

At least the ring was perfect. Suzanne Huntington had helped him pick it out. Honor's birthstone, sapphire, with some diamonds around it. Suzanne had blinded him with science about the cut of the stones and the setting and blah blah blah. He'd taken in one word in ten. But even he could see that it was nice.

Honor's pretty mouth fell open as she lifted the lid of the box. She held it and looked up at him. She wasn't putting it on her finger.

She was a woman who valued words. He could persuade her with words, he knew he could. Except none were coming to him. Not one.

"Honor?" he croaked.

She smiled up at him. But, fuck. She wasn't saying yes. She wasn't saying no but she wasn't saying yes, either.

Everyone was openly watching, some with their chin in their hands, like watching a series on TV. Only the kind of series where the lead character gets whacked in the first season. Sweat trickled down his back.

"I promise to watch my cholesterol and eat meat no more than twice a week and to eat vegetables at every meal!"

There. All his cards on the table.

She carefully and slowly removed the ring from the box and put it on her finger and stood up. Taking her own sweet time about it.

"Well, in that case, darling, yes!"

The shouts and cheers and whistles rose to the rafters.

Dear Reader,
I hope you enjoyed **Midnight Renegade**.
If you did, I'd appreciate a review on Amazon or
Goodreads.

To read an excerpt from Nick and Kay's story,
Midnight Fever, please turn the page.

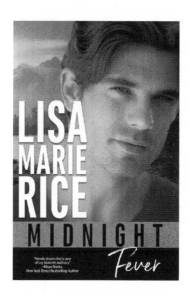

One

Portland, Oregon

"You're a hard woman to catch, Dr. Hudson," Nick Mancino said, smiling. Well, not really smiling, more like a baring of teeth. His dark eyes seemed to penetrate her head. "Missed you by five minutes in DC."

Kay Hudson suppressed a sigh as she looked at the handsome face scowling at her. It would be easier if he weren't right. She had been avoiding him, though not because she didn't want to see him. Nope. He'd featured in many erotic dreams. They'd been dancing around each other for months and it was entirely her fault that this was the first time they were actually together in the same room.

And what a room—elegant, hushed, candlelit. The Lounge offered the finest food in the Pacific Northwest. She'd eaten here several times before with her good friend, Felicity Ward. They'd laughed and eaten superbly well.

Not that she was hungry. Her stomach cramped with anxiety and the thought of food was slightly nauseating. She hadn't even been able to order her meal, something she usually enjoyed.

Nick had missed her by five minutes in DC. Yeah. She'd gotten word that Nick was arriving and had escaped out the back door as he walked in the front. And she'd deliberately come into Portland last month the day after he'd left for a job. She'd been avoiding him for a while now.

Not because she wanted to. God no. Who wouldn't want Nick Mancino? *Just look at him,* she thought. He was elegantly dressed—definitely in her honor because she knew he preferred sweats and jeans—but the white Armani shirt, Versace tie and blue-black Hugo Boss suit couldn't hide the fact that that hard body wasn't meant for boardroom suites. It was meant for midnight raids.

And sex.

Nick exuded toughness and self-reliance, the kind of

guy who wouldn't back down from anything. More than capable of defending himself. No one needed to protect Nick, least of all her.

In ordinary times, at least.

There wasn't any physical danger Nick would refuse to meet, but there was the question of fairness. Nick had had a brilliant career by being smart and brave and amazingly hard-working. He'd become a Navy SEAL and then a member of the FBI's elite Hostage Rescue Team.

Such hard things to do. They were things he'd earned a million times over. She didn't want to hurt a career he'd worked so hard for.

As long as he was in the FBI, she could ruin his life with what she was doing. If things went south, she might have to run for her life, and every single person she'd had dealings with before disappearing would have their lives turned inside out. He'd live under a perpetual cloud. It would ruin his career.

But Nick wasn't with the FBI anymore. As of last week, he was with Alpha Security International, a big security company in Portland. A good place to be, with good people. Felicity worked there, and said that the bosses at ASI were reasonable men. Nick would definitely not be penalized by an association with her. Not at ASI. They'd be on her side, and his. So now she could allow herself contact with him. Briefly.

Nick was still airing his grievances. "And I missed you by about an hour in New York last month."

"Mm." That had been careful timing, too. Nick had

been on a job and had found out from her grandfather that she was in New York. She'd checked out of the hotel early, missing him by half an hour.

"I could almost think you're avoiding me, Dr. Hudson."

His tone dripped sarcasm. The "Doctor" was overkill. Particularly considering the incendiary kiss they'd shared back when Nick was helping to save her beloved grandfather, who'd been kidnapped by a former Russian FSB officer. He'd moved his lips to her ear and breathed "Kay," and every hair on her body had stood up. It would have gone beyond that kiss—which had almost been enough to give her an orgasm—straight into sex, but she had put a stop to it. Wrong time. Wrong place. She'd been worried sick about her grandfather.

But sex was definitely in the cards.

They were off to a good start. He was interested, she was interested.

As a matter of fact, she'd never been as aroused and attracted to a man like she was to Nick. He fascinated her. And—icing on the cake—she liked him. A lot. And—the cherry on the icing on the cake—he wasn't a jerk. So, she made room to have Nick Mancino in her life.

Then her professional life blew up in her face. Each time she ran away from him it was because something scary was happening. Something that showed that things were very wrong in her world.

"Not avoiding you, Nick," she lied, looking him

straight in the face.

His eyes were mesmerizing. Dark and intense, set in a dark and intense face.

He stared at her as if she were under interrogation. He was good at interrogations, too, a master. She was a scientist and had no clue how to dissemble.

Too much. His intensity was too much. Kay dropped her own gaze and watched the patterns her fork tines made in the damask tablecloth. This was painful. She could actually *feel* her heart hurting, like someone was crushing it under an immense weight.

Nick reached over and placed his hand on hers, stilling it. His hand was fascinating. Dark and calloused and sinewy with strength, nicked with scars. He'd already had two careers as a warrior and was starting a third. He was a warrior in every line of his body. He was walking testosterone and oozed it out of every pore. Even his hands.

Kay was under intense pressure, about to do something that would blow her existence to smithereens. These past weeks, as she'd contemplated steps that would ruin her life, perhaps forever, she'd remained calm. All the permutations of the steps she had to take had been slowly and carefully considered.

Her job sometimes required that she hold pipettes of nature's most dangerous creations in her steady hands. In a level-4 biolab, with clumsy, thick rubber gloves, she handled life's worst enemies—pipettes of Ebola, Marburg, rabies. It was possible that one day she'd be asked to handle smallpox, and she'd be okay with it. But this? Nick Mancino's rough, scarred hand over hers? It made her tremble.

She finally looked up, met his eyes.

"You *have* been avoiding me, Kay," Nick repeated. His jaw muscles clenched. "Don't deny it."

She couldn't deny it anymore, because it was true. There was nothing she could say that wasn't a lie. Nick was a walking lie detector, anyway. He could smell lies at a hundred paces, like sharks could smell blood in the water.

Kay opened her mouth and then closed it. She huffed out a breath, tried to smile, looked him in the eyes. "I'm here now."

Nick blinked and a slow smile grew on his face. He lifted her hand to his mouth and kissed the back of it. "Yes, you are."

He could feel her hand trembling, she knew. Nothing escaped his notice. He'd been a SEAL and then a member of the FBI's elite Hostage Rescue Team. He wasn't going to miss the fact that the hand he was holding was shaking.

Looking away from him was impossible.

"May I top you up?" Kay jumped at the intrusion. The waiter, hovering. He'd introduced himself when they'd arrived, but she couldn't remember his name. She could barely remember her own.

"Thanks." Nick leaned to one side as the waiter poured another glass of an excellent merlot and waited for Kay's glass to be filled again. She took a sip, barely tasting it, then another. And another. Dutch courage, her grandfather called it. God knew she needed any kind of courage there was on offer.

"Your *antipasti* will be coming shortly," the waiter offered in a delicious Italian accent that might even have been real. You never knew. He had Italian good looks—thick black hair shaved at the sides and luxuriant on top, sharp cheekbones, a soul patch, brown eyes with ridiculously long lashes, which he actually batted at her. His eyes twinkled.

A real hipster hottie.

She looked from him back to Nick, whose eyes weren't twinkling at all, and who had absolutely nothing trendy about him. Clean-shaven, short-buzzed hair and he definitely wasn't batting his eyelashes at her. As a matter of fact, he was staring at her narrow-eyed.

It wasn't even a contest, she thought. The waiter thought he was cute, but he looked like a puppy next to Nick. Maybe even from a different, wussier species.

"Fine." She smiled, forcing the edges of her lips up, trying to remember how to smile. She'd almost forgotten how. There hadn't been much to smile at these past weeks.

The server glided away and reappeared two minutes later, sliding long white porcelain rectangles filled with tiny bruschette, fried stuffed olives, sage fritters, ramekins of goat cheese soufflé and tiny pesto-filled mozzarella balls. Nick didn't say a word and didn't break eye contact with her as the plates were placed in the center of the table.

They sat there, staring at each other, until the server

discreetly coughed. Kay glanced away from Nick. It was surprisingly hard to do, like wrenching something that was stuck. Nick was an eye magnet.

Two small square hors d'oeuvre plates appeared in front of them. "Enjoy," the server said, a trace of irony in his voice.

Enjoy.

Yeah, that was the kicker. She'd been avoiding Nick, trying her best not to even think of him, and by rights, she shouldn't even be here this evening. She had something dangerous to do tomorrow morning, and then she would probably disappear forever, and why the hell had she agreed to dinner with Nick?

Because, well, she enjoyed the hell out of him. Her grandfather was FBI, her father had been a judge, so she was used to tough guys, but Nick was something else entirely. Like he'd invented the tough guy persona—super tough, capable, absolutely mesmerizing. When she was with him, he threw a force field of sex and protection around her. It was as if he bent gravity. She'd loved every single second she'd ever spent with him and she'd thought of him constantly, even while running away from him.

Nick picked up his fork, speared a mozzarella ball and frowned at her. "Eat," he growled.

She sighed, picked up her own fork, put a hot stuffed olive on her plate and pushed it around. Her stomach was closed, there was no way she could eat anything. Every muscle in her body was tense, tightly knitted. It felt that if she put food down her throat, it would just bounce right back out.

He made a gesture and she put the olive in her mouth. Chewed. Swallowed. It was delicious, a little ball of warmth sliding down her gullet and into her closed stomach, which opened, just a little.

"Drink," he growled, and she took a sip of wine, which tasted like sunshine and joy.

He narrowed his eyes at her, only gleaming darkness showing. "That wasn't so hard, was it?"

Yes, it was hard. This whole thing was hard.

God, he looked so amazingly sexy. The soft over-head lighting picked out the edges to his face, his hair so black it looked faintly blue. He was so fixed on her it felt like a spotlight had been turned on. Kay wasn't used to being under the intense focus of a man like this— usually she was the focus of bland attention by bland males. Fellow scientists, the odd pharmaceutical company executive or CDC manager. All men who basically found money or power or science more interesting than she was.

Nick was hotly focused on *her*.

Nick was the most fascinating man she'd ever met, she was half in love with him, and she was going to take a leap into an abyss from which she might never return.

"Whoa there."

She looked up, frowning. Nick had put down his fork and gently pinched her chin. He rotated her head left and right, checking her out. His scowl was gone, replaced by something that looked like worry. Only that was crazy. Nick Mancino didn't do worry. Everything in his world was under his control.

His eyes held hers. "What's wrong?" That deep voice was gentle, and for some insane reason, she had to blink back tears.

She tried the smile again. Practice makes perfect. "Nothing." She lifted her head, hoping to escape those strong fingers, but he held fast to her chin. He wasn't hurting her but he wasn't letting go either.

"Bullshit," he said, his voice still gentle.

This was a very bad mistake. She should go before she broke down in tears and told him everything. Which would be an even worse mistake, because Nick Mancino would not approve of what she was about to do, and when he disapproved of something, there were consequences.

So—get out of here, fast, she told herself, running through possible excuses that didn't sound insane. Headache, stomach ache, vague female complaint. That last one should do it. No guy wants details on female problems.

"I, ah." She coughed to loosen a tight throat. "I don't feel too well. I think I should go."

Nick barely registered her words. He was studying her face the way a sniper studies the battlefield. "You don't look well," he said finally. "You've got bags under your eyes and you're very pale underneath your makeup. God knows you're still beautiful—nothing less than a gunny sack over your head would change that—but there's something wrong." He drew his hand away slowly, making it a caress. "What's wrong, honey?"

Kay blinked. Her heart had given a huge thump in her chest when he'd used the term of endearment. Oh God. This was getting out of control. She should get up right now and walk out. Nick wouldn't follow her if she made it clear that she didn't want him to. But that was the thing—she wasn't capable of simply getting up and leaving. And she was certainly incapable of pretending she didn't care about him. In her state, nerves on edge, with sleepless nights and worry gnawing at her every single moment, she didn't have the strength to pull it off.

But she had to do *something*. She'd found it possible to resist tough-guy Nick, but this gentle Nick, dark eyes watching her with sympathy and something else… Nope. Couldn't do it. The truth was out of the question, but she could skirt it.

"Work," she said, her voice slightly hoarse. She cleared it. "Work. I'm having some issues at work."

His black eyebrows drew together. "Considering what you do, that's really alarming."

You have no idea, Nick, she thought. "It's more admin stuff than anything else," she lied. "My boss is being…difficult and is making my life hard. It's a little depressing."

Depressing didn't begin to cover it. She might have stumbled upon a plan to burn down the world.

"I'm good with guns," Nick said. Which was an understatement. He'd been a sniper as a SEAL and as an FBI HRT guy. "Want me to shoot that son of a bitch who's bothering you? Say the word and consider it done." His face was entirely deadpan, as was his voice.

Kay hesitated a beat then smiled. It was shaky, but genuine. "That was a joke," she said. "Wasn't it?"

"Nah." He speared a mozzarella ball and put it up to her lips. "I meant it, but let's pretend I was joking. Though whoever your boss is, he has worse weapons at his disposal than I do." He shuddered. "Any guy who deals in smallpox and Ebola scares me more than I could scare him." He nudged her mouth. "Open up and eat."

Kay opened her mouth and he gently placed the ball on her tongue. It was delicious and went down like a dream. Her stomach had been closed for weeks, but now it just opened up like a flower.

The entrée arrived. Beef ragout on a bed of pappardelle for Nick. Gorgonzola cheese risotto for her. The dishes looked amazing and smelled even better.

Nick wound strands of pappardelle with ragout around his fork and put it next to her lips. She chewed and swallowed. God. Food like that should be illegal.

It was the food but it was also Nick himself. He'd offered to off the bad guy and it was such a tempting thought, except she wasn't too sure who the bad guy was here.

But beyond that, Nick was definitely someone to take your woes to. She couldn't take this particular woe to him—that was her burden to bear—but in general, he was made to lift burdens from people, and not just with his sniper rifle. There was something about him— that tough guy, protective attitude—that made her feel better.

"Attagirl," Nick said approvingly when she began to eat. "See what the thought of me whacking your boss does? Brings your appetite right back."

Kay smiled.

"That's more like it," he said. "I thought you'd forgotten how to smile."

She'd thought that, too. "Haven't forgotten," she said. "Just not much to smile about lately."

"You shouldn't have avoided me." Nick shot her a dark, intense glare. "I'd have made you smile. Guaranteed."

And just like that, heat shot through her, a scalding wave from head to toe, like a sun blossoming inside her, under her skin. She had very fair skin, and she knew beyond a shadow of a doubt that she was blushing bright as a stoplight. Though in childhood her skin showed exactly what she was thinking, she'd learned to control it. Or thought she had. And now, just when she needed control most, her fair skin betrayed her.

"You like that thought." Nick leaned back in his chair, never taking his eyes off her for one second.

Kay closed her eyes and drew in a deep breath, let it out.

"Yes," she sighed. "Apparently, I do."

She didn't dare open her eyes because she knew what she'd see—a smug male face. After a long moment's silence, she finally opened them and saw Nick looking at her soberly. Not smug, not smirking, even though he'd alluded to...well, to sex. The eight-hundred-pound gorilla at the table.

He drummed his strong, thick fingers on the table-cloth once, eyes dark and serious. "What's wrong, Kay?" he asked, that deep voice gentle and controlled. "And don't say you don't know what I'm talking about."

No, he understood far too much, was way too perceptive for her to lie right now. "I can't—I can't talk about it," she said finally, after a long silence.

He drummed his fingers once more, thinking about it. If there was one thing a former Navy SEAL, former FBI HRT guy understood, it would be what he'd call "opsec". Operational security. What she knew and what she suspected hadn't been classified as secret because it didn't officially exist, was pure supposition, but it was a bombshell nonetheless. And certainly not something she could share now.

"Okay." Nick continued watching her, face expressionless. "I can't argue with that. So, you won't tell me—"

"Can't," she interrupted. "Can't tell you."

"All right." He bowed his head in acknowledgement. "Can't tell me. I respect that. God knows I've got enough stuff of my own I can't talk about."

I bet, Kay thought. Just about every mission of his as a SEAL would remain classified until the sun went nova.

"Just tell me this. Give me this much." His jaw muscles hardened, the skin over his temples hollowed. "Someone bothering you? Harassing you?"

She might be driven into lifelong exile, she might be tossed into the deepest dungeon in the world, she could lose everything she had worked so hard for.

Her head dropped. "Not quite in the way you mean, but...yes."

Nick was silent.

Surprised, she lifted her head.

He waited another beat. "That stops," he said. "Right now."

Actually, it did. Not because of something Nick could do, but because of what she was about to do. She was stepping into danger...but it was almost better than the last few weeks of agonizing heartache as she slowly came to the realization that someone in an institution she worshipped had sold out and had her best friend killed.

Whatever was to come, at least she wasn't tormented by doubts. Whatever was to come, she was going to face it head-on.

So, yeah. It stopped, right now.

"Thanks." Kay smiled wryly.

He cocked his head, studying her. "I can't ask and you can't tell. That's about it, right?"

She nodded, throat tight.

Oh God, how she *wished* she could unburden herself. How she wished she could open up, tell him everything, walk him through how she got here, alone and lost.

Nick was smart and, above all, Nick thought strategically and tactically. Kay was lost in this world. Her

LISA MARIE RICE

world was science, the world of truths. Eternal truths. A world of things that could be proven. Two plus two equals four had been true before humans walked the earth and would be true to the end of time. The beauty of science was its clarity. If scientists didn't understand the truth, it wasn't nature's fault, it was theirs. The universe was clear and straightforward, even down to quantum physics. It was people who were opaque and contradictory and often made no sense at all.

"Something I have to deal with myself," she said. "You can't help me." Actually, no one could help her.

"I can't help you with the science thing," Nick admitted. "But I can beat someone up for you. Easy. I'd enjoy it, too."

A laugh burst out of her, a little intense bubble of emotion that brought tears to her eyes. *Whoa.* She coughed and looked away, blinking furiously. If only it were so easy.

For a second Kay was so tempted to lay all her problems before him, put everything in his very large and very capable scarred hands. Nick would know what to do. And now that he was out of the FBI, his career couldn't be ruined.

But that would be so unfair. Kay had a heavy burden to bear, and it was hers alone. Nick was a good guy, but he'd already helped her out so much. He'd helped save her grandfather, her only family.

Nick was interested in her—he'd shown that. He'd made it clear he'd like an affair. But sex didn't mean he wanted to take all her baggage on board. It would be

354

like lifting a thousand-ton anvil, all for a quick lay.

Though with Nick, maybe it wouldn't be so quick...

Heat blossomed through her again, a blast of it so strong it was like a hand at her back, pushing her forward.

Sex with Nick.

So.

There it was, out in the open. In the back of her mind, she'd been thinking of sex with Nick for a while now. It was, possibly, the reason she'd agreed to dinner tonight. Kay wasn't used to her subconscious tripping her up, but there it was. Her glands leading her around instead of her head.

Well, why not?

Who would it hurt? Her, actually, because it could only be a one-night stand, and Kay didn't do those. She'd never had an affair that was only sex. A night of passion then disappearing forever...ouch.

Plus, she thought Nick might like something more. A two-night stand, maybe, at a minimum. A week-long affair, perhaps. Nick wasn't known for his long-term relationships, but he wasn't a player, either. He'd want something more than slam-bam thank you, sir, which was basically all she could offer.

But one night...oh man. Payback for all the long, lonely nights wrestling with this huge, writhing *thing* at the center of her life. Nights spent staring at the ceiling, slowly coming to terms with the fact that someone in an institution she admired was fundamentally evil, way beyond anything she could ever imagine.

Nick knew about that kind of evil. Grandfather Al knew, too. They knew what humans were capable of. Their enemies were the scumbags of the earth. Terrorists, rapists, murderers, abusers, the corrupt. Men whose coin was pain and fear.

Kay's enemy her entire life had been completely different. Her enemy was nature itself. She was going to be a brick in the wall that cut mankind off from its worst enemies—cancer, heart disease, muscular dystrophy. All the illnesses the flesh was heir to.

Disease, illness, plagues—they'd always been so horrible, killing millions and millions of people throughout history. Smallpox alone was one of the most terrifying things on earth. And yet…it never failed to astonish her that people could be more dangerous than disease. More murderous, capable of much greater damage.

But Nick had known that for a long time.

She'd always thought of herself as brave. She worked in a bio-safety level 4 lab encased in body protection as strong as a space suit, but one tiny tear, one leak and she would die a horrible death. That was bravery.

Nick was braver.

She'd been so afraid these past weeks. Her heart constantly thrummed a drumbeat of terror. She'd end her day exhausted, sticky with the sweat of anxiety. Which was exactly how she woke up in the morning, too. Heartsick and terrified.

Nick wasn't afraid of anything. She knew that about him. He'd done astoundingly heroic things. She didn't know this from *him*. He never talked about it, ever. She knew it from her grandfather and from stories her friend Felicity passed on from her lover, Metal, and his guys. The guys in Nick's new company, who'd been his teammates in the SEALs. The consensus was that Nick was a really good guy, one of the rare ones. Hard-headed, yes, stubborn as they come, but brave as a lion.

Nick the Lionheart! a teammate had yelled when Nick had run across an open field of fire with a wounded soldier in a fireman's carry, bullets pounding the sand at his feet. Nick had thrown the wounded teammate over the threshold of the sandbag bunker and then tumbled over head first, bullets following him. Nick stood immediately, took up a station at a break in the wall of bags and started calmly picking off enemy targets, totally unmindful of the fact that a bullet had passed through the meaty part of his thigh.

Nothing ever rattled Nick.

What would it feel like to be like that? To be so fearless? To feel up to any possible physical challenge? She'd never know. But…maybe she could get close enough to him to borrow some of his courage. Touch that strong, tough body all over, feel him inside her…

Another bloom of fiery heat.

His eyebrows drew together in a V shape. She'd turned beet red again. He must be wondering whether she suffered from some kind of mental or hormonal disorder.

Maybe she was. Nick Lust Disorder.

"So," he said casually, leaning back. "Is that a yes?

Want me to beat someone up? Whack someone for you?" His tone was light but his face was deadpan. Tough and utterly inscrutable.

She sighed. "I wish." If only this was the kind of problem you could shoot your way out of. Pity bullets couldn't kill viruses.

They'd eaten their way through dinner, though she'd left most of hers on her plate. His had disappeared and she'd yet to take a bite of hers. He took her spoon out of her hand, dipped it into the creamy panna cotta and held it in front of her lips. When she opened her mouth, he slipped the spoon inside and she nearly fainted from the sugar rush.

"Again," he insisted, heaped spoon at her lips. He watched as the spoon entered her mouth, pulling it out slowly, empty. His face was dark and hard. "Jesus." He looked like he was in pain.

It nearly made her smile. "It's just dessert, Nick."

He wasn't smiling at all. "Not the way you're eating it, sweetheart. You're making this pure sex."

Kay blew out a breath. This was so unfair. She wasn't trying to be sexy, though…well, with Nick Mancino across the table from her, staring at her with dark, narrowed eyes, it was hard to think of anything *but* sex.

"Sex," she whispered without even realizing it. The word was in her head, in the cloud of pheromones swirling around her, even in the panna cotta. It was in the molecules of the air.

Nick wasn't a fidgety man, but he froze into immobility. "What did you say?"

What? What was he talking about?

His face was a mask of tension. "What did you say?" he repeated.

What had she said? Kay ran the tape in her head back a minute and there it was. What she'd said.

Sex.

What was she thinking of?

"Sex," Nick said. His dark eyes glittered. "You said sex. I heard that. Distinctly."

Kay swallowed and nodded.

"So…" He scooted his chair closer. "Does that mean that sex is on your mind? The idea rolling around your head as a possibility? Say, in a completely theoretical and abstract way?"

"Not theoretical," she whispered through a scratchy throat. "Not abstract."

Nick's face tightened and he looked at her intensely, like looking through a screen door at something from a long distance away, uncertain of what he was seeing.

"Not theoretical," he repeated. He took the large, snowy-white linen napkin off his lap and threw it on the table. "That means practical. You're thinking sex in a totally non-abstract and non-theoretical way. With me."

She nodded.

His eyes were like lasers piercing into hers. The cords in his neck stood out, his jaw clenched.

This was crazy. She was sending out huge signals— like flares on a dark night—without thinking about the consequences. Careful, steady Kay, who always thought before she spoke, was now opening her mouth and wondering what would come out next.

Totally out of her control, as if her mouth was separate from her, run by someone else.

"Yes," she whispered.

You might also enjoy:

THE MIDNIGHT TRILOGY
1. Midnight Man
2. Midnight Run
3. Midnight Angel

The Midnight Trilogy Box Set

THE MEN OF MIDNIGHT
1. Midnight Vengeance
2. Midnight Promises
3. Midnight Secrets
4. Midnight Fire
5. Midnight Quest
6. Midnight Fever

MIDNIGHT NOVELLA
Midnight Shadows

Woman on the Run
Murphy's Law
A Fine Specimen
Port of Paradise

THE DANGEROUS TRILOGY
Dangerous Lover
Dangerous Secrets
Dangerous Passion

THE PROTECTORS TRILOGY
Into the Crossfire
Hotter than Wildfire
Nightfire

GHOST OPS TRILOGY
Heart of Danger
I Dream of Danger
Breaking Danger

HER BILLIONAIRE SERIES
CHARADE: Her Billionaire - Paris
MASQUERADE: Her Billionaire - Venice
ESCAPADE: Her Billionaire - London

NOVELLAS
Fatal Heat
Hot Secrets
Reckless Night
The Italian

About The Author

Lisa Marie Rice is eternally 30 years old and will never age. She is tall and willowy and beautiful. Men drop at her feet like ripe pears. She has won every major book prize in the world. She is a black belt with advanced degrees in archaeology, nuclear physics, and Tibetan literature. She is a concert pianist. Did I mention her Nobel Prize?

Of course, Lisa Marie Rice is a virtual woman and exists only at the keyboard when writing romance. She disappears when the monitor winks off.

58469083R00217

Made in the USA
Middletown, DE
07 August 2019